Irvin Schuller

Murder at the Grammar School

Irvin Schuller

Murder at the Grammar School

Novel

Translated from the German
"Mord am Schiller-Gymnasium"

Bibliographic information of the German National Library:

The Deutsche Nationalbibliothek lists this publication in the German National Bibliography; detailed bibliographic data are available on the Internet at http://dnb.dnb.de

© 2021 Erwin Schüller (pen name: Irvin Schuller)

Author's homepage: www.erwin-schueller.com

Proof-Reading and editing: Duncan Thorburn

Cover: Julia Schüller / Erwin Schüller

Printed and published by: BoD – Books on

Demand, Norderstedt

ISBN: 978-3-7534-9607-8

*For my friend Friedemann,
who was taken from life all too soon
in a tragic traffic accident,
and whose own experiences
inspired me in part to write this novel.*

This novel narrates dramatic events and actions, some of which take place at a grammar school in the town of Lundenburg in the south of Germany. The name 'Schiller Grammar School' does not refer to any existing school. Places as well as persons, actions and facts described in the novel are fictitious. In some places there may be circumstances similar to those in the novel. However, any similarities with real persons or events would be unintentional and purely coincidental.

1 Working Late

A sultry midsummer evening descended like a great shroud over the city centre of Lundenburg. Despite the onset of dusk, it still felt like a sauna. Around the school all the tables in the street bars and coffee shops were full. It was the end of the day and people were looking for ways to cool down with drinks and ice-cream.

Despite the heat, there was loud laughter and a babble of voices everywhere, especially from schoolchildren and students who were looking forward to the upcoming summer vacation. The city traffic slowly and steadily pushed past the school. Again and again the line of cars stopped at the zebra crossing in front of the building. One might have thought that today, with this record heat, all of Lundenburg wanted to go downtown.

The huge school with its small bell tower, which gave it a touch of ecclesiastical dignity, lay quite deserted in the middle of the bustling city centre. The janitor of the Schiller Grammar School, Mr Maier, stood casually in front of the building in sloppy work clothes, smoking a cigarette, his eyes gliding over the facade. On the first floor you could still see light through two windows.

The boss is working overtime again, he thought, and just before nine in the evening! "Well if he enjoys it, why not," he murmured and went on. He took a leisurely stroll around the schoolhouse. Next to him on a leash, his pit bull terrier, which he had acquired some months previously in order to feel more secure during night inspections of the premises. He had recently been threatened by three shady characters whom he had surprised conducting a drug deal in the car park. The whole area was considered unsafe in the evening. The train station was only a five-minute walk away and drug dealers and petty criminals loitered after dark. But the area was also under surveillance by the police, who regularly patrolled from around ten o'clock in the evening. Mr Maier checked the main entrance door. It was locked. He went on satisfied. He then lit another cigarette and strolled comfortably across the extensive grounds with its sports facilities and large play areas. It was turning dark.

Headmaster Lochberger was sitting at his desk on the first floor. He stared at his notebook, now and then typing on the keyboard, and looking at his Excel charts. His slim and sportsmanlike figure straightened up occasionally when he went to his office cupboard to take out a folder. With his grey suit, light blue tie and well-groomed grey hair, the sixty-year-old might have been mistaken for an insurance salesman.

His office consisted of two rooms A large anteroom with two workstations for the secretaries and his actual office, with a seating area for meetings and his personal workplace with a desk and cupboards. A connecting door led directly to the copy room, which was also used by the teachers to prepare lessons. However, this door could only be opened from the headmaster's office . The boss did not like to be disturbed.

There was no one else in the brightly lit office but from the copying room one still heard the humming and rumbling of the machine. Lochberger noticed this, but paid no further attention. Teachers often stayed there until late at night producing teaching material.

He looked at the wall clock. It was already five to nine. He had promised his wife earlier that he would be home around half past nine. He would have to call her again and tell her he might be a little late. Next week there was a teacher's conference and he had a lot of documents to prepare. An urgent need forced him to pause briefly. He got up, left the office, and walked down the long corridor to where the teacher's toilets were, about a hundred meters away down on a lower floor.

As he hurried back after a few minutes, the door of the copy room was just opening and Mr Strasser, one of the Spanish teachers, came out with a stack of copies. Behind him came Mr Baum, a friend of Strasser's and a teacher of German. Both were accompanied by Mr Pobler, the longest-serving colleague and also a philologist. The headmaster was a little annoyed to see them at that time because they were not people he enjoyed meeting, especially as they repeatedly had expressed a clear opposition to him, instead of sharing his informed and well-considered opinions.

"Well, what's going on here this evening. What are you still doing in the house," he asked the men in a somewhat gruff tone.

"I still had to make a few copies for the project next week," replied Strasser. Baum followed up. "We work hard and are not afraid of a night shift, Mr Lochberger. And why are you on duty so late?"

"Well, our headmaster works day and night. That is an old Prussian virtue, dear colleagues," Pobler said cheerfully and ironically.

Lochberger stopped and looked at the group sceptically.

"Next week is our conference, there is still a lot to do. But you could have done your tasks earlier. At this time nobody should be in the building, we decided that at the last general conference. If you don't remember then read the minutes from time to time. I wish you a pleasant evening!" said the headmaster angrily and disappeared into his rooms

"The same to you," Pobler called after him. "And don't work so hard, it's not good for you!"

Pobler laughed out loud. "Our Lochi doesn't get enough of his Excel spreadsheets. At some point he'll get a heart attack because of overwork. What about you, are you going for a beer?", he asked Strasser.

"I can't, unfortunately. I'm going on a date right now."

"Oh, the man is now plunging into the nightlife," Pobler teased. "You could introduce her to us. We also want to see a beautiful woman once in a while. What do you think, Franz?"

"Yes, definitely, it is your duty as a good colleague not to keep your conquests a secret."

"Okay next time, I promise, but unfortunately it won't work tonight, please understand. I have to go. See you tomorrow!"

Strasser ran down the stairs. His colleagues followed him at a leisurely pace, their conversation echoing through the stairwell for a while.

Lochberger had stepped to the window in his office and was peering out into the school forecourt. In front of the building four students were playing football. Maier, the janitor, stood smoking next to the dishevelled figure of a drunk man who spoke loudly to him with a wine bottle in one hand and a cigarette in the other.

My goodness, Lochberger thought. Rabble and incompetent people everywhere. Strasser, Baum and Pobler, who should have been dismissed long ago had it been up to him, along with that lazy janitor. But unfortunately he was the head of a state school and not the boss of a private company. And these state officials and employees, it was practically impossible to dismiss them. At best they could be scared away, which sometimes was successfully achieved, so that the teachers in question voluntarily applied for another school and then eventually left. He had succeeded in this a few times but unfortunately these three men, who formed a permanent nest of resistance against him, had stayed on. Fortunately Pobler and Strasser's terms had now expired. They would soon both retire and so the problem had largely resolved itself.

But what are these disagreeable people doing here in the building at this time, he wondered suspiciously. They have all day to make their copies! He hurried back to his desk to continue working. His screen asked for the password and he entered it but only a blue screen appeared saying, 'A virus was found, the system is restarting and checking for viruses'.

Strange, he thought. Where could a virus have come from. After all, they had the best virus scanners on the market at his school! Lochberger was alarmed. He was pressed for time and wanted to finish some presentation slides that night.

He waited impatiently to continue working. The computer had now restarted but instead of the usual start screen there was another warning message from the virus scanner.

'Virus found on drive E:', the program reported and immediately issued the name of the malware: 'Tequila'.

"For God's sake," Lochberger muttered to himself. That was the last thing he needed now, he hadn't had an incident like this in years.

Lochberger was a mathematician and computer scientist so the whole thing didn't seem to be an insoluble problem. The scanner had identified the virus and would now destroy or block it and he could continue to work.

When he displayed the contents of his SD card with the file explorer, however, he got a real fright. All the data was unrecognizable. There was only a mishmash of confused characters, everything was practically illegible. He opened a file as a test and the same picture also appeared there. The contents were illegible. All he could see was a wild jumble of characters of all kinds.

The malware had obviously changed all of his files.

Now the headmaster realized that he wouldn't be able to get anything done that night. This sudden incident was completely puzzling. But the school had provided for such cases. There was a maintenance contract with a private service provider for data processing. Mr Alumno would have to do a night shift to restore his data. He was about to pick up the phone when it started ringing. It was his wife calling to ask him when he was going to come home.

"I'm leaving straight away, Monika, but it will take a few more minutes. There is a little problem that I still have to solve, but I'll be right there."

Then he called the number of the specialist and the answer came from Mr Becker, an Alumno employee.

"Good evening, Lochberger here, I know it's after nine o'clock. I'm sorry to have to disturb you at this hour but it's an emergency. Can I speak to Mr Alumno?"

The speaker on the other end of the line explained that his boss was not there at the moment but he himself could probably help. He asked about the nature of the problem.

Lochberger briefly described the situation and that he could not continue his work because of a sudden virus alarm. He was puzzled because everything had been perfectly normal before his toilet break. Becker assured him that the problem could be solved. Mr Alumno would later analyse the situation remotely. The virus search would then be carried out thoroughly with several scanners, which would guarantee that nothing would remain. However, there was one drawback. The steps taken since the last automatic backup at eight o'clock may have been lost.

"I can manage without the work of the last hour if necessary, but it would be nice if everything else could be restored," Lochberger said.

Mr Becker's voice sounded confident, saying that the matter would be dealt with quickly and if necessary Alumno would work until tomorrow morning. He himself would only be in the office until Alumno returned but he expected him to be back at any moment.

"You are my saviour, Mr Becker," said the headmaster. "I have some urgent things to do. Next week we have the teachers' conference and I absolutely have to finish some documents."

Mr Becker said the whole thing wouldn't be a problem and the headmaster should now think about the end of the day instead of worrying.

"I know. My wife is waiting, she called me earlier. So I will be back at school tomorrow around eight if you have any information for me. Thank you for your help. I hope you succeed in finding a solution."

Mr Becker said goodbye with the assurance that everything would be fine the next day. Lochberger switched off his phone and took a deep breath. Thank goodness there was this maintenance contract with Alumno Data Technology. He had already needed it a couple of times for difficult cases and although he was very familiar with computers and was also an experienced programmer there were always situations where he could not do without some external support.

This incident was mysterious and unique. He had never lost data on an SD card before. He always bought high quality cards and exchanged them regularly for safety's sake. He now checked the data on his hard disk with the scanner and could not find anything conspicuous. So the virus had only attacked his data card? This contradicted all his experiences. He thought hard. How could a virus possibly access his SD-card? On his school system? Hardly. Everything was protected by state-of-the-art security. So, on another computer? But he hadn't used his card on another computer! Everything was just fine before he went to the toilet. Wait a minute! Strasser, Baum and Pobler were just here making photocopies next door. Did they have anything to do with it? A suspicion arose in him and he got up and went to the connecting door to the copy room. He pushed against it, and lo and behold, the door opened. So someone had tampered with the lock and the connection between the copy room and the headmaster's office had been open all the time.

It now seemed clear to him that the virus attack on his data card was no accident. Obviously, these teachers had caused this. Probably to annoy him. So out of sheer badness or simply a prank because hardly anyone could get any other benefit from it. The card contained his business letters and documents, diagrams and evaluations, as well as the source code of his latest software modules.

So the destruction of his data was a mere act of harassment and an attack on his professional success, on his triumph at the next general teachers' conference, an attack on his beloved school reform project 'Schiller FIX – fantastic – innovative – excellent'.

Only someone who hated him and wanted to harm him could do something like that and the only people who could be considered as the authors of this deed were Strasser, Baum and of course Pobler, with all of whom he had had angry confrontations several times over the past few years for various reasons. He raged and snorted angrily, then finally shouted, "These stupid idiots. But wait, I'll get them." Lochberger sat down at his secretary's desk, booted up the computer and wrote an email to his deputy, Manfred Degen.

Hello Manfred, short information about EDP. I became the victim of an attack tonight, my notebook was contaminated by viruses. I was briefly out of my office around nine o'clock and when I came back five minutes later Strasser, Baum and Pobler had just come out of the copy room. Allegedly they had made some photocopies.

Back at my desk I wanted to continue my work but my computer reported a virus and my data was all gone, my SD card is a mess. I suspect that these colleagues have infected my notebook. Apparently they had tampered with the lock and my office was accessible from the outside all the time, so they could enter when I briefly went to the bathroom.

I have already called Alumno. They will take care of my computer by remote maintenance tonight and eliminate the viruses. If you see the colleagues mentioned, give them a good talking to! See you tomorrow, Reinhard.

At 9:25 pm Lochberger packed his briefcase to finally drive home. His wife would be waiting for him. When he had all his things packed, he left the notebook switched on on the desk, including the data card, so allowing the technician to have access. After turning off the light, he left the office and closed the door behind him.

The stairwell was still illuminated. He was surprised that the janitor had not yet shown up as normally the building was empty from 9 pm and the light should have been switched off. You have to have a serious word with the man again, he thought angrily. He must be dismissed, he doesn't follow instructions and is constantly missing and he also seems to be drinking. In a bad mood he walked down the stairs. The evening had gone differently than planned. All that remained was to hope that everything would work again the next day.

He unlocked the back door and carefully opened it. His silver-grey Audi was parked outside. Nobody else was in the car park, which was dimly lit by the street lamps. It was good to be careful around here at night. Drug dealers and their customers were often hanging around. He flicked the switch and the light in the stairwell went out. He was about to go out of the door when he heard a sound behind him. Just then he felt a hard blow to the head and everything went black and silent.

2 Alert

Alex arrived at his temporary home around eleven o'clock that night. He had been living with Ulla for a few days after he had closed his own flat in Lundenburg because of his imminent move to Bavaria. After all, he would be a pensioner from next month and wanted to spend his retirement in the old farmhouse he had bought in Dorflingen. Ulla had been sceptical at first and had described the idea of living in a village in the country as "stupid". However, after seeing the house with her own eyes, she soon gave up her resistance and said that she could now imagine moving to it the following year when she retired.

His partner was asleep when he went to bed. He was very excited and happy about the successful action against Lochberger. And of course glad about the money. That night he slept restlessly and woke up at around half past five, quite exhausted. He tried to get back to sleep but knew that Ulla would get up around 6 am to get ready for work, which kept him awake. Just before six the alarm clock rang and his partner got up and shuffled into the bathroom. He pretended to be asleep because the last thing he needed now was a conversation about his late arrival. He managed to fall asleep again when the phone suddenly rang in the hallway. He heard Ulla pick it up and answer.

"Yes, please wait, I'll get him," he heard her say. Who could want to speak to him so early in the morning? Ulla was already in the bedroom and said only very briefly, "Phone for you."

"Who is it?"

"I don't know, a woman. She didn't give her name."

Alexander went to the phone and picked up the receiver. "Strasser," he said.

The voice of Monika Lochberger was heard on the other end of the line. He was startled. Thinking quickly he spoke aloud the name of one of his female colleagues.

"Oh good morning, Ms Zander. What is so important that you call me at six in the morning?"

Monika immediately recognized his little trick with which he wanted to hide her identity from his partner. She spoke softly, almost in a whisper.

"I have to speak to you very urgently, before school starts. Don't ask questions now, you can tell your friend that you have to do morning supervision because a colleague is ill."

"Oh," he said, "good of you to remind me, I would have forgotten that. The early supervision. Yes, the plan was changed yesterday afternoon. I did not see that, thanks for letting me know."

"You are doing very well," said Monika. "Please come to the swimming pool at exactly seven o'clock. I will be in the parking lot behind the building. It's a blue VW Golf. Then we can talk."

"Okay, all right, Ms Zander, thanks for the info. I'll have to get ready quickly. I wouldn't have had any lessons until the second period. See you later. Bye Ms Zander."

Alex hung up and went to the bedroom to get dressed. His girlfriend followed him and stood at the open door with her right hand on her hip.

"Why did that woman call you at six in the morning?"

"You heard it, there was a change in the substitution plan and I have early supervision and have to be at school by seven. I'm glad she called me, otherwise I would have got into trouble with the boss again."

"Was this Ms Zander also at your booze up yesterday?"

"No, she wasn't. I was having a drink with three English teachers who are visiting our school. Don't be so suspicious, that's terrible."

"If you always told the truth, I wouldn't have to be suspicious. But I don't have time for long discussions, I have to go to the office. Will I see you tonight?"

"Of course. I'll be there after six o'clock. We could actually go to the beer garden. It is forecast to be warm and dry."

"We'll see. We can decide that tonight."

Ulla left the apartment at six forty-five and headed for work. Five minutes later, Alex closed the apartment door behind him and drove the three kilometres to the indoor pool. Behind the baths he saw the blue Golf with the final digits 33 on the license plate. The parking lot was quite empty at this time and there was little chance that anyone would recognize him. He parked next to Monika's vehicle and got out. At the same time she opened the passenger door and he sat next to her, leaned over and hugged and kissed her passionately.

"Monika, you scared the hell out of me this morning. Now I'm curious to see what news you have. Has your husband noticed anything about the theft?"

She fixed him firmly in her stare and tried to register every expression on his face.

"I would now first like to hear from you what exactly happened last night."

Alexander looked at her in astonishment.

"Well, I can tell you that quickly. I was in the copy room from 8 pm and had prepared the connecting door to your husband's office so that it wasn't really closed. I was then able to go from the copy room to your husband's office unnoticed. Then I waited for him to leave his office. I hoped he would go to the bathroom. That was finally the case around nine o'clock. I took my prepared SD card, quickly went to his notebook, exchanged the data cards and disappeared back into the copy room. It didn't take thirty seconds."

"Splendid, you did a great job," said Monika, smiling at him tenderly and giving him a passionate kiss.

Alex continued. "Then suddenly my colleague Baum came into the copy room. I was a little scared. But he didn't notice anything, he wanted to make some copies. We then came out of the room together, and our colleague Pobler was standing in front of it. At that moment your husband came back from the bathroom. There was a brief exchange of words and then he was back at his door and disappeared into his office. The two colleagues wanted to invite me for a beer but I refused, mentioning that I had a date. I quickly left the school building, the two colleagues were following slowly. I got into my car, drove three hundred metres to the Matterstrasse intersection and parked the car. Then I called you and waited for Daniel, but he was late. It was after ten o'clock when he got to me."

Monika listened carefully and watched him closely.

"Well, everything went really well. But something else, you haven't read a newspaper or heard the news this morning?"

"No, I usually read the paper at breakfast, and that was cancelled today because I had a conspiratorial meeting with Ms Zander." He grinned. "Did your husband have any suspicions about me?"

Monika looked at him with a relaxed expression. "My husband didn't say anything and he won't say anything either."

Alex grimaced. "What do you mean by that?"

"My husband is dead," said Monika, staring at Alex sharply.

Alexander didn't seem to understand.

"What do you mean, dead?"

Monika smiled coldly now and couldn't hide a certain satisfaction.

"He's dead and you don't seem to know about it. Then I'm glad I didn't fall in love with a murderer."

Alex seemed completely unimpressed on the outside, but enjoyed Monika's admission of love very much and kissed her.

"Please don't tell me ghost stories early in the morning. I still don't know what you mean?"

"My husband was murdered last night."

Now incredulous astonishment was expressing itself on his face.

"What, that's not possible!"

"It's true. But maybe it's better that way."

She paused, put her right hand on his left and looked at him tenderly.

"That's terrible, of course. How did it happen?"

"I don't know, but when my husband didn't come home, I got restless and at about eleven I went to the school to get him. Then I found him lying on the floor in a pool of blood. Someone had beaten him to death."

"That's horrible. I don't know what to say. Who could have done such a thing?"

"I don't know, I'm completely at a loss. But I'm glad that you have nothing to do with it."

"But I ask you, do you seriously think I could have done that?"

"No, of course not. I know that you are a kind and sweet guy." There was a pause, they hugged each other.

"My condolences," said Alex after a while.

"Thank you," Monika continued in a different tone from which a trace of fear could be heard.

"But there is a problem now. You seem to be one of the last to have been inside the school with my husband until late at night. In principle, you are under suspicion. You will be questioned by the police. You must have an alibi."

She looked worried and distant at the same time.

"Of course, we cannot say that you spent the evening with Daniel, because that would raise questions, and he is known to be one of Messerschmidt's employees, so there must be no connection. Can you get an alibi somewhere, Alex?"

He thought for a moment.

"Maybe Ulla. However, we are currently experiencing certain tensions and she distrusts me and fears that I am cheating on her."

"Try to talk to her and make peace. A watertight alibi is vital for your survival. Otherwise there could be in serious trouble. The police won't hesitate if there is a suspicion of murder," said Monika.

Alex looked at her in dismay, and at that moment he realized that he had a real problem and had to solve it alone.

"How can I best reach you if necessary?"

"Definitely not over the phone. My connections and conversations may be monitored because the police will suspect me. After all, I inherit everything. You can send me a letter, if absolutely necessary, but no emails, OK?"

"OK. I hope everything works out."

"I hope so, too. The police department will interrogate me soon.

After all, I will benefit from the death of my husband." She leaned over to Alex, pulled his head towards her and kissed him long and passionately.

"Give it time and then nothing stands in the way of our future."

They tenderly said goodbye to repeated vows of love and then parted. Alex was stunned as he watched her drive out of the parking lot.

3 A Visit from the Police

I was just getting out of the shower when the doorbell rang. I wasn't expecting anyone. It was just before 8 am. Maybe it was one of the neighbours? I came out of the bathroom and went to the house intercom.

"Hello, who is it?" A deep male voice answered.

"Police sergeant Schmidt. Are you Mr Alumno?"

I winced and said, "Yeah, what's up?"

"Could we speak to you for a moment?"

I couldn't suppress the distinct anger in my voice. "I just got out of the shower and I'm in a bathrobe. It really is a very inappropriate moment. What is it all about? Couldn't you have phoned me first?"

"We called you earlier but you didn't answer," said the policeman.

I had indeed always activated the answering machine overnight and this morning I forgot to switch to normal mode.

"We have a few questions for you. It's pretty urgent, but if you can't manage at the moment, you are welcome to come to police headquarters later."

I thought for a moment. In the late morning I wanted to keep the appointment at the Schiller Grammar School, but I could probably arrange it beforehand.

"Well, I could come in about an hour. Who should I contact and where exactly?"

"You know our headquarters at 22 Friedrich Engel Street?"

"Yes, yes, I know."

"Good, then report to Commissioner Sauer there, room 212."

"Okay," I said. "But tell me, is it maybe about the red light that I ran recently?"

"No," said the voice on the other end. "It is a crime and you will only be interviewed."

"And in what matter?"

"I can't explain that to you right now. I ask for your understanding."

"Well, see you later."

I hung up and went back to the bathroom. Police visit at eight in the morning! You can't even take a shower in peace, I thought. What do they want from me? A testimony? A crime? I haven't seen anything, I haven't heard anything! Give me a break! On top of that, it was embarrassing that the police were standing in front of the house. Probably the other residents saw them. And then there would be gossiping and grinning again.

I opened the bathroom window and in fact there was a patrol car down there. The policeman in uniform was just getting into the vehicle. Such a stupid story. That will give them something to talk about. My good reputation is extremely important to me. I'm a freelancer, my reputation is the basis for my livelihood and I might be ruined if even a slight suspicion were to fall on me as a result of such a silly incident.

A crime? Probably a misunderstanding or a mix-up. Annoyed, I finished washing and got dressed because I wanted to get the police visit over with as quickly as possible and then visit Mr Lochberger at his school.

Yesterday evening, after Lochberger's telephone conversation with Becker, I had carried out remote maintenance on his computers and had actually found a virus on his SD card. An old virus that had appeared twenty years ago and destroyed files of all kinds. How this had happened was beyond me. Actually, the infection was only possible by using the data card in another infected computer. In fact, only the data on the SD data card of the headmaster was affected. Neither on his hard disk nor in other areas of the entire school network were any pests found. This indicated that my hypothesis was correct. Lochberger had probably put his card into another computer at home or elsewhere and caught the virus there. I was able to restore most of his data and play it back on the data card. So the headmaster's notebook was okay again.

I got dressed, made myself a coffee, and tried to get rid of my bad mood. Police visit before breakfast! One was spared nothing!

I have nothing against the police, especially not against the German police. They work correctly and you know that there are laws in this country that protect you from arbitrary actions. As a former immigrant, I particularly appreciate that. In Argentina, where I was born, there had been terrible conditions under the military dictatorship a few decades ago, similar to what happened in the Third Reich in Germany. At that time policemen came to the front door at four in the morning and picked people up for an interrogation, a 'testimony', and often these people never came back. They disappeared without a trace and were often murdered.

Thankfully, my mother left Argentina with me before the military dictatorship came to power. We arrived in Berlin in 1955, when I was just three years old. I never got to know my father, my mother was a single parent.

When my mother met Helmut, a Berlin entrepreneur who wanted to marry her, in Buenos Aires in 1955, she accepted the offer and moved to Berlin. However, things did not work out.

The man was still married at the time, going through a divorce, but the matter dragged on and his wife tried to prevent it. For two years we lived with Helmut in his spacious villa and my mother was waiting for the divorce decree, which was repeatedly delayed. I didn't care at the time. I couldn't really understand it anyway. For me the new circumstances were pleasant and exciting. We had a large garden and there was a dog I loved to play with and the maid Carina spoiled me a lot. Helmut was obviously quite wealthy and in his Mercedes we would often drive to Lake Wannsee on weekends or go hiking in the area.

It was a great time and I learned German very quickly. Until I was three years old I had only heard and spoken Spanish. When we moved in with Helmut, he made the condition that only German was to be spoken at home.

"The boy has to learn German, otherwise he won't get very far here. You can still teach him Spanish later on," Helmut had said to my mother. That was indeed very far-sighted of him and a wise decision, although it quickly made me forget the few bits and pieces of my mother tongue, and my mother stuck to his guideline to only speak German to me. Unfortunately, she didn't think about teaching me Spanish later on. It wasn't until my studies that I started to deal with this language myself. My mother only mastered a few bits of German when she moved to Berlin and had to learn it with great difficulty, practically learning it with me at the same time.

The whole thing was actually a running joke in our family history. My mother's mother was a German Jew and emigrated to Argentina in 1931 with her Spanish friend and later husband Joaquin, for fear of the Nazis, which she recognized very early on as a danger. My grandmother had to learn Spanish at the time, and when her daughter, my mother, was born in 1932, the only language spoken at home was Spanish, because my grandfather was a Spaniard and they lived in Argentina.

As a result, my mother grew up without any knowledge of German and the few words that she might have heard from her mother as a baby were quickly forgotten. In two successive generations, a child in our family has not learned the mother's language, which is a strange thing.

After more than fifty years in Germany, my mother couldn't speak German correctly. The only thing I could accuse her of was her lack of seriousness. She never really dealt with German grammar. She constantly made mistakes that would have been accepted from a beginner but which I found embarrassing for someone who had lived in the country for so long. But she was always a loving and good mother and I owe her a lot. So what do a few grammar mistakes mean. In Berlin, where people spoke a dialect, hardly anybody noticed it anyway.

Unfortunately, the wedding never happened, because Helmut was killed in a tragic traffic accident in 1958. It was a great shock and a hard blow for both of us. So my mother kept her maiden name Alumno, and that is the reason why today I still have this Spanish name although I'm a German citizen.

As a freelancer in Germany, I have often found that my name built up certain barriers. I would have had easier access to customers as 'Emil Schulze' or 'Hans Schmidt'. When people hear 'Winfried Alumno' many people pause and then ask me where I'm from. My name triggers a certain suspicion and only when I cross this first threshold do people realize that I am an ordinary German citizen. Indeed my mother officially changed our nationalities in 1970.

My grandmother, who emigrated in 1931, was called Katharina Feigenbaum. I would have preferred the name Feigenbaum and it would have opened some doors more easily to me in my life in Germany than the somewhat exotic name Alumno. But I have come to terms with it and at my age I no longer have any ambitions to change much in my life.

My small company for computer networks has been going very well for years. I have no reason to complain. I am fine here and I often watch TV reports about Argentina with regret and a certain pain. It's awful to see how this once rich country has been run down. So many people there are living in poverty and misery.

I cannot be grateful enough to my dear mother, who unfortunately died last year, for bringing us to Germany back then.

A glance at my watch interrupted my train of thought. It was time for me to prepare for the visit to the police headquarters. I slowly finished my coffee and got ready to go out.

4 An Interview

"Please do not put through any phone calls for the next sixty minutes," Commissioner Sauer said to his secretary, who had just left his office. Opposite him sat Mr Degen, the deputy headmaster of the Schiller Grammar School in Lundenburg, a man in his mid-fifties, with a friendly face, broad-shouldered and strongly built.

"Nice that you could come so quickly," Sauer began the conversation. "It's really incredible what happened there."

"Yes, we are all stunned, it's terrible," Degen replied.

"Do you have any initial suspicions? Was there any colleague who had special conflicts with the headmaster?" asked the inspector, frowning.

"No, we can't figure it out at all. There was always a little friction among some colleagues but nothing out of the ordinary. In professional life there are always conflicts. It won't be much different here with you, I suppose."

"Yes, of course, although it seldom happens that people kill each other because of it."

The commissioner grinned a little maliciously about his own joke.

"No, I cannot imagine that one of my colleagues could have done such a thing," said Degen, defending the honour of his profession.

"Oh, you know, you can imagine a lot when you've been a policeman for thirty years. You don't necessarily have to carry out a murder personally. There are enough people who do quite a lot for money."

"Are you thinking of a contract killing? That sounds a bit too fantastic to me."

"Well, at the moment I can only quote Socrates: I know that I know nothing", he said with a grin and then continued. "We have to go according to plan if we want to get anywhere, and I need your help to do that."

"I would like to assure you of that, Mr Sauer."

"So let's start with last night. How long were you at work yesterday?"

"I left around five o'clock."

"And where were you at the time of the crime, between half past nine and half past ten?"

"Well, you will get to the point in a moment..."

"Every teacher is asked these questions, and I can make no exception for you."

"Quite clear, Mr Sauer, I was home from eight o'clock, with my wife, and we had friends visiting us."

The commissioner noted down each answer.

"Can you tell me the names of your visitors? We have to check all the details of our interrogations, it's just routine."

"Yes, I understand. Mr and Mrs Kiesberger came to visit us. They live in Lundenburg, Herzog Street."

"Thank you, I have noted that down. Your boss was at school very late at night? Did that happen often?"

"Yes, indeed, but not quite as late as yesterday. He usually left between 7 pm and 8 pm."

"Were there other colleagues in the school last night, and if so, until when?"

"I can't really answer the question exactly, we never know who is in the building and who isn't. Colleagues come and go when it suits them, I mean outside of class times."

"So you don't know whether Mr Lochberger was alone in the school building last night, shall we say from eight o'clock?"

"I only know that apparently three colleagues were in the copy room right next to the headmaster's office until around nine. They must have been making photocopies."

"I see, and how do you know that?"

"Mr Lochberger wrote me an email at about a quarter past nine in the evening, in which he claimed that he had been the victim of an attack and that his notebook was infected by viruses."

The superintendent frowned and looked questioningly at Degen.

"Wait a minute, let me explain. The boss went briefly to the bathroom around nine o'clock. When he came back, the teachers Strasser, Baum and Pobler had just come out of the copy room and were obviously about to leave. Everyone said goodbye to the boss. When Mr Lochberger then wanted to continue working, his computer sounded an alarm because of a virus attack. The data on his SD card had been destroyed. He believes that the three teachers had infected his notebook during his absence."

The inspector had listened intently and looked sceptical.

"It's an interesting story but it sounds a bit odd. Do you think it's even possible?"

Degen shook his head, obviously undecided.

"The whole thing sounds like a stupid childish prank but it would be possible. However, I don't see how this incident could be connected to the murder."

"I can't see that at the moment, either. What can you tell me about these three colleagues? Did they have any conflicts with your boss?

Just tell me what you can think of."

"Well, there was a bit of trouble from time to time with them, that's true, but I really wouldn't classify them as potential murderers."

"You shouldn't do that at all, dear Mr Degen, you shouldn't rate anything but help us to put this puzzle together. How have these colleagues been in their dealings with their boss, in your opinion?"

"Well, there were certain initial problems with Strasser. He started school relatively late, almost exactly fifteen years ago. Late means that he was already fifty years old and actually had no school experience."

"How did that come about?" asked Sauer.

"After his state examination, I think that was at the beginning of the eighties, Mr Strasser did not get a teaching position and then started working elsewhere, in adult education."

"And why was he suddenly accepted into the school service after that?" the detective asked.

"After the turn of the millennium, there was a significant shortage of Spanish teachers. Spanish had suddenly become fashionable among students and there was a demand that had not been foreseen. Strasser had studied Spanish, so he was hired out of this acute shortage of teachers."

"And then, did he integrate well into the school?"

"Yes, at first things didn't always go smoothly but those were actually minor things, of no great importance. Mr Strasser was rather reserved, but he got along well with the students."

"And what about Baum and Pobler?"

"Well, Baum was a bit stubborn and had a couple of fights with the boss, but I can't tell you more about it. And Pobler, as the longest-serving colleague, has taken some liberties, including some insubordination, but it was all just talk. I can't imagine that there is still potential for aggression for any acts of violence."

The Commissioner grinned. "Everything sounds terribly harmonious. So, in your view, was there nothing serious that could somehow justify a particular hostility between these teachers and their boss?"

"Well, no, I wouldn't say hostility, but I do remember that the boss occasionally reprimanded some colleagues quite harshly because a class test was supposedly wrongly graded or because some students complained about unfair treatment and so on."

"I see," the superintendent muttered and adopted a thoughtful expression. "Does a headmaster have the time to check students' class tests?"

"Usually not, but if a student complains to him then he has to investigate the matter. But otherwise I don't know anything. As I said, there were minor things and there are always colleagues with certain problems and then a boss has the task of rebuking the colleagues concerned and putting them back on the right track."

"Did you sometimes have the feeling that maybe he wasn't always being tactful enough?"

Mr Degen smiled, a little embarrassed and then said that certainly everyone had their own style in dealing with other people and sometimes the impression was created that the boss was a bit authoritarian and even intimidated some colleagues. But everyone had their own way of doing things, which was ultimately a question of style, and he didn't want to comment on that.

"You don't always make friends behaving like that, do you? Have any teachers left the school recently? Were there early retirements or transfers to other schools?"

Mr Degen thought for a moment and then said that there were a number of colleagues who had moved, mostly for family or personal reasons. Some employment contracts had been terminated prematurely over the past few years because some colleagues did not want to work until they reached the statutory age limit. The superintendent grinned mischievously.

"I find that difficult to understand. Do these people have such dream jobs and want to quit early!"

Mr Degen was grinning too now. "Well, you can join us as an intern for a month on a trial basis. Let's see if you are still talking about a dream job."

"It was a little joke," the inspector apologized. "I know that being a teacher is tough these days."

Mr Degen shrugged his shoulders in agreement.

Now there was a knock on the door. Mr Sauer called, "Just a minute," got up, went to the door, opened it a crack and exchanged a few words with a man and then came back to his desk.

"The next person is already here. This murder gives us a mountain of additional work," groaned Sauer. "I want to come back to these three colleagues you named, Strasser, Baum and Pobler. Is there anything else that might be of interest to us?"

"I don't know, but, Mr Strasser, by the way, is leaving early at the end of the school year, one year before reaching retirement."

"I see." The inspector thought about it. "Do you think this early departure from school has anything to do with his antipathy towards his boss?"

Mr Degen considered and pulled the corners of his mouth down and hunched his shoulders as if to express that it was difficult to say.

"It has just occurred to me that there was once a letter that Strasser wrote to the boss, that was about a year ago. He made very negative comments about him which were almost insulting."

The superintendent raised his eyebrows. "Interesting. Could you send me a copy of this letter?"

"Yes, sure, I'll email you a copy."

"Thank you. Well, we will talk to all the teachers personally. Another question. How is access to the school building regulated? Can every teacher enter the school building at any time?"

"Yes, that's the way it is. The building is locked by the janitor in the evening at around 6 pm but the colleagues all have a key and can enter the school building at any time of the day or night."

"Without doubt this is a security risk, you don't have any entrance controls?"

"That's correct."

"Then anyone could have gotten into the school building yesterday evening. For example, some vagrant. Wouldn't an electronic entry control be a sensible thing?"

"Yes, but as is so often the case here, finances are the decisive factor. We have no money for that and the country does not want to provide any funds for it. Such an electronic system can easily run into tens of thousands of euros."

"I see. That is difficult to implement."

Mr Degen agreed. "Security is certainly a hot issue. Anyone can walk into any school building at any time and in the past few months we have had several cases of homeless types who tried to get into the school toilets. I'm not sure whether this concept of open school buildings will really be sustainable in the long term."

Mr Sauer raised his eyebrows with a critical look. "Your boss might still be alive if there were such entry controls."

Mr Degen was silent and made a gesture of helplessness.

"My son," continued the inspector, "was in the USA for a student exchange last year and told me that the entrance doors to the school are locked during class and that there are even security guards."

"Yes, I know that. Our colleagues always tell us that when they return from the United States. But these are different cultures and such a concept has so far not been implemented anywhere in Europe."

"Good," said the superintendent raising his left hand in a gesture that indicated that he couldn't figure out the whole matter at all.

"I will try to interview all the members of staff in the next few days. The school holidays will start soon. Do you think it is possible that I can speak to everybody before the holidays start?"

"I don't know, there are certainly some who are leaving on their first day of vacation."

"Could you perhaps send a circular letter to the staff and tell them I'd like to speak to those people right at the beginning of the week?"

"Yes, certainly. I will then email you the list of these colleagues and then you can arrange everything else."

"Great, that's how we'll do it. Thank you for your visit, Mr Degen, we'll stay in touch. If you find anything new that might be of interest, please call me immediately or write to me, here is my card."

"Thank you, I will. By the way, I'll be here for the next two weeks. We haven't planned our vacation until mid-August so you can reach me at home anytime."

"Well, then let's try to shed some light on this and I hope that from the further conversations with your colleagues there will be more clarity in the matter. There must have been an enemy or a motive, a murder doesn't usually come out of the blue, so we have to find the motive and that will be our first and foremost goal. Thank you again for your help, Mr Degen."

"You're welcome. Have a nice afternoon, Mr Sauer."

"Well, nice afternoon is easy to say. I'll have the press conference later at four pm. The press is incredibly curious but I won't be able to tell them very much today. See you then, take care."

5 So Many Questions

My apartment was not far away from police headquarters, so I walked there. I wasn't quite comfortable with the whole thing, and I hadn't the slightest idea about what the police wanted from me. While pondering this question, the only thing that occurred to me was the red light, but the officer had talked about a crime. The police headquarters, resembling a great glass palace, was already in front of me and I asked at reception for Commissioner Sauer. "Second floor, room 212," the officer said curtly, without changing his expression. I took the elevator and went up to the second floor. These public buildings always seem repulsive to me. Long corridors in ugly shades of grey, many locked doors behind which fates are decided. Here and there individuals sat in front of the rooms waiting to be let in. I stood in front of room 212, read the nameplate, hesitated a few seconds and then knocked twice.

"Just a minute!" I heard a strong male voice from inside and immediately afterwards the door opened a crack. A grey-haired head pushed through the doorway and looked at me questioningly.

"Hello, my name is Alumno. I have an appointment with Mr Sauer," I said.

"Hello Mr Alumno," the official replied in a friendly manner, without coming out from behind the door. "I'll be right with you, but please have a seat. I have a meeting at the moment, it won't take long. I'll call you in."

I nodded in agreement, the door closed again and I sat down on one of the three wooden chairs. The little table next to me was bare, a few magazines would have been nice. At the left end of the seemingly endless corridor, two older women were sitting in front of another office. I had never been here in this new building. Luckily I rarely have contact with the police.

There was an incident a few years ago where the police really got on my nerves. Policemen kept coming to me for weeks and repeatedly demanding testimony about a robbery that happened at night in our residential area. One night around one o'clock I heard screams from outside. A woman was calling loudly for help. I was still awake and opened the window, but couldn't see anything. The cries for help could be clearly heard from somewhere nearby out in the dark. Nobody else seemed to hear this. No other window opened, apparently everyone was sound asleep. When the woman's screaming didn't stop, I called the police emergency number. The officer on the phone said he was going to send a patrol car right away, and he asked for my personal details. After that, I went to bed. The yells from outside stopped immediately after I had called, and then I fell asleep but about an hour later my doorbell rang. I staggered towards the intercom, drunk with sleep. Two policemen wanted to speak to me about my emergency call. I was really upset about being dragged out of bed in the middle of the night but I pressed the button for the front door. Two young officers stormed upstairs. I let them in, otherwise they would have woken up the other residents of the house by talking loudly in the stairwell.

"I didn't call the police to get me out of bed at night," I complained.

"We're sorry," said one of the two uniformed men, "but we're looking for that woman you heard screaming. We haven't found anything in the area. Can you tell us a little more? Did the woman say anything? Where exactly do you think the cries came from?"

"If I knew more I would have already told you on the phone," I growled sleepily and in a bad mood. "And no, I have no idea where the screams came from. They seemed to come from somewhere nearby but I can't tell you which way and I haven't seen anything either. And next time I will think carefully about making such a call again if I am to be woken up afterwards at two o'clock in the morning."

The officer apologized for the disturbance. He had hoped to learn more. After all, a crime might have occurred. The two of them left me again and stomped down the stairs. Everything was quiet again, but I couldn't sleep for hours.

Of course, the neighbours in the building had woken up at that time and the next day a nosy busybody asked me what was going on and why the police had come to me.

So I was asked to tell the whole story several times to the entire building, and when, the next day, it was in the newspaper that a young woman had been attacked and robbed nearby, the excitement was of course great and the police came again, to record my statement. The policemen didn't come just once but several times, although different ones came each time and they kept asking the same questions, which almost drove me to the edge of distraction. That was five years ago. At that time I swore to myself that in the future I would simply ignore any screams from women at night. And now these annoying people want a testimony from me. I just want to know about what? A crime? The whole thing must be a misunderstanding. The door to room 212 suddenly opened and a tall man of about fifty who looked familiar to me, came out. He greeted me briefly by nodding his head but took off with a quick pace and had already disappeared into the stairwell when I realized that it was the deputy headmaster of the Schiller Grammar School who had just stormed past me.

"Come in," called a resolute voice from inside and I closed the door behind me. The superintendent rose from his chair, came up to me, and shook my hand. "Sauer, very pleased to meet you. Nice that you could come, it's relatively urgent. I'm sorry you had to wait a bit, there is a lot going on here today. Have a seat."

"I'm really curious to see what's so urgent. This morning your colleague on the intercom gave me a hint that it was a crime, but I don't know what I have to do with any crime."

"So much the better," said the Commissioner with a slight smile. "I have prepared a few questions and I would ask you to answer them spontaneously."

I nodded and looked expectantly at the Commissioner.

"First question: do you know a Mr Lochberger?"

"Yes I know Mr Lochberger," I said. "He is one of my business partners."

"Can you briefly describe the nature of your business relationship?"

"With pleasure. Mr Lochberger is the headmaster of the Schiller school here in Lundenburg and we met two years ago when the school's computer network was being expanded. The teachers there encountered certain technical problems and I was asked to help expand the network. Networks are my speciality, I am a freelancer. This is how my maintenance contract with the school came about and since then I have been there several times to help out with difficulties."

"And how did he appear to you personally, what would you say, was he friendly or perhaps difficult to deal with?"

I was puzzled. "Why do you use the past tense when you are talking about him? He called my company last night and I want to visit him at his school later."

The inspector was apparently a little embarrassed and apologized.

"You are right, one has to be careful with the language, so I correct myself: How does he appear to you personally, are there any problems in dealing with him?"

"No, none at all. There have not been any difficulties so far. On the contrary, it has always been a very constructive cooperation. He is a personable guy and has an understanding of the subject matter, that is, of computers. And that of course makes cooperation easier than if you have clients who understand little or nothing about the matter."

"You have just said that you spoke to him on the phone last night. What was it about and when was the call?"

"Well, I didn't talk to him personally, but my employee, Mr Becker was on call last night, he conducted the conversation and then told me about it. Mr Lochberger had problems with a virus attack on his computer and the data on his SD card was illegible, a malware had destroyed it, and so he called us. It was around a quarter past nine. He asked Mr Becker to fix his computer via remote maintenance. I came home about five minutes after this call and then I took care of the matter right away. But now I'm curious why you are asking so intensely about my relationship with Mr Lochberger and his school."

"You haven't read or heard any local news today?"

His question worried me.

"That is actually true. I haven't had the chance because your people rang my doorbell shortly before eight and asked me here. What is it that I could have read in the newspaper?"

The superintendent raised his eyebrows and announced the unpleasant news.

" The headmaster of the school was attacked."

"What? That is not possible!" I was upset.

"Unfortunately it is. And now we're trying to find out who could have done it."

"I understand, and how is Mr Lochberger now?"

The inspector tightened his lips. "He was fatally injured."

"For God's sake," I said. I was really shocked.

"Well, that's probably how everyone reacted who knew the man. The question now is who could have had an interest in killing him? By the way, where were you between 9:30 and 10 pm?"

"I took a walk from about half past eight to twenty past nine and then I was at home without interruption. As I told you, I came home about five minutes after the headmaster called. My colleague Becker was in my office until shortly before 10 pm and I was busy with the remote maintenance of Mr Lochberger's computer until about half past ten, as can be seen from the maintenance logs."

The Commissioner took notes of the statements and continued with the interview.

"Do you know anyone of the teaching staff?"

"Yes," I replied, still dazed by the bad news. "I know the deputy headmaster, Mr Degen, who is also always there for the network administration. I also have an old friend from our school days who teaches there, namely a Mr Strasser."

The commissioner didn't change his expression and asked further.

"Yes, I've heard the name Strasser before. How would you describe Mr Strasser and his attitude towards the school and especially towards the school management?"

I thought about it for a moment, Alexander had told me some of the internal goings on of school life when we occasionally met for a beer and in fact he had sometimes scolded the school management and especially expressed his anger at the headmaster quite openly. But now was probably not the time to disclose such details.

"I know relatively little about Mr Strasser's attitude towards the school management. I can't remember him talking to me about it."

"Well, I'm a little surprised. You are close friends, aren't you?"

"Yes, we have known each other for many years and meet occasionally to exchange ideas."

"How often do you see each other on average?"

"Well, I would say about once or twice a month, depending on the circumstances. We go out to dinner and chat a little."

"But I imagine Mr Strasser also talks a bit about the school every now and then, right?"

"Of course we tell each other something about work. We are in very different worlds, me in data processing and he as a language teacher. There are not too many overlaps and yet it is sometimes interesting to catch a glimpse of a different professional field."

"When was the last time you saw your friend Mr Strasser?"

I thought for a moment. "That would be the weekend before last, on Sunday evening."

"And did he mention anything about conflicts with the headmaster or school problems?"

"No, on the contrary, he was happy about his imminent retirement and we talked about the future and what we would do in the remaining years of life."

"Okay."

The superintendent cleared his throat and now looked very serious.

"Mr Alumno, we contacted you this morning because we requested the telephone connection data and could see from it that you were Mr Lochberger's last phone contact. Perhaps your employee noticed something during this phone call that could help us. Please ask him if he heard someone else in the background or whether anything else struck him as suspicious."

"I'll ask him but I think he would have told me if anything had been suspicious. The headmaster was of course quite nervous because he suddenly had this virus attack on his computer and could no longer work, but Mr Becker was able to calm him down again. We have experience with such things. Something was strange, though. The virus on the headmaster's data card came from the nineties."

"That's too complicated for me. Please explain, how does such an old malware get onto the headmaster's computer when such great virus scanners are installed everywhere?"

"I wondered about that too," I said thoughtfully. "In my opinion, there is actually only one possible explanation. The headmaster must have used the data card in another infected computer and caught the pest there. All attacks via the school network would have been blocked by the system."

The Commissioner took notes.

"Is it also theoretically possible that someone could have taken the data card from the headmaster's computer and put it into another infected computer?"

I pondered for a moment.

"In principle, it would be possible. But of course the question arises here as to the purpose of this operation. Why would someone do such a thing? A prank by a student might be conceivable. But why would a murderer stage such a fuss. That seems to me very absurd."

"Well, there is no direct connection with the murder at first," admitted the inspector. "But maybe the perpetrator just wanted to keep the victim at work for as long as possible. He probably assumed that Mr Lochberger would try to solve the problem that same evening and that he would be in the schoolhouse until late at night."

"Possible, but the whole thing seems a bit speculative to me."

"Well, I'll tell you something now. When you knocked on my door earlier, Mr Degen from Schiller Grammar School was sitting here with me. He told me that Mr Lochberger wrote him an email yesterday at a quarter past nine, in which he claimed that the teachers Strasser, Baum and Pobler had somehow put this virus onto his computer when he was briefly out of his office. Lochberger immediately suspected the men mentioned because no one else was in the school. The connecting door to the copy room was not locked, the door handle had been tampered with. Furthermore, Mr Strasser apparently had written a letter to his boss about a year ago, which Mr Degen rated as rather offensive and in which a certain hostility can be seen."

I was dismayed by this and looked embarrassed.

"I don't know anything about that. Don't say that you suspect Mr Strasser of murder!"

"At the moment everyone is equally under suspicion. Every teacher in the school, every student, the janitor, even the cleaners," the inspector tried to reassure me. "But I want to talk to all of the teachers as soon as possible."

"Well, that will be the best, I'm sure," I said.

"Really a strange story. A virus attack would be outrageous, but a murder, completely impossible! I have known Mr Strasser for many years. He certainly could not have killed anyone."

"Anyway, we urgently need a conversation with him. On Monday we want to talk to as many teachers as possible. I hope that I'll see him then, too."

I nodded and looked worried.

"From my side that's about it for now, Mr Alumno. Your explanation about the virus infection and so on was very helpful, that's not always easy to understand for a layman like me. Thank you in any case. Can I reach you within the next few days, if any questions arise?"

I nodded. "Yes, actually I'll be here the whole of August. I don't like to travel in the high season. So I'll definitely be in Lundenburg until the end of August."

"Very well, then we'll stay in touch and if you can think of anything else, give me a call, will you?" We both rose from our chairs. We said goodbye with a handshake and I made my way home.

My head was buzzing with everything I had just learned. Was it possible that Alexander was involved in a crime, even murder? It seemed incredible to me. But of course I was also very surprised about this virus story. However, there was certainly a reasonable explanation for that. It was grotesque that they wanted to blame my friend for this. Maybe the other colleagues Mr Sauer had mentioned were behind it. I decided to investigate the matter and speak to Alex soon and ask him to dispel all suspicions through an open and honest conversation.

6 A Staff Meeting

The deputy headmaster stood in the hall of the new building and waited for the chaotic babble of voices of the teachers to subside. The main edifice had been closed by the police for forensic investigation, and eighty chairs had been set up in the annexe to hold the briefing at this makeshift meeting place. Daylight penetrated unhindered through the glass roof of the modern structure and with it the solar radiation, which was already causing the temperature on the upper floor to rise to over thirty degrees. Since its construction over ten years ago, students and teachers had been sweating in class in the summer. Air conditioning had not been installed as being too costly, and the windows could only be opened towards the school garden, the street noise being too loud at the front. In warm weather everyone hated the place, which the local press had praised as a "pearl of modern architecture" at the inauguration. The architect Dr. Hans-Balthasar Neumann had even received the first prize for his idea of a concrete block with a glass roof and wooden cladding.

Gradually the noise subsided and the staff noticed that Mr Degen wanted their attention.

"Dear colleagues," he began his speech. His voice sounded pained and somewhat gloomy. "You all know that our Headmaster, Mr Lochberger, was murdered last night. We are all stunned at the moment and can't understand how something like this could happen at our school."

He looked around the hall. The teachers were all very serious, some looked sad and some faces showed tears.

"These dramatic and sad events," continued the deputy headmaster, "demand that we have to change our program for the last days of the school year. This morning I had a conversation with the police and was instructed to tell you that all colleagues of our school are hereby summoned for an interview. In view of the short time until the start of the holidays, no written summons will be sent. With this message to you today, the invitation is deemed to have been completed and I will send this information to all colleagues again today by email. Please note the attendance list and make a note so that we know who is missing today and must therefore be informed separately."

He paused briefly and looked for the list. "We and the police are faced with a riddle. At the moment nobody has the slightest idea who might have committed this crime. The police are hoping for help from us, and that's why it is so important that all of you attend these interviews before you start into the holidays. Don't get me wrong, we are to be heard as witnesses, not as accused. However, the Commissioner,

Mr Sauer, told me today that at the moment, in principle, anyone who had access to the school building is suspect."

Mr Degen cleared his throat and reached for the glass of water on his table.

"In particular, I was told to ask you about the intended start of your vacation. The reason for this is simply that those people will be the first to be invited for a police interview, while the others will be invited later. I would therefore ask you to put your names on the list that is now circulating and to make a note of when you want to leave. Those who are leaving early will then be invited to the police interviews on Monday of next week. The lessons on Monday, that means our planned projects, can only take place here. The old building is temporarily out of bounds due to the police investigation. All colleagues who can go outside with their groups should please do so, otherwise we cannot get by with the premises here. Wednesday of next week is our last school day with the issuing of certificates. We will do this according to plan, but the small party in the afternoon will be cancelled in consideration of current events. Let me summarize again. We are all asked to appear for the interviews with the police and I must warn you not to take this lightly. As I said, in principle, each of us is suspect. So please attend. From Monday morning a list with the names and appointments will be placed outside the headmaster's office, so everyone will know when it will be his or her turn."

There was now a noticeable agitation among the teachers. Many were talking in hushed tones to the people sitting next to them.

"Please be patient, we will soon be at the end of our meeting. Do you have any questions?"

The senior teacher Willig stood up and spoke. "I would like to say three things. Firstly, in many conversations with my colleagues, I was asked again and again why our headmaster was at the school so late last night? You could perhaps say something about that, Mr Degen. Secondly, of course, after this terrible act, the subject of security has come to the fore for all of us. Many of the colleagues I have spoken to say that they now feel unsafe here on the school premises, especially when, for example, they have afternoon classes and there are only a few people in the school. And thirdly, in connection with this, the question of whether we shouldn't limit the time of evening access to the premises to a relatively early time, say around 6 pm, simply for security reasons."

Mr Willig sat down and Mr Degen spoke again. "To your first question, why Mr Lochberger was at school yesterday at half past ten, I can only answer that he was obviously preparing documents for the general teachers' conference on Tuesday, where he was to have spoken, in particular about the success and the evaluations of the courses of our Schiller FIX program up to now. This meeting will be postponed till September. Mr Lochberger was often in the school for a long time in the evenings but as far as I know he usually went home between 8 and 9 pm. Why he was here until so late yesterday, I can't say for sure. And on your other points, it's good that you brought them up. I had almost forgotten. In the school management we have actually decided that with immediate effect the school may no longer be entered after 7 pm, or that everyone must have left by that time, at the latest. The main building is already sealed by the police and the locks have been replaced. Our janitor is instructed to make an inspection at seven o'clock and he will also take his dog with him, for safety reasons. So please make sure, 7 pm is the absolute closing time. Anyone who is in the school afterwards is guilty of an official offence and, moreover, he would also undermine our security precautions.

And most importantly, of course, please always lock the door when you leave or when you arrive late in the afternoon. This applies from 5 pm onwards. Nobody should be able to come into the school unnoticed."

Ms Pfeifel, sitting at the back, got up to speak. "That is exactly the point that we have often discussed. There are no entrance controls. It's scandalous. There is nothing like that in any medium-sized company, let alone large companies. That also shows how little education is worth to us as a society. We just accept it that anyone can simply walk into the building without difficulty because no one will prevent him from doing so. An intruder can easily hide and then wait until everyone has left. This situation is untenable and I would argue that we should consider how we can change this state of affairs at the start of the school year, after the holidays. It's a bad joke if the police now suspect us teachers of having something to do with the murder, while the buildings are open to everyone at any time and there is no control whatsoever. I just can't understand it. What does the management plan to change this situation?"

Mr Degen looked helpless. "You all know that we have spoken about this topic many times, and all of my attempts with the regional council have so far been unsuccessful because we were told quite clearly that they cannot establish special regulations for our school. If such an entry check is really necessary then it would have to be introduced nationwide and that would run into tens of millions of euros.

So we will hardly get any help from the regional council. If we want to change anything, it must be a private initiative that we would have to carry out on our own. But I don't know at the moment how that would work or how we could get the funds for it. I hope the teaching staff can come up with some ideas on this. Please think about it in the next few weeks, then we can discuss this at the beginning of the new school year and maybe we can find a solution. Any more questions?"

Mr Degen looked around expectantly. No more raised hands could be seen.

"Well, then I hereby dissolve the meeting and point out once again that the circulating list should be filled out by everyone and that the list with the police appointments will be displayed from Monday. I wish you all a good weekend and hope that all of you will be able to cope with this severe blow. It is indeed a very painful experience and it will probably keep us busy for a long time. Get home safely. See you on Monday."

Some colleagues got up in a hurry and pushed their way through the fully occupied entrance hall to the exit while others stayed seated and talked. There was a considerable level of noise within a very short time and discussions were going on everywhere.

"Well, I don't understand why Lochi had to stay until midnight," said the senior teacher Pobler to the person next to him.

"It's only in the evenings that you find any peace and quiet here, and he wanted to concentrate on his projects undisturbed," replied his counterpart, Mr Strasser.

"Oh. He had peace and quiet all day. Always locking himself in his cubbyhole. He didn't even notice what was happening here at school."

"Well, that's an exaggeration. He always had appointments for meetings, I think he did have a busy schedule," said the third person in the group, Mrs Woller.

"If you ask me, it's all excessive ambition and pathological. No sensible person sits at a desk at night and stares at a computer. The man lacked balance, he was overly ambitious," Pobler exclaimed excitedly.

Senior teacher Otter spoke next. "Yes, he was keen on success, but above all he wanted to prove to us in the next conference that his project is so wonderful."

"Schiller FIX, fantastic, innovative, excellent. That's a big deal, honestly," mocked Mr Pobler ironically. "Lochi was a mathematician, and for those guys minus times minus equals plus. That's the only way to understand the whole thing. That means, a reform with a big minus multiplied by a headmaster with the same minus results in a plus according to this calculation, namely Schiller FIX."

His listeners grinned, but Strasser said, "But the vast majority were in favour, so it's pointless to complain about it."

Pobler gave his colleague a sharp look. "A majority in favour, what nonsense! The majority chickened out and abstained, that's what it was! In the first vote for this so-called Hinterwalden model, only twenty-three out of eighty voted in favour, seven were against, and fifty voted by abstention. That is how the decision came about. Majority? No way! Lochi has always been good at manipulating the whole team here."

"Well, it's your own fault if you allow yourself to be manipulated. I voted against it," shouted Hochstetter from the left side.

"Yes, you are one of the few who have guts enough to oppose the school administration but the others are scared shitless."

"Now don't overdo it," said Strasser. "I also voted against it, by the way."

"I know," said Pobler appreciatively. "But I am not exaggerating, it is a fact, and..." - now he spoke more softly, almost in a whisper - "look at our staff council. What are they doing, buying drinks and sweets for events but when the going gets tough and you need help to enforce something against the school management, you don't hear from them, do you?"

"Come on now, you're exaggerating, you're in a bad mood again today," said Woller. "Go home to your wife. Maybe there will be something good to eat for lunch."

"I suppose," replied Pobler, "but Lochi doesn't need anything to eat, he has eaten enough for one lifetime."

"Hey, steady on," muttered Strasser, "that's a dreadful thing to say. It sounds like you're happy about his fate."

And Hochstetter said with a grin, "Well, that's suspicious, I think I'll have to tell the police, that Mr Pobler made such derogatory comments."

"You bullshitter," said Pobler, "don't mess around with the cops, otherwise there's going to be trouble, my friend."

Strasser looked astonished and rebuked the opponents: "Stop this nonsense, it will probably be best if we all go now. Almost everyone has gone and we are still sitting here as if we had nothing better to do."

The proposal met with general approval and everyone stood up, packed their belongings and left the hall, continuing the discussion. Strasser and his colleagues were just about to go outside when the thunderous voice of the deputy headmaster rang out:

"Messrs Pobler, Baum and Strasser, please come and see me in the parents' office."

Alexander Strasser suspected something and he felt a chill running down his spine. Pobler grumbled to himself: "Now he's going to ask us whether we killed Lochi because we were in the school house so late last night."

Baum laughed sarcastically. "That would really be the last straw!"

Mr Degen stood in the long, dark corridor where the staff room, technical and conference rooms were located and waited for the colleagues who slowly came up to him.

"I would like to speak to you briefly, gentlemen, and I will invite you in one by one. Let's start with you, Mr Strasser."

"Have a seat," said the deputy headmaster after he had closed the door.

"You were in the school building for a relatively long time last night, Mr Strasser."

"Yes, that's true, I still had a lot to copy for the project days."

"I want to get straight to the point," said Mr Degen. "There is an email from Mr Lochberger written at a quarter past nine on the night of the murder, in which he claims that his computer was infected with viruses. At least, that malware suddenly appeared on his data card, and he writes that he suspects you and the other two colleagues because you were in the copy room next door until 9 pm. What do you think of that?" Strasser was appalled by this revelation and couldn't hide his shock.

"Well, Mr Degen, you don't think I have anything to do with the murder, do you?"

"No, I don't. But at the moment it's not about the murder. It's the boss's SD card."

"I really don't know what you're talking about," Strasser said excitedly, "I don't know anything about any SD cards, I was just in the copy room and made some photocopies."

"Mr Lochberger went to the bathroom at around 9 pm. Until then his computer was working without any problems. When he came back you had just left the copy room, right?"

"Yes, that's correct. I had finished my work and came out of the room when Mr Lochberger came towards me. Mr Baum and Mr Pobler were there, too."

"After a short break from work, Mr Lochberger noticed a virus attack on his computer. He also noticed that all the data on the SD card was illegible and that everything had been working without any problems before he left his office."

"That could have been anything. Why did he suspect us then?"

"There was nobody else in the building except you, and the head-master found that the connecting door to the copy room was open, so he suspected that one of you was the culprit."

Strasser had turned pale and he was obviously very uncomfortable.

"I have nothing to do with it, believe me."

"The question is whether the police will believe you too, Mr Strasser. The facts are already out, and there is a certain amount of suspicion against you."

"Suspicion of what," shouted Strasser excitedly?

"Are you trying to blame me for the murder?"

Mr Degen was silent and seemed to be thinking. Strasser saw Degen's penetrating look, waiting for an answer. He was in a bind, what to do? He lost his train of thought. He had to get rid of the suspicion of murder at all costs, but now to admit the data theft would suddenly make him the prime suspect.

"I'm sorry, all I can say about this accusation is that it is false. I have nothing to do with the headmaster's computer problems."

"Good, I take note of your statement. Then I will talk to the next person. I wish you a nice weekend."

"The same to you, Mr Degen".

The deputy headmaster showed the man out and then took the other two colleagues for a one-on-one interview. Pobler roared indignantly and furiously when he was confronted with the suspicions.

"Well, Mr Degen, you know, that's the height of insolence. I've been at this school for thirty years, and now you dare to question me? I'm not ready to continue this conversation alone. I demand the pres-ence of a staff council, who is then supposed to testify and record this imposition. I have nothing more to say at the moment, Mr Degen. Good afternoon."

With that he rose without further ado and stormed out of the room.

"Ridiculous theatricals," he called out to his waiting colleague Baum. "It's like a bloody kindergarten here!"

Meanwhile the deputy headmaster was standing in the doorway and asked the last person to come to his room.

"Mr Baum, Mr Pobler tends to have emotional outbursts. I hope we can talk calmly and objectively. You were in the copy room with Mr Strasser yesterday evening around 9 pm, is that correct?"

Mr Baum answered in the affirmative.

"There is an email from Mr Lochberger last night in which he claims that his computer was tampered with while he was briefly in the bathroom and that he suspects you and the other two colleagues. It seems the door connecting the copy room and the principal's office was open. Someone had tampered with the door handle. What do you think of that?"

"I can only say that I have nothing to do with it at all. The accusation is quite absurd and fits well with the twisted mind of Mr Lochberger, who apparently sees mainly enemies among his staff and therefore behaves often with hostility towards them."

Baum looked challengingly at the deputy headmaster.

"I'm sorry, that's all I have to say and it is sad that there is such a level of suspicion at this school. I am not ready for further questioning now. I will give my statement to the police on Monday. Goodbye, Mr Degen."

Degen looked puzzled when Baum got up and left the room straight away. That was a complete success, thought the deputy principal and went to the staff room to check the incoming emails before he left the school.

7 Monika's Statement

Monika Lochberger had correctly suspected that the police were in quite a hurry to talk to her. Around eleven o'clock in the morning her doorbell rang and two plain-clothes officers stood outside the door.

"Good afternoon Mrs Lochberger. We are from the Criminal Investigation Department. We'd like to ask you a few questions." They both had their identity cards out in front of them.

Monika glanced at them. A Mrs Steiger and a Mr Graf stood before her. She nodded.

"First of all, our sincere condolences on the death of your husband. Could you spare a few minutes?"

"Yes of course, please come in."

She led the officers down the hall into the large living room and asked them to sit down.

"Mrs Lochberger, we know that the shock of this incident is, of course, very recent, and we only want to question you briefly. Perhaps you can remember something that will help us find your husband's killer."

"I understand completely," said Mrs Lochberger. "Please ask your questions. I will of course do everything I can to help you."

"First of all, at what time did you speak to your husband last night, by telephone."

"That was just after nine. I called him and asked him why he still wasn't home. He said he had a problem with his computer and that's why he was late, but he wanted to leave in the next few minutes and come back."

"And what happened?"

"Well, of course, I know he likes to forget the time whenever he's brooding over his work. When he still wasn't here at 10:30, I called the school again, but he didn't answer. Neither did he answer any calls on his mobile. It rang a few times and then the answering machine came on. I was a bit worried, and when there was still no message from him in the next few minutes, I became concerned and drove over to the school, which is only ten minutes away from us. His car was still parked in the teachers' car park but all the lights in the building were off. I pulled into the car park, I have a key for it..."

Inspector Graf interrupted. "You have a key to the car park. Do you also have a key to the building?"

"No, only for the car park. I occasionally drove my husband to work or picked him up, so he got me a key."

The two officers nodded in agreement. Mrs Lochberger continued.

"So after I'd parked my car, I tried to see if the back door was open, and in fact I managed to get in without a key, it was not locked. I turned on the light and I got a terrible shock. My husband was lying on the floor in a pool of blood. I tried to talk to him. He was on his front. I felt his face, but he looked lifeless, I could not feel a pulse either. I immediately called the emergency services and asked for an ambulance and the police. I was not sure if my husband was dead or just unconscious. Five minutes later a patrol car arrived, the ambulance arrived shortly afterwards. The doctor could only confirm his death. Your colleagues from Homicide and Forensics came and searched the entire area for clues."

She took a deep breath. One could feel the memory stirring in her.

"Mrs Lochberger, do you have any idea who might be behind this murder? Did your husband have any enemies?"

"I really cannot imagine who could do such a thing. And I am not aware of any hostility. He actually always tried to get along with everybody reasonably well, so I don't think he had any adversaries."

"Of course, we will interview all the teachers at the school, but after initial talks with the deputy headmaster, Mr Degen, there are no indications of serious hostilities among the staff. We must therefore include the possibility that a stranger may have entered the school and committed this murder. However, the motive is still completely unclear to us. Do you know if your husband had a wallet or purse with him?"

"Yes, of course, he never left the house without it. He always carries it in his jacket, in his breast pocket, and inside he has his ID, driver's license, credit cards and cash. You didn't find that on him?"

"No, we didn't find any papers on his body. Do you remember if he had his wallet with him?"

"I really wasn't looking for it. I was so shocked and concerned about his condition, I didn't check his jacket pocket."

"That would mean, however, that we are dealing with a robbery-homicide. Do you know how much cash your husband usually carried around with him?"

"Usually around a hundred euros, but he always had a credit card and an EC card."

"Well, that's all for now, from our side. Here is my card with phone number and email address. If you think of anything that might help us, please let us know immediately. And please send us the details of your husband's credit and debit cards. It's possible the killer used them to make purchases."

"Yes, thank you for the information. I'll send you the numbers later. I hope you find the murderer soon."

"We will do our utmost," said Inspector Steiger. Her colleague Graf added, "We will stay in contact with you and inform you as soon as there are any new developments."

"By the way, if you wish, we can send you a member of our psychological service. They are trained to help victims to process traumatic experiences. You can also contact us by phone if you don't want to decide at the moment."

"Thank you very much but at the moment I prefer to be alone. If it's too much for me, I will gladly accept your offer and call you."

"Mrs Lochberger, once again our condolences and as I said, our offer of help is available."

She led the officers to the front door and said goodbye. She stood in the open door until they got into their car and drove away, then closed the door and sighed.

8 Press Conference

Shortly before 4 pm Commissioner Sauer went down to the basement in the elevator. He was quite nervous and also a bit annoyed about this case, which would absorb all resources over the next few days. The conference room was already rather full with an estimated twenty journalists and television people present. TV cameras were being set up and journalists were standing around in the room talking.

Sauer went to the lectern and greeted those present.

"Good afternoon, ladies and gentlemen, please take your seats, our press conference will start in a few moments. We are still waiting for your colleagues from Southwest Television, who will be a little late due to traffic problems."

One of the employees put refreshments on the tables and the journalists sat down and started opening their laptops.

The journalist from Southwest Television just then came in with his cameraman. Sauer went to the door, shook his hand and exchanged a few words with him. The tripod was unfolded and the camera was set up. Sauer slowly walked back to his lectern and looked around expectantly. The murmuring slowly subsided and the journalists all concentrated on the speaker.

"Good afternoon, ladies and gentlemen, we can actually start now. I would like to welcome you most warmly to our press conference today, the occasion of which is unfortunately a very sad one. Last night, between nine thirty and ten o'clock, Mr Lochberger, was murdered in the Schiller Grammar School. The headmaster was killed by blows to the head with a blunt object. The murder was discovered last night at about 11 pm, when the victim's wife arrived at the school to check on her husband, whom she had been expecting at home long before.

Our specialists arrived at the school before midnight and began the forensic examination. For reasons pertaining to the case in question, I cannot give you any details about the status of the ongoing investigations at the moment.

However, we have found traces that we suspect might possibly lead to the capture of the perpetrator or perpetrators. However, all this is still very speculative. Further investigations will naturally focus on the question of a murder motive.

All the teachers at the school will be questioned in the course of the next few days. So far, talks with staff members of the school have not revealed any indications of motive. However, it is still too early to reach a final verdict on this.

As you can understand, this appalling murder has caused a terrible shock at the school and in the whole town of Lundenburg. Mr Lochberger leaves behind a wife and fifteen years of successful work at the Schiller Grammar School, where he has implemented a major educational reform concept entitled 'Schiller FIX - fantastic, innovative, excellent' over the past seven years. This project has received very positive reports in numerous media, and not least due to the successful management of the school, Mr Lochberger was able to increase the number of pupils by fifteen percent over the last few years.

I would like to take this opportunity to express my deepest sympathy to the entire school, colleagues, parents and students. As things stand at present that is all I can say. You are now welcome to ask questions but please understand that I cannot go into too much detail while the investigation is still ongoing."

Mr Sauer nodded and ended his presentation which was answered by the journalists by knocking approvingly on the tables. Some hands were raised and the round of questions began. Mr Sauer pointed to one of the journalists.

"Can we rule out that any strangers could have entered the building at night through an open door?"

The Commissioner answered.

"The entrance doors are locked by the janitor every evening at about six o'clock, and he said he did so yesterday as well. But since all teachers have keys to the building, it is quite possible that someone went into the school afterwards and forgot to lock it again. Unfortunately, we do not yet have a complete overview of who was in the house last night and we hope that our interviews will reveal this. OK, here in front, the gentleman with the red tie."

"Wouldn't it be necessary to draw immediate conclusions from this incident and ensure that schools have effective entrance controls in the future? In recent months, we have heard of cases where vagrants or other persons of dubious character have walked into schools and used the toilets there, or at least tried to do so. There have also been cases of harassment of pupils by persons from outside. Now we have a murder case. How long do we have to wait until you decide to secure the schools effectively? After all, we live in an age of terrorist attacks."

The journalist was obviously very agitated and it showed in his voice. Mr Sauer replied with a shrug of his shoulders and made a gesture of helplessness.

"I am well aware of this. We have had such discussions on a number of occasions. I know that in the USA, for example, access to schools is very strictly regulated. There, nobody gets into a school building without a security pass. This is a political decision, and it has to be solved at a political level. As police, we can only give advice here, but it would certainly be helpful if pressure could be brought to bear on the decision-makers from parents or teachers, or even from the press." The Commissioner smiled expressively here and looked around the room. "Then perhaps something could change. I'd like to encourage you to report on it, ladies and gentlemen of the media. It can do no harm if the public takes a closer look at the subject. At the moment, the situation in the whole of Germany is the same as it is here. In principle, anyone can go into any school during the day, and that was, by the way, the problem during the rampage in Winnenden a few years ago. Namely that the violent offender also had free access to the school. Now the gentleman to the left of the 'Lundenburg Voice'," shouted the Commissioner.

"I would like to join the previous speaker in taking the subject a little further and asking you all a question first. In the last twenty years, have any of you ever visited a company with more than a hundred employees? Have you been able to simply walk into the company building or was there perhaps a doorman who checked you or perhaps even an electronic lock which could only be opened with an ID card?"

The journalist paused and let his eyes wander over the room. Everywhere there was nodding and mumbling.

"The Schiller Grammar school has about one thousand students. There's no establishment in all of Germany that would operate without entrance controls. Why do the teachers put up with that and let themselves and the students be treated like third-class citizens by politicians? I think that this is an absolutely dreadful situation and I would like to know from you, Mr Sauer, whether you now intend to use this terrible crime as an opportunity to address the government with clear demands."

The Commissioner was visibly uncomfortable when he replied to this question.

"You are absolutely right in your criticism. We have already discussed these problems in detail among our colleagues and have decided to take action on this issue and make corresponding demands on our members of parliament. Of course, after this terrible incident, there can be no easy way to continue."

"Now the gentleman, no, the lady at the back, yes, in the back row in the green blouse," the Commissioner indicated.

"Can't we increase police presence around schools at night? If staff are working late at night, they are of course particularly at risk.

Wouldn't it then make sense to have special surveillance around schools in the evening hours? Especially since the station is very close by and educational institutions often become a meeting place for shady characters in the evenings?"

"You are absolutely right, but we have been doing that for quite some time now. There have been numerous arrests of drug dealers on school grounds or in the immediate vicinity in recent years. So we do in fact have an increased presence around the schools in the evenings, but obviously we cannot go to the headmaster's office and ask him once every hour if everything is okay."

There were no more raised hands to be seen, which the Commissioner was quite happy about.

"We will of course keep you up to date. All of you will be informed daily by email as soon as new information becomes available. Should any important breakthroughs in our investigations be indicated, we will hold a new press conference. At the moment, however, it doesn't look as if a solution to this case can be expected in the next few days. Thank you very much for coming and I wish you a pleasant evening. Thanks again and have a safe journey home."

The journalists applauded and some got up from their seats. Others were still hammering texts into their keyboards. The meeting slowly began to break up, while the Commissioner stood in the entrance area and talked with various reporters.

9 The Beer Garden

After the conversation with Mr Degen, Alex had left the school building stunned. Thoughts rushed through his head.

It had suddenly become clear to him that he had put himself in an extremely difficult situation. The business with the headmaster's computer had aroused suspicion against him. If someone found out that he had stolen the card, he would be threatened with legal proceedings. Even worse, however, was the danger of being accused of murder. The other two colleagues would certainly not be considered as suspects. They had only been in the school building for a short time and then went to a pub together. He, on the other hand, had been alone at the scene of the crime for a long time and after leaving the school he had had no contact with anyone except Messerschmidt's helper, who brought him the money. He was in desperate need of an alibi for the time of the crime, which was even clearer to him now than before.

His partner Ulla was the only one who could help him. He wondered if she would be willing to do it. In the last few months they had had many arguments and conflicts and the relationship was at times on the brink of collapse. He knew that he was to blame in the first place because he had started an affair with an old acquaintance and Ulla had discovered this after a few weeks and intended to leave him. Only with a lot of effort had they survived this crisis, among other things with the help of a counsellor, where they talked for a few weeks and decided to try again.

So now he needed an alibi from her but what could he tell her to convince her? That he had had a beer with some colleagues after school? Then she would want to know the names, and she was quite capable of calling these men to check his statements. She was extremely suspicious since his slip up six months before and that was a huge problem now.

He couldn't tell Ulla that he had stolen the data card, so he could hardly say that he had waited for Daniel until after ten o'clock to hand over the card and collect his fee. But what if he did? She would probably condemn the whole thing as criminal and then there would be no alibi.

She might have swallowed his story about having a drink with the three Englishmen but if not, he could not provide convincing evidence. So for the moment he was still without an alibi.

He could not expect any help from Monika Lochberger either, because she could hardly testify that she had spent the evening with a teacher from her husband's school while waiting for her husband.

He drove out of town in his car and took a long walk through the woods to clear his head. The longer he thought and brooded about the matter, the more hopeless his situation seemed to him.

Ulla was already back from work when he arrived home.

"Hello, Ulla," he greeted her and tried to hug her, but she pushed him away. "I'm cleaning and my hands are dirty. Be careful."

He handed her a small bouquet of flowers which he had hidden behind his back, smiled at her kindly and struck an encouraging note.

"Darling, why don't you stop cleaning until tomorrow and I'll help you. Let's go to the beer garden, the weather is perfect."

"Thanks, that's nice," she said, smiling happily at the flowers.

"Yes, dinner would be nice now. I'm glad the week is over," she said then. "I'll just change my clothes."

The beer garden of Dionysus was very busy. Most of the fifty or so tables were already taken when they arrived there around 7 pm. In the shade of the old chestnut trees, the customers sat, filling the place with loud chatter.

They found an empty table, sat down and ordered their drinks immediately, as the waiter went scurrying past.

"Ah, the weekend at last", Ulla said and gave a deep sigh.

"Yes, I'm glad too", Alex agreed, "it's been an eventful week."

"Say, there was a murder at your school. I read about it in the paper today."

"Yes, last night someone killed the headmaster in the schoolhouse. It was awful."

"That's terrible! Who could have done such a thing?"

"Nobody knows."

"This is just like in American crime novels. And that in Lundenburg! I don't dare go out at night any more!" Ulla said nervously.

Alex looked worried.

"The unpleasant thing for me is that I was late at the school and now of course I'm under suspicion."

"What? You're not serious, are you?"

"I'm afraid so."

Ulla waited for him to continue. "What's happened? Talk to me."

"Nothing happened, but Lochberger has always had it in for me, especially after the somewhat angry letter I wrote him last year."

"Of course, that wasn't very clever. It's obvious you didn't make yourself popular by doing that."

Alex was silent and looked at her regretfully.

"And you think," Ulla continued thoughtfully, "you will now be connected with the murder? Why did you spend so much time in the school? That is suspicious, isn't it?"

"You're absolutely right, that's what I'm afraid of. I came out of the school building at ten past nine and the headmaster was still working at that time. According to the newspaper report, the time of murder was between half past nine and ten o'clock."

"Yes, and why did you come home so late yesterday, it was already half past eleven? You didn't have anything to do with the murder, did you?" Ulla asked worriedly.

Alex rolled his eyes and gave a deep sigh.

"You're not seriously asking that now, are you?"

Ulla remained silent and shrugged.

"When I came out of the schoolhouse, I met three Englishmen in the car park who had been staying at our school for a week. They are three young colleagues who were doing an English project with us."

"And?" Ulla asked curiously.

"We talked a bit and then we decided to have a drink together. We went to the Horse Stable bar. They didn't know the place and I wanted to show them something typically German, something special. We went there and it was packed, we almost didn't get a seat. You know that you can't actually go there without an advance booking."

"And then you all had a drink together?"

"Well, time just went by really fast and suddenly it was a quarter past eleven, so we left. They flew back to England this morning. Yesterday was their last day, so they were glad they could celebrate a bit in the evening."

"All right, but then you have an alibi, because you must have been seen there, right?", Ulla asked.

"I'm afraid not. Last night was so crowded that the bar staff will hardly remember individual faces. I didn't know any of those present, at least none that seemed familiar to me."

"And the three English guys? They're witnesses who can testify."

"In principle, yes, but I only know their first names. I have no other information about them, I know only that they come from three different places in England. It will be very difficult to find them again."

"That's pretty stupid. What are you going to do?"

"That's what I've been wondering. Anyway, it's too risky for me to rely on anyone having seen me in the bar. If no one remembers me, I have no alibi and could be held responsible for this murder."

Ulla frowned and shook her head.

"Of course, we can't risk that," she said. "What if I said you were with me all evening from 9:30 on?"

Alex looked as if he had suddenly won the lottery.

"That's a great idea, that's the solution, darling."

"Of course, I risk being charged with perjury because in a murder trial I'm sure I'll be sworn in. I don't know if I can risk that," she said thoughtfully and fixed Alex sharply.

"Darling, if you don't help me then I'm in real trouble. Without an alibi I'm lost."

"This is bad for you," said Ulla with an icy tone in her voice. "One can only hope the police believe you."

"Oh, please, you don't really believe I'm a murderer, do you?"

"No, I don't, but I don't believe the story about the Englishmen either. By the way, you could have called me last night, so I wouldn't have spent hours worrying and waiting for you. Of course I remember how you had a fling six months ago with that girl. You were supposedly having a drink with your colleagues."

"I beg you," Alex interrupted her desperately.

"No, I have the feeling that you're lying to me again, and if that's so, then it's high time you told me the truth because I don't want to build our future life on lies," she said.

"But, Ulla, have you gone completely mad? I'm not seeing another woman, I swear it. I love only you and I promise you it will never happen again. I simply forgot to call you yesterday. I'm sorry, please forgive me."

Suddenly the whole beer garden seemed to be shouting, "Hello Mr Strasser, hello Mr Strasser!" Alex spun around. A group of students of his ninth grade class rushed towards his table, calling out to him. When they reached his table they giggled awkwardly, four girls and a boy. Alex was embarrassed by the whole thing, he hissed at them, "For heaven's sake stop shouting. The whole town doesn't have to know that I'm here. What are you doing here anyway?"

"But Mr Strasser, don't be so unfriendly, we were just pleased to see you," said Andrea, one of the students reproachfully. "We wanted to have a Coke. That's not forbidden, is it?"

"Yes, it's okay, I just didn't want you to shout so loud. It doesn't give a good impression, Andrea."

"Okay, Mr Strasser, we will be quiet. We wish you and your wife a nice evening. Bye." And the group left as quickly as they had appeared and sat down at an empty table on the other side of the beer garden.

"These are the joys of being a teacher," Alex said resignedly to his companion. "Above all, you don't have any privacy when you live in the same town."

"Well, they didn't mean any harm, they are just children," Ulla defended the pupils.

"Hello Mr Strasser," said a deep voice behind Alex. Only this voice did not sound familiar to him. He turned around. Ulla stared at the man standing behind her boyfriend.

"Good evening," said Alex. "Have we met before?"

"No", said the strange man. "I was having dinner here with two colleagues of mine, they have just left. I was still chatting with the waiter and then I overheard these young people calling your name. I believe you are Mr Strasser from the Schiller Grammar School, aren't you? But I don't want to bother you tonight, when you're enjoying the evening with your wife."

"My fiancee, Frau Schulze," Alex said with an insecure expression.

"No harm meant, Mr Strasser. My name is Sauer, Commissioner Sauer. I'm busy with the Lochberger murder case, hence my interest in you teachers."

He grinned and went on:

"No offence. I'll say goodbye, but I wanted to ask you, are you still here next week or will you spend your holidays elsewhere?"

"No, I have planned my holidays for later on, so I'll be here."

"Oh, good. Then I'd like you to come and see me on Monday. I hope all your colleagues will be there."

"Certainly. I'll see you then."

"Well, have a nice evening and a nice weekend."

"The same to you, Commissioner," said Alex.

Alex waited until the Commissioner was far enough away.

"Bloody hell. Do you realize now that they're already on to me? He wants to see me on Monday and interrogate me about what happened at school and why I was there so late. He thinks I might be the killer. I need your help. Otherwise I could spend the next few weeks in custody. Is that what you want?"

"Of course not. All right, you were at my place at a quarter past nine, and we spent the rest of the evening at home. Are you happy now?"

"Ulla, this is about our very existence, not satisfaction. You know that I love you and I want to spend the future with you. If you want that too, you've got to help me," Alex pleaded.

"This sounds like blackmail," Ulla said with an indignant look. "I will think it over carefully. I won't make any promises. By the way, tomorrow I'll be in Munich with Inge. We can continue our talk on Sunday."

Alex gave her an angry look and then growled resignedly. "It's getting late, let's go."

10 A Call for Help

Saturday morning was sunny, just like a photo from a holiday brochure. Blue skies, birds singing, balmy air, it was wonderful. I was sitting on the balcony having breakfast and reading the newspaper. In the local section I found another report on the murder of the headmaster. Apparently the police had not yet come to any conclusions. The speculations ranged from a drug addict, as they were to be found in the area and especially at night, to a student who wanted to take revenge for not passing his final exams. The latter, however, seemed to me a bit far-fetched. No student could be so miserable and stupid that he could let himself get so carried away as to commit a murder and thereby destroy his own future.

In the middle of my thoughts on this subject my telephone rang. It was Alex. I was amazed to hear his voice at this early hour.

"Hello Alex," I said. "It has been a while since I heard from you. I'm reading the newspaper and the article about your school. Nasty business, huh?"

"Yeah, it's terrible." Alex said. "I wanted to talk to you about it. But I know it's very early and you're probably still at breakfast, I don't want to disturb you. Can I stop by your place today?"

"Sure, I'm home. I have nothing to do. I don't think I'll be going out until this afternoon. What time do you want to come over? How about in about an hour?"

"Oh, yeah, that'd be great. If it really suits you, I'd like to come by around eleven."

"Great. I'll look forward to seeing you then."

I had not asked what exactly it would be about but after the Commissioner asked me yesterday about Alex, I suspected that it might have something to do with the police interrogation. A bad premonition came over me.

But probably Alex just wanted to talk about the whole thing and maybe find out if the Commissioner had said anything to me about him. Well, I would see what was on his mind soon enough.

At the moment I didn't want to deal with the subject any further and instead enjoy the beautiful summer morning. It would be a hot summer's day again. Now at about 10 am the thermometer was already at twenty-four degrees in the shade and I had the awning out because otherwise I wasn't going to be able to stand it for long on this south-facing balcony.

The sun shone from a most beautiful blue sky. In the garden below, the janitor was busy pruning the rose hedge and in the house next door on the ground floor Mrs Kraft was sitting on her terrace. She was having a pleasant breakfast with her adolescent son, and now and then I heard scraps of conversation. It was the epitome of a nice summer morning and I could have sat there for a long time, lazy and satisfied, if two wasps hadn't suddenly appeared out of nowhere and surrounded me aggressively. I took a small bowl from the table, dipped a spoon lightly into the honey jar and placed the spoon with the bowl at the other end of the table, hoping that the two annoying insects would settle down there. The trick actually worked and I could once again devote myself to my contemplative idleness.

I like to sit on a balcony with a nice view, especially when it is quiet. My work is quite hectic and tense, and peaceful contemplation is the best relaxation therapy for me.

This evening I had intended to pick Susanne up from the airport, having previously planned a long weekend together. But last night she had cancelled everything as an urgent appointment had come up. So we would not see each other until the following week.

We have had a weekend relationship for fifteen years. There were a lot of discussions whether we should or could move in together but there are some obstacles. She has her clients and business relations in the Hamburg area and I, on the other hand, am in the Stuttgart area and since we are both freelancers, losing our current business partners would be a significant economic disadvantage for both of us. And then there is the question of whether we would really be happy, being together permanently. I admit that I have gotten used to living as a single person,without the need for constant agreements about every little thing. A spontaneous life with lots of work and also a lot of peace and relaxation within my own four walls, without having to fear nerve-racking discussions or even arguments.

In this way, what was originally conceived as a temporary arrangement has become a permanent provisional one to which we have settled in quite well. We see each other every second weekend either in Hamburg or in Lundenburg, and it is always a great pleasure to be together again and the time spent together is a joy for both of us. There is no routine, except on holiday, when we travel together for two or three weeks. Then we get a foretaste of what it would mean to live together permanently and are then usually quite satisfied that we can withdraw into our own four walls again and throw ourselves into our work.

Marriage or no marriage, that was a frequent topic in the first years of our relationship. In the meantime the issue has resolved itself. We are both financially independent and professionally committed.

Neither of us wants to move, neither wants to risk disadvantages. Besides, we were both married before and both lived to regret it.

My cell phone suddenly rang and interrupted my train of thought. It was Alex.

"Hello Winfried, what's going on at your place, I'm standing in front of the door and have been ringing for five minutes. Didn't you hear me?"

"Oh, I'm sorry, I'm sitting on the balcony and actually I didn't hear the bell. Just a moment, I'll open the door."

I let him in and we went to the balcony.

"Long time no see," I began. "It's been two weeks, I think!"

"Yes, that was when we went to Dionysus' together, where I was with Ulla last night."

"How are you two doing? I haven't seen her for almost a year."

Alex had an embarrassed expression.

"We've been going through a crisis for some time now. Somehow I can't get along with that woman. I think we're too different."

"Maybe so, but I'm not the best judge of that. I hardly know her. Sometimes I have the feeling that you are hiding her from me."

"You may be right. I don't feel comfortable with her around other people. The way she behaves or even talks. It sometimes alienates me without always being able to say exactly what it is."

"Well then, I can imagine that you would rather not appear in public together. Can you talk through your difficulties?"

"Unfortunately not. She is incapable of an open discussion about problems. As soon as something comes up between us, she freaks out and panics and then she claims there are no issues, that I'm just making them up. On the contrary, she says that everything is wonderful and that my constant criticism is destructive."

"Well, sounds a bit neurotic, what you're telling me. Do you want to stay together?"

"I am not sure about that. She is always talking about our future and how she wants to live with me permanently. All my hints that I need more space and less relationship, she answers with hysterical reactions. I don't know what to do any more."

"What did she say about your move to Dorflingen? After all, you'll be over a hundred and fifty kilometres apart!"

"Well, she was against it at first. It was too remote, too rural, but after several visits there, she found the house and the surrounding area very beautiful and said she could imagine living there after all. Next year she's retiring and wants to move there with me."

"You should have sorted out your problems by then. I'm sorry that things aren't going so well with you. I thought it was a pity that you broke up with Sylvia. She was actually a very smart and nice woman. I never understood why you just left her."

"Don't remind me," Alex said with a sigh.

"I was blinded at the time and also had the impression that Sylvia and I were stuck in a rut. It was just a feeling of dissatisfaction and the routine. Everything seemed to be so entrenched and then on holiday I probably got into boisterous spirits and I slipped into a relationship which, in retrospect, proved to be problematic."

"This problem can be solved, if you want. I could try to mediate between you," I suggested.

"Well, maybe I'll take you up on your offer," Alex said. "But I didn't come to you today because of that or because I wanted to..."

He got stuck and was obviously looking for the right words.

"So what is it?" I asked, somewhat impatiently.

"It's about the murder at the school. I think the police suspect me because I was there until nine on Thursday night and the headmaster was killed shortly after."

"Yes, of course it looks a bit suspicious", I said. "But besides that, you seem to have been hostile to your headmaster."

"What gave you that idea?" Alex asked startled.

"I spoke to the Inspector yesterday. He invited me because I had a close professional relationship with the headmaster, since I was in charge of his computer system. I was therefore questioned and he asked me a few things about you. He had already spoken to the deputy headmaster and knew that Mr Lochberger had written an email to Degen on the evening of the murder around a quarter past nine, in which he claimed that you and two other colleagues were still late in the school and that you had loaded a virus onto his computer. He suspected you because there was probably no one else in the school and the connecting door to the copy room was not locked. The door handle must have been tampered with."

"Damn it," hissed Alex.

"What do you think of that?"

"I admit it. I contaminated his data card with a virus."

I felt as if I had been struck on the head.

"But why, what was the point?"

"I wanted to play a prank on my boss, to spite him, as revenge for the humiliation I had suffered from him for years."

I shook my head and frowned.

"Where did you get such a stupid idea?"

"I'm retiring from school in a few days. This was my last chance for a little revenge."

"Sorry, I feel this sounds a bit silly. One might have expected this from a student, but from you?"

"Yes, I know I made up a stupid prank, I know that now, but I have nothing to do with his death."

"I believe you, but you must convince the police, not me. You must have an alibi stating where you were after you left the school. All that matters is whether you were in the school building at the time of the crime, which according to the newspaper report is between 9:30 and 10 pm. That won't be a problem, will it?"

"Yes, that's exactly the problem, Winfried. I left the school just after nine o'clock and, I'm embarrassed to tell you this now, I took a little trip to the red light district out of frustration with Ulla."

Now I was really surprised by this confession from my friend.

"And did you meet any girls who could testify that they talked to you?"

"It didn't come to that. I first went to a Stuttgart strip club and watched the girls but couldn't decide to talk to one. Then the whole thing suddenly repulsed me and I drove back to Lundenburg around eleven. At a quarter past eleven I was at home and Ulla was already in bed."

"So no one saw you between 9 and 10 pm who could testify to that?"

"That's right. I spoke to Ulla today but told her a different story, namely that I had had a drink with three Englishmen. Ulla doesn't believe my story. That's why she refused my request for an alibi for that evening. She suspects that I was with another woman. I can't tell her that I was in a strip joint."

"This is really a very awkward situation," I said and was at the moment quite perplexed about the difficulty my friend had got himself into.

"Why were you at school for so long anyway?"

"I was making photocopies."

"You're a worse workaholic than me," I grinned at him.

"Normally I wouldn't, but the copies for the end of term project still had to be made."

"Yes, and what are you going to do now," I asked him, probably showing by my facial expression that I thought the whole thing was pretty hopeless.

"I wanted to ask you, if you can help me."

Alex looked at me expectantly.

"If you could confirm that I was with you and that we had a beer together, it would be all right."

"I'd like to do that, Alex, but there's a catch."

"What's that?"

"Commissioner Sauer specifically asked me yesterday when I last saw you. I told him that it was the weekend before last. Which it was. Now I can hardly claim that you were with me last night, because he would notice and call me out on it."

"What a bloody mess!" Alex cursed to himself. "That's really awful! What do I do now?"

"I guess you have no choice but to tell the truth."

"But that doesn't give me an alibi, and whether the police will believe me, I don't know."

"I see no other way," I said. "Besides, nowadays there are highly sophisticated forensic methods for catching a murderer. I assume that forensics will do their job in your case too."

"But I'm afraid they'll lock me up on initial suspicion and I may be in custody for months. It would kill me! Don't you think we could stick to that story about our beer together last night?"

"Alex, please understand, I can't get caught up in contradictions, and this would be inconsistent with my first statement. If it went to court, I would be sworn in, and I would have to change my original story or be convicted of lying under oath. It's too risky for me. A freelancer who gives false testimony can pack up. Word gets around very quickly and you are then no longer trustworthy. So please do not ask too much of me. If I had not already spoken to the Commissioner, the situation would have been different, but he has taken note of my statement. I cannot possibly make a completely different claim now."

"Okay, I understand your point, I'll have to think of something else."

"Why don't you talk to Ulla again and pull out all the stops? Maybe you can make her change her mind."

"I guess that's the only solution I have left," Alex said resignedly.

"And how far on are you with your move," I asked, in order to change the subject.

"It´s all done. Two boxes are still there with kitchenware and other stuff I don't need any more. The new tenant saw the things and was interested in them. Oh yes, my diaries are still there. I wanted to store them with you because I'll be in the south for months in winter. Someone might break into my house and I would feel uncomfortable if my private notes fell into other people's hands. By the way, after the holidays I wanted to have a house-warming party in my new home in Dorflingen. You'll come, won't you?"

"Of course I will. You can count on it."

"Well, I'll be going then. I hope I can convince Ulla."

"I'll keep my fingers crossed. Call me and let me know how everything went."

"On Monday I have to see the inspector. The police have summoned all the teachers for questioning. I'm dreading it."

"It'll all work out, don't worry too much. If you're innocent, they can't hurt you."

"Well, you still have blind faith in our justice system, don't you?"

We said goodbye, and I looked out the window and watched Alex walk to his car, still puzzled. I hoped that he could convince his girl-friend to help him in this difficult situation.

11 A Crisis

Alexander was desperate. Shortly after Sunday breakfast, his girlfriend Ulla confronted him again and attacked him with tirades of jealousy and suspicion. The call from his mysterious colleague on Friday morning had driven her crazy. She kept asking him inquisitorially about the details of his alleged restaurant visit with the Englishmen and he didn't seem to convince her. He got entangled in contradictions and finally she turned on him.

"It is now quite clear to me that you are deceiving me. You think I am stupid, don't you? It was exactly the same thing last year, you lied to me and behind my back you met that Greek woman. You can get lost. And you can get an alibi from your new girlfriend, but don't count on me. And if you think that I will continue to be cheated on and if you don't change from the bottom up, then it would be better to end our relationship immediately. I don't feel like carrying on like this any more."

Alex got angry. He was outraged at these accusations.

"You know what," he said, "I'm fed up with your constant accusations and your insane jealousy. I wasn't with another woman yesterday. I told you that a hundred times. Maybe you should get psychiatric help. And if you want to keep on hounding me with these stupid accusations I'm going to pack up and go."

"So His Majesty is preparing to move out. That's perfect. She's probably already prepared you a room at her place. You can leave at once. I can live very well without you. I don't need a lying ass like you. Take your things and get out of here now. Leave the keys in the mailbox."

He was amazed and upset by this unexpectedly violent reaction. At the same time he felt a wave of relief. He hadn't expected that this very conflict-laden and problematic relationship with Ulla would end so quickly. However, he could not show his secret joy, instead he shouted angrily, "Hysterical bitch, I'm leaving with the greatest pleasure, so that I'll never have to listen to your ravings again." Ulla was already at the front door, clutching her handbag.

"I wish you all the best for the future," she said sarcastically and slammed the door behind her.

Alex felt as if he had been struck on the head. He hadn't been able to foresee this quick decision and he couldn't believe that she would deny him the alibi outright. What should he do now? He had the police interrogation on the following day and he was one of the first to be questioned. He couldn't prove that he wasn't in the school at the time of the crime. Even worse, if anyone had seen him sitting in his parked car near the school until after ten o'clock, that would definitely be used as evidence against him.

Who could help him now? Was there any possibility at all? He considered and went through the list of his acquaintances and friends but they were either working at school or were out of the question for other reasons. After all, it did mean asking a lot. Would he give an alibi to someone he didn't know very well and thus run the risk of a false statement? No, he had to admit that.

He regretted the whole thing, it was a nightmare. What a crazy idea to steal the headmaster's files! And all for a miserable ten thousand euros. Basically pocket money! That in itself could get him a prison sentence. And then there was the murder. That shouldn't have happened. Who could have foreseen it? It should have been the perfect crime. It was sheer madness and probably for him the end of life as he had known it up to now.

At the forthcoming interrogation it would come out that he was at the school in the evening with Lochberger. He couldn't prove how long he had been there, so consequently he would be placed under suspicion of murder and therefore he had to expect to be remanded in custody.

Should he really go to jail? Under no circumstance! If he perhaps...

But there was no point in fantasizing, he had to make decisions. He had to get out of here, that was clear, and as soon as he was gone they would issue warrants for his arrest, probably all over Europe. Where could he go? Alexander pondered this for a long time, and it quickly became clear to him that he could only escape successfully if he got himself false papers. He had enough cash, but that also had to be organized. He didn't want to walk around with several thousand Euros in his pocket. Furthermore, it was to be expected that his accounts and credit cards would be blocked and then he would be finished very quickly. With his motorhome he could not drive through Europe. The vehicle registration number and type would very quickly put the police on his trail.

The best thing would be to sell the campervan. It was of no use to him now, but how could he find a buyer and at such short notice? He could ask his friend Winfried, who had already expressed the wish for one. He decided to talk to him as soon as possible. Time was pressing.

12 Travel Plans

My cell phone rang while I was driving through Stuttgart. It was just before noon and a peaceful Sunday midsummer mood lay over the city.

Alex was on the phone. "Hello Winfried," Alex said in an apologetic tone. "I'm sorry if I'm bothering you again, we saw each other only yesterday, but it's something urgent and I have to leave tomorrow for some time and I wanted to discuss a few things with you. Are you available now or this afternoon?"

"I'm just on my way for a little hike to the Bear Lakes. If you feel like coming out, join me and we can chat while we hike, how's that?"

"That's a great idea. It'll do me good too, if I get some fresh air. I'll be there in 20 minutes. Is that okay?"

"That's great. I'm looking forward to our hiking together. See you soon. I'm in the first parking lot. There should be some free space."

Half an hour later we were walking on the forest path along the lake shore. Out there the air was pleasantly cool and smelled aromatically of forest plants and conifers. It was a warm summer's day and numerous hikers trudged around the lakes, ducks and swans were on the water and the birds were chirping.

"So, what are you up to, you said you wanted to go away? But just now, when tomorrow all the teachers are to be questioned? Wouldn't you rather give your statement first?"

"Winfried, I've thought about it for a long time, but I have no chance of getting out of here in one piece. I have no alibi for the time when the murder took place. Ulla has thrown me out and won't help me. If I can't name anyone as a defence witness, then all suspicions are pointed at me and I'll be locked up. I don't want to take that chance. So I'm leaving. I hope they catch the killer soon. When they do, I can come back. Not before."

"I think it's madness," I said. "Where are you going? They'll look for you all over Europe. If you're wanted for murder, mug shots will be published, you won't remain undiscovered for long."

"I know, and that's why I have to take some precautions. First, my motorhome. If I drive around in it, they'll catch me right away. They just have to look for my license plate number. Which brings me to my first question. I want to sell the RV, and fast. Would you be interested? It's two years old, you can get it for a good price. Or else I'd ask you to sell it for me. I'll give you power of attorney and the papers."

"I'd like your motorhome," I said. "But you can't just sell it on the spur of the moment. And I might feel guilty about taking advantage of your plight."

"I've thought it over. I want to sell it."

We talked about the car for a moment. Alex had bought it two years ago and fulfilled this long-cherished wish. I told him that I didn't have a large amount in cash at the moment, but he said that he would prefer me to pay small amounts over a longer period of time anyway, because he didn't want to travel around with so much money.

"Well, but do you really want to get rid of this vehicle so suddenly? You'll regret it, and after a few weeks you'll be very sorry."

"I guess so," Alex said thoughtfully. "But we could arrange a buy-back option, say for a year. So if all goes well and I am safe again, I could buy the car back for the same price. In the meantime, you could use it for free."

"That's an irresistible offer, I have to admit. And how much do you need cash in hand right away?"

Alex said he didn't need anything right now, but they might freeze his accounts if the police put out a warrant. So he would rather leave the money with me and get smaller amounts every month and the best way to do that would be with a credit card in my name. I replied that this could be done. I happened to have a Visa card that I hadn't used for months.

"Great. That solves one important problem: the supply of cash."

"Also, I'll need a new identity if possible, but you probably don't have any advice for me, right?"

It was all happening a bit too quickly now, and I wanted to clarify some basic things with my friend.

"Before we get into the realm of crime stories, tell me exactly what happened. I have read the newspapers. I know that your headmaster has been the victim of a murder attack. I know that they haven't caught the murderer yet and I know from you that you were at school until 9 o'clock in the evening, in the room next to his. Now you claim that you are under suspicion of murder and have no alibi. Yesterday you told me that you came out of the school at about nine and instead of going home to your girlfriend, you were supposedly hanging around dodgy entertainment venues. 'I hear the message well, but I lack faith.' That's what your friend Goethe would say."

"Come on, don't be such a prude. Have you never visited a strip joint in your life?"

"When you're twenty or thirty you do all sorts of things, but we're not that age any more, are we?"

"Yes, we are," he said defiantly. "I told you yesterday that I was furious with Ulla because she had made me so angry with her damn stubbornness and morbid jealousy. That's why I wanted to get to see some nice girls and have a little chat."

I couldn't wipe the grin off my face.

"And then, did you meet a nice lady and have a nice chat with her?"

"No, I told you yesterday. I was in a bad mood, watched a couple of strippers, but got fed up after a while and went back home."

"And that's why you don't have an alibi now. One of those women must have seen you or maybe talked to you. I can't believe you hang around a place like that for an hour and not be seen by anybody. You can tell me a lot of things, but I don't buy it."

"Then just let it go."

"No, you're not getting off that easy. Your job now is to go back there and ask those ladies if they remember you being there on Thursday night. You put on the same clothes, it'll jog their memory."

"Now that's a really completely crackpot idea. I'm not going to run around that joint again and ask each of the girls if they remember my pretty face because I was there three days ago. They'll laugh their asses off or think I'm a complete lunatic."

"If I were you, I wouldn't care what they think of me. If your pro-spects for your continued existence are to end up behind bars, I'd rather be laughed at by three dozen girls than take that risk. If you want me to go with you, I can explain to them what it all means."

"That's kind of you, Winfried, but I think we should forget it, it's complete nonsense!"

"But to flee headlong and arouse the suspicion of the police, that's not stupid!"

"Stop your sarcastic remarks, please."

"We've known each other for ages, almost fifty years. But I've never seen you behave in such a reckless and crazy way. That starts with your long stay at the school. What were you doing at the copy machine until nine at night? In this beautiful summer weather. That's not normal. You always tried to finish school as early as possible. If you ask me, there's something wrong, I just don't know what it is yet, but I can't get rid of the feeling that you haven't told me the whole truth and this supposed act of revenge with the virus also seems a bit unbelievable."

"For God's sake, are you starting to suspect me now, too? I might as well take a rope and hang myself from the nearest tree."

"This is not about suspecting. You want me to help you, and I'm happy to do so, as much as I can. But I do mind being told half-truths or fairy tales, and your strip club story is a fairy tale, right?"

Alexander did not answer, as a group of walkers approached us and our conversation was not intended for the public ear.

"The Commissioner asked me about the fact that you had obviously shown hostility towards the headmaster before. He told me about an insulting letter you wrote to him. If that is known at your school, then why on earth do you have nothing better to do than to stay in the room next to your headmaster until nine o'clock in the evening, both of you alone in the whole school building, no one there. It's just screaming to the heavens, don't you see it? Is it any wonder they suspect you?"

Alexander kept silent and stared at the ground.

"Why were you really at school so late at night? The police will ask you that in any case, and not just once. Be assured they will ask you that a hundred times, and your explanation with the photocopies is not very convincing. They won't believe it. I am your friend and not a policeman. If you want me to help you, it would be good if you gave me a little more insight into what really happened."

I was gradually talking myself into a state of indignation and anger.

Alex looked at me with a grim expression on his face for only a moment, something seemed to be working inside him, but he remained silent.

"You don't want to talk yet. Well then I'll tell you something new that may surprise you."

Alex glanced over at me with a sceptical look.

"Lochberger called me on Thursday night at a quarter past nine."

Now a look of horror came over his face.

"What? Why did he call you?"

"I suppose you know that I have a maintenance contract with him for all his computers, that is, for the school administration."

"Yes, you told me," said Alex and looked at me suspiciously.

"He called us because his notebook suddenly didn't work. When he came back from the toilet, his notebook wouldn't start. He was pretty desperate, but my employee Becker calmed him down and promised to have it fixed for the next morning."

"And did you manage that?"

"Yes, after two hours it was fine again. However, I noticed that the notebook constellation was not quite the same as before the malfunction."

"What do you mean?"

"Someone obviously replaced the SD data card ."

"How could you tell?"

"Every computer on the net is logged in detail. Every data carrier has an ID, and it changed suddenly. There's a log entry at two minutes past nine. The SD card was removed from the notebook and another data card was inserted immediately afterwards. The cards have different identifiers. The exchange of the cards probably happened during the headmaster's toilet break. At seven minutes past nine, five minutes later, according to the log file on the computer, work was resumed. In other words, you not only downloaded a virus to his computer, but also stole his data card. And what did you do with the stolen SD card? After all, your headmaster had stored his work files on it and they were obviously very important to him."

I looked over at Alex. He suddenly seemed a bit pale and stared at me.

"Don't you think it's about time you told me the truth now," I asked him.

Alex stopped and looked at me, embarrassed. "Okay, you win, there's no point in pretending any more."

"Well, I'm listening."

He began falteringly and reluctantly to explain what had happened that night and he admitted the theft of the SD-card. He also told me all about his cooperation with Lochberger's competitor Messerschmidt, confessing that his motives were greed and revenge. I now understood why he had no alibi, since he had been waiting in his car near the school at the time of the crime until Daniel, Messerschmidt's employee, came to pick up the stolen data card.

I was shocked by this confession.

"That looks a little bleak," I said after hearing the whole story.

"But I can't understand it. You had your working life behind you, a carefree retirement before you, and now you go and do something like this? After all, you have worked honestly all your life and have not done anything crooked. Why do you have to get involved in a crime so close to the beginning of your retirement?"

"A crime!" he returned in a scornful tone. "You're exaggerating…"

Now I lost my temper and my tone of voice became sharper.

"My dear friend, it seems that to this day you are still unaware of the gravity of your actions. Of course, data theft is a criminal act, and in the context of an employment relationship, all the more so. You might even be deprived of your retirement pay or have it cut because of serious infidelity to your employer. Where's your intelligence, anyway? This Messerschmidt has waved ten thousand euros in front of your nose, and you turn off your brain and think you have to start a second career as a thief?"

I was talking myself into an angry mood, angry at my friend's obvious obtuseness.

"I wanted to take revenge on this guy who had made my professional life hell for years with harassment and insolence. And it all would have worked out wonderfully if he hadn't died."

"So with your sense of wrongdoing, it's not far off," I said. "Theft is not a trivial offence, and there is no right to revenge, either. You've got some strange preconceived ideas, which are just ridiculous. Even if everything had gone according to plan, your headmaster would have been informed by me about what I told you before, namely that his computer had been manipulated. Of course he would have suspected you. I don't know if you could have been convicted, but you surely would have gotten into a lot of trouble, one way or another. I'd feel more comfortable if you could at least acknowledge all this."

Alex had become very meek now.

"You talk like a prosecutor," he said.

"A District Attorney will tell you very different things, my friend, but I can't accept that my best friend has so little insight into right and wrong."

"I wanted to supplement my pension fund, but I see now that the whole thing was a stupid idea. The question is, what am I going to do now?"

I looked over at him with an agitated expression on my face, my sermon had obviously had its effect. After a short break I continued.

"I see two options for you, and both are not very pleasant. You go to the police and report what you just told me. Then they will either believe you and charge you with theft and breach of confidence. That could result in two to three years in prison if you don't get off on probation. But if they don't believe you, then you will probably be in custody for suspected murder, and everything else is difficult to predict."

"And what would you advise me to do?"

"Difficult question," I said. "If I were you, I wouldn't want to go to prison, of course. Personally, I don't believe that years in jail are meaningful either, it would hardly make you a better person. If you were a stranger, I would say 'Off to jail with him', but as your friend, I can't recommend it. Prison life would probably destroy you."

"So I can assume you'll help me escape?"

"What choice do I have? I couldn't sleep any more if I had to visit you in prison."

There was a pause in our conversation. We had circled the lake in the meantime and were on the opposite side near the little self-service restaurant. There were many walkers on the path. On a Sunday that was normal and the forest area at the Bear Lakes was a popular destination for outings.

One could hear a brass band playing music in the distance now. I invited Alex for a beer and we slowly walked the last two hundred yards to the garden restaurant where most of the tables were already taken. We waited in the queue of the self-service restaurant for a few minutes and each of us got a beer and some Bavarian sausages with pretzels. Back in the open air we were lucky, because a table had just become free, which we then occupied.

It was a magical summer Sunday, the July sun shone from a cloudless blue sky. Children ran back and forth on the grass, and dogs frolicked exuberantly around their owners. The brass band music resumed, marching music sounded across the wide meadows and Alex and I toasted the future with our beer mugs to the sounds of the Prussian march 'Old Comrades'.

This future did not look very rosy for my friend at the moment, that was pretty clear to both of us. But I wanted to do everything to help him escape, because I was convinced that he was not a murderer and I hoped that the perpetrator would be caught soon. Then Alex could come back and the problem would be solved.

"You raised the subject of a new identity or identity card earlier. Maybe I know something. This might surprise you," I said after a break, when we had finished our snack.

"I am curious," Alex said inquisitively and wiped the beer froth from his mouth.

"It's a long story, but I'll make it short. I once worked as a student for a scrap dealer as a driver for about two weeks. He had a criminal past as a fence and arms dealer and had connections to certain people in Stuttgart's old town. I came to the guy through the employment office's job placement service. Years later I used to meet him in Stuttgart from time to time and usually exchanged a few words with him. Most of the time he was hanging around in the area between Leonhard Church and Austrian Square, and he also told me that his son, who was about my age, had gotten into the scrap business.

The last time I saw the old man was about thirty years ago, and I had completely forgotten about him in the meantime. But as luck would have it, two years ago I got a call from a guy who needed help with his computer network, and he needed it very badly. The address was in Stuttgart's old town behind the Leonhard Church, a somewhat rundown neighbourhood. However, the guy had set up a very nice apartment with an office on the top floor of this building. His business was scrap metal, and while I was tinkering with his computer, he talked about how his father had built it all up, but had died a few years before.

Somehow I got the idea that his father might be the man I had worked for as a driver, and it turned out to be true. We started talking. He told me a lot about his father's career as a scrap dealer. I soon solved his network problem and the man was very satisfied. We chatted about this and that and he told me that he would also like to help me anytime if I needed papers, he could always get them. At that time I really wasn't interested in that but I said jokingly that it was of course good to have a way out in case I had to disappear under a false name and I would get in touch with him."

"That's a crazy story," Alex wondered.

"If you want, I can call him. He's probably still living there. It won't be cheap, he said something about a thousand euros for a new ID with a passport and a driver's license."

"That would be great, Winfried. It'd give me a good night's sleep, and then I could leave soon. I have to take new photos tomorrow. I'll shave my beard off. A little change won't hurt."

"Well, it's Sunday today, and the hearings start tomorrow. Time is running out. What do you want to do tomorrow morning?"

"Well, I could go to my GP in the morning and get a sick note. That would give me two or three days. But then I'll have to leave."

"Looks like you'll be taking an extended vacation."

"Do you think you can get the papers in three days?"

"I don't know, we'll see. If not, I'll have to mail them to you somehow. But make a list of everything we have to do. So there's your campervan, we need the sales contract, the registration, and then the financial business. Anything else? How will you travel, by plane or train?"

"I'll take the train. They don't have passenger lists."

"You can take my son's car, he won't be back for 6 months. He's in the US at the moment, and his Golf is just sitting there."

Alex was amazed and very happy with my offer, and we made our way back. At my place we sorted out the last things and I gave him the credit card in my name. Alex wanted to be prepared for all eventualities, and would leave the next day if the circumstances required it. After our evening together, Alex didn't go back to his apartment, but stayed with me in the guest room. He gave me his keys for the old apartment and also the keys to his new home in Dorflingen in the Bavarian mountains. I promised him that I would take care of everything.

13 The Commissioner Takes Stock

On Monday morning, there was an almost endless stream of visitors at the police headquarters with a constant coming and going of teachers from the Schiller Grammar School. The Commissioner had estimated ten minutes for each conversation, which meant that he could listen to six persons per hour, as did his colleague Muller. Since the teaching staff consisted of around eighty people, it would take at least a full day to interview everybody. But the police officers worked single-mindedly and almost non-stop.

The first interviews began at 9 am. By four o'clock almost all of the sixty teachers had been questioned. Some of them were on sick leave, some of them had not shown up despite having been invited. The Commissioner wanted to deal with them personally in a follow-up meeting the next day. Alexander Strasser was among those who had not appeared. The Commissioner had particularly high expectations of Strasser's questioning and he was somewhat surprised that this man, against whom he secretly had strong suspicions, had simply called in sick.

At three o'clock in the afternoon the Commissioner met with his colleague Rainer Muller and they exchanged interim results.

"Well, what are your first impressions, Rainer?" Sauer began the conversation.

"Not much," answered Muller, "but at least some people said that there was a certain dissatisfaction among the teaching staff with the headmaster's management style. Allegedly some of them left the school in recent years because they no longer liked it there under the leadership of Mr Lochberger. But he has also got followers."

"Yes, I've heard the same thing. I also noticed that most people avoid making their own statements and instead said they have heard this and that about him."

"Exactly, or that there are rumours in the school, etc.. It's all very vague."

"By the way, I'd like to see a list of those who left school in the last few years. We'll have those people checked out if they have moved away."

"I've thought about that."

"And what about conflicts or hostilities against the headmaster?"

"Some colleagues said that this new concept at the school, called 'Schiller FIX', is rejected by a large part of the staff but the headmaster, by virtue of his position, imposed it on the school, so to speak."

"Yes, I heard something similar. But it was said that the teachers did not look into the matter soon enough. In an early vote on this project, it seems that a large majority abstained so that a minority of the staff who supported the headmaster in the vote, prevailed. So this new concept was introduced without a real majority behind it."

"This is called democracy. If the majority abstains then these people should not complain afterwards when a minority takes the decisions. But have you understood what this 'Schiller FIX' is all about? I didn't quite understand it."

"I had it explained to me by two teachers who said pretty much the same thing, independently of each other. This 'Schiller FIX' is an abbreviation for 'fantastic, innovative, excellent'. It is, so to speak, a reform concept with which the headmaster wanted to distinguish himself as a great pedagogical innovator, as the Einstein of grammar school education. The main idea of this concept is to make part of the lessons available for so-called free courses, meaning, lessons on subjects that normally do not even exist in the classroom. These can be courses associated with play and crafts. Creative things such as painting or pottery, or sports activities. Even extra tuition in various subjects."

"Well, that sounds quite positive. A teacher explained something similar to me. So where is the disadvantage or the drawback?"

"The time for these free courses has to come from somewhere because you can't simply increase the amount of timetable hours. And these extra lessons are taken from the core subjects, for example English, French, mathematics. So instead of four, there are now only three hours of instruction per week."

"So that's the secret of the great FIX. But wait a minute. My son is now in the seventh grade and is learning English in the third year. If he now only has three hours a week instead of four, I don't think he's going to be able to do that. He has a lot of grammar problems and he's not the fastest."

"Yes, this argument has actually been put forward many times. There seems to be some truth to it, as you just said. The children who are not so bright will probably fall behind if there are only three lessons in the core subjects instead of four."

"And what do the friends of this glorious new model say about this?"

"They say that all students with problems will get personal tutoring in the so-called free courses, which are regularly held in the afternoon."

"Well, I don't know. That seems a bit counterproductive. So, first you take away an hour from the children in each core subject and thus the opportunity for sufficient exercises and repetition and then you repair the damage by putting the poor victims into tutoring courses. I don't find that very convincing."

"Yes, but of course you are not a teacher and you have little knowledge about methodology and didactics. By the way, this model is not completely new. It has already been successfully put into practice in a small village in the Bavarian mountains, at a small school in Hinter-walden. This is why the experts here speak of the so-called Hinter-walden model. The headmaster went there twice with some of his staff to see for himself this concept on site. As a pioneer, so to speak, he wanted to bring it to a large urban grammar school."

"That may be all very well but why should my son be taught according to such a model when, as a result of these cuts in hours, he will later lack 25 percent of the time normally needed to grasp and learn a certain subject?"

"You may be right. Of course some parents have asked this question, as have some teachers at the Schiller Grammar School, as we now know. There was a lot of bad feeling there, especially since the timetables got extremely complicated by these extra classes. Some of the staff also complained that they suddenly had to teach a lot of additional pupils from different years because of the this. They felt that this was an extra burden, not to mention the disrupted timetables. That's what I've heard time and again as a criticism and that was already a relatively strong reason for a certain hostility towards the headmaster and his management team."

"I can completely confirm what you say, that's more or less what the teachers told me. However, I didn't hear anywhere that someone might have had murderous intentions for these reasons. And as far as personal hostility is concerned, everyone kept a low profile. But I have heard the name Alexander Strasser a few times. He wrote a nasty letter once and he did not hide his critical opinion of the school management."

"I had this Strasser on my list, but he didn't appear today. He called in sick. The man gives me a very suspicious impression. He was at the school until around nine o'clock on the evening of the crime, allegedly making photocopies. The headmaster seemingly took a short break for a visit to the bathroom and then, on his return to his office, discovered that a virus was on his computer. He suspected Strasser and two other teachers, who were all still in the house at that late hour. That's all we know at the moment. Whether Strasser and Co. actually introduced the virus into the headmaster's computer is still unclear. But it would also be difficult to understand why Strasser first carries out a virus attack and then beats the headmaster to death."

Mr Muller laughed out loud, the Commissioner looked at him disapprovingly.

"Muller, a little more seriousness please."

"Excuse me, boss but sometimes you really have a funny way of saying things."

"This scenario is hard to imagine. Strasser is about to retire. He'd be deranged if he killed his boss at this moment."

"Yes, I agree with you. But after thirty conversations with teachers today, I wouldn't be surprised if one or two of them weren't so clear in their heads. Just look at the reform that the headmaster introduced with so much fuss, against all objections that the quality of teaching might suffer."

"Well, the changes in quality can only be seen after a few years, if at all. And then the author of the reform already enjoys his retirement. But that is another matter. Back to Strasser. The fact that he once wrote a nasty letter to his boss does not seem to me to be an indication of murderous intent. In general, I don't see the motive here."

"And what about the other two teachers who were also at the school in the evening?"

"We interviewed them both. They left school together shortly after nine and then went to a restaurant in town for dinner. They have also named witnesses who can vouch for them. They don't seem to be suspicious."

"Antipathy and occasional anger and friction are not motives for murder, are they? And nobody has ever called Mr Strasser deranged."

"You can't always tell. We'll need a psychological report, if necessary. Besides, there are also murders committed in the heat of passion. Perhaps the headmaster saw Strasser in the house and confronted him about the virus. The argument escalated and Strasser struck him."

"Well, you can speculate about all sorts of things. But I can hardly imagine that this teacher was the murderer. That somehow doesn't make sense. But why doesn't he come to the interrogation like his colleagues? That makes him suspicious, of course. And the fact that he was at the school for so long on the night of the murder, that's also strange."

"Well, we must question this Strasser as soon as possible. Write him an email. We don't have time for correspondence now. And give him a deadline. It's urgent. He has to be here tomorrow morning, let's say at ten o'clock at the latest, otherwise we'll just threaten him with an arrest warrant and a house search. We'll have to intimidate him a bit."

"What if he hires a lawyer and pleads sickness and incapacity?"

"We'll just have to proceed differently, but I don't think so. If he hired a lawyer now, he'd be even more suspicious."

"Okay, I will write to him and tell him that he is expected here at 10 am tomorrow. Have you spoken to the headmaster's wife?"

"Mr Stark was there. He spoke to her on Friday. She appeared calm. She wasn't too upset by her husband's death. She seemed almost indifferent."

"Could she have had an interest in his untimely demise?"

"It's hard to say. We know too little about their marital relations so far. But in any case, she is the owner of the software company for which the spouse produces the software."

"What! Are you saying that Lochberger had time to produce software in addition to his headmaster´s job?"

"Looks that way, at least that's what the deputy told me. Apparently his boss wrote most of the school administration software himself. The company is in his wife's name. A civil servant is not allowed to have lucrative jobs on the side."

"We have to take a closer look at this. If the wife is the owner of the company, then the death of her husband does not really change anything for her. But maybe there is a life insurance policy. We should also clarify that. As a general rule, spouses are always suspect in the event of death."

"There is something else we have to check. If Lochberger was active as an entrepreneur, then he probably also has competitors. So far we still lack any information on this. A competitor could also be an enemy and possibly be considered as a suspect."

"Well, I think we have enough to do for now. Put our new employees to work on all this information. I'd like to get a clearer picture by noon tomorrow, before I interview Strasser."

"Alright boss, we'll get whoever did this. So far we've tracked down everyone who thought they could commit a murder in Lundenburg."

14 Panic

Alexander sat on the sofa in Winfried's living room with his tablet in front of him. He read the latest news and made notes for his upcoming trip. Fearing police persecution, he had sought shelter with his friend. He didn't want to go back to his apartment, because there he expected the police to turn up at any moment. Besides, the apartment was already practically empty and he would have had to be content with an uncomfortable overnight stay on an air mattress.

This morning he had been to his doctor and had feigned terrible stomach pains in order to receive the desired sick note. He had then sent it by email to the school and the police headquarters.

Afterwards he had shaved off his beard and put on old horn-rimmed glasses, which he had not used for years, but with which he could still see well enough. With such a changed appearance, he had gone to a photo booth and had taken the passport photos that Winfried needed to order the new ID.

If he hadn't had to wait for his new identity papers he would have left the previous night. He was on tenterhooks and it was clear to him that it wouldn't be long before the police started looking for him.

A new message just came in on his tablet. He opened the mail program, it was a message from the Lundenburg police headquarters.

Dear Mr Strasser, your sick note was delivered today. Nevertheless, we must ask you to come to the police headquarters tomorrow, Tuesday, at 10 o'clock for questioning. This is an examination of witnesses in a murder case and is very urgent. The summons can only be waived if you present a medical certificate stating that you are unable to attend a ten-minute interview due to a serious illness. In this case, a bedside interview would be arranged.

If you disregard this request and do not appear at the appointment with Mr Sauer in room 212, we would like to caution you that your immediate compulsory presentation will be requested from the public prosecutor's office. In addition, you must expect a considerable fine if you do not comply with this urgent request.

Damn it, thought Alexander, so it's starting now. I can't sit and wait any longer. I must leave tonight, then I'll be in France before midnight and out of reach of the police for the time being. Winfried will have to send me the papers. He said that it would take about three or four days until they were ready. I can't wait that long under these circumstances.

His friend wouldn't come home until late that night, but it wasn't really necessary to wait for him now. They had discussed all the essentials the previous evening and this morning. Winfried had offered him his son's car, for which he was very grateful, because otherwise he would have to take the train and be very limited with his luggage. But this way he could take a lot with him without having to worry about the size of his suitcase. After all, he would be away for a long time, he reckoned about one or two months. He had given Winfried the keys to his house in the village together with a power of attorney to use his house or, in case of a longer absence, to rent it out. He had already moved in the last few weeks and there was nothing left in the old apartment in Lundenburg, with the exception of a box of diaries, which Winfried was to pick up and keep with him.

The diaries had been his private records since he was eight years old, and he did not want these documents to fall into the hands of the police during a house search. For a while he had considered destroying these diaries entirely but then he shied away from the idea. There were many hours of his life in these records and sometimes he himself had taken out and read one or other of them concerning some stage of his past with great interest and was amazed at what life had demanded of him and what he had experienced, with all its ups and downs.

Winfried, his best friend, was supposed to keep his notes and read them. They were safe with him. He could pass the diaries on to his daughter Margret, who had been living in Australia for ten years, if the worst came to the worst. His contact with Margret was unfortunately limited to occasional emails at Christmas or on birthdays. His ex-wife had been successful in alienating his daughter during and after the divorce and the close contact they had had in her childhood was basically lost.

The diaries were in a way the quintessence of his entire life, and when he looked at the balance of his own life in this way, it sometimes seemed as it had been nothing but a permanent failure on all levels. What dreams he had had at twenty or twenty-five! He had written them all down in his diaries as expectations for the future. He wanted to become a writer, a journalist, a freelance artist, a musician, although at that time he had not yet decided on one of these paths. In any case, he wanted to do something extraordinary, become famous, influential and of course wealthy. Those were the dreams of his early twenties.

The reality of his later life however looked different. He had become a teacher at a grammar school, married too early and in addition, to a woman who did not suit him very well. Then suddenly he was a family man and breadwinner and was responsible for a little daughter. After the state examination he was not able to get a teaching position and had had to make his living in other ways, including working for an insurance company . Suddenly he had had to face the harsh reality that was miles away from his original dreams and had nothing to do with artistic creativity, bohemianism and the idyllic world of literature.

Divorce, erratic relationships and a permanent struggle for existence as a freelance computer trainer, that was my glorious everyday life for years, he thought. On top of that came an expensive business failure. Goodness, there is hardly a mistake I haven't made. And now, at retirement, I'm stupid enough to get involved in crooked deals. With one foot already in jail and if I'm not careful, soon with both feet, possibly for life. Oh Alex, you complete idiot, what have you gotten yourself into? He had spoken the last sentence out loud.

The balance of his life? He laughed sarcastically. A sad record, let's not talk about it, he thought and got up to pack his personal things. He then carried the suitcase and the rest of the luggage out to the car and stowed his things in it. It was an older Golf, but it was still in good mechanical condition. An old tent and the air mattress were already in the trunk, so he could definitely stay in a camp-site somewhere or camp in the open if nothing else was available. It was now high season all over Europe. In July and August it would probably be difficult to stay overnight in most places. Winfried had thought of everything and equipped him with the necessary camping equipment. He was really a great friend.

Around 7 pm he was ready to go, wrote a short farewell note to Winfried and put the new passport photos next to it. He also wrote a few words of farewell to Monika, addressed and stamped the envelope and then got into the car. He slowly backed the Golf out of the drive-way, took another look at Winfried's house, and then headed for the highway to France, stopping at a mailbox and posting the letter to Monika.

15 The Diaries

When I came home around seven, I immediately noticed that the car was gone.

Had Alex left already? The note on the kitchen table made it all clear.

Hello, Winfried. I had to leave urgently - details on the tape.

A tape cassette was beside the sheet. I put it in my machine to listen to it. Alex explained to me why he couldn't wait and and that he had left in a hurry. He had forwarded the summons from the police by email to me for information. Again he explicitly asked me to go to his apartment and pick up the package with the diaries. The two remaining boxes contained things that he had left for the future tenant's use, as he had agreed with him. But in no case should I wait too long, otherwise the next tenant could have access to his diaries as soon as he moved in, or the police could search the apartment and confiscate them. I should send him the identification papers by registered mail to an address he would tell me. At the moment he did not know where he was going. In case of anything urgent he would send me an email with an encrypted attachment. We had agreed on a password to exchange messages in case of emergency, without strangers being able to read them.

So now it had actually happened, he was on the run. I immediately corrected myself and replaced the term 'on the run' with 'on vacation'. He was now on holiday for an indefinite period of time, and I hoped that the police would quickly clear up the case and so allow him to come back home soon.

His request to get the diaries out of the apartment was understandable and it was also clear to me that this really had to happen without delay because at the end of the week the next tenant was expected to move in. In addition, there was the danger of a house search by the police if Alex did not appear the next day for an interview. So I decided to settle the matter that same night. It was still too early now. I wanted to wait until it got dark to avoid being seen.

In the meantime I turned on the TV. The news was just starting. Mass protests in Hong Kong, protests in Bolivia, clashes between demonstrators and police in Venezuela, unrest and civil war-like conditions in Iran, bomb attacks in Iraq, and looting in France by demonstrators.

One could get the impression that the world had gone off the rails, and not just since today. But the really big issue, apart from all these violent clashes, was the climate issue. Everyone was now talking about climate change and everything revolved around it.

Of course, the subject is an explosive issue and I am not one of those who deny global warming, as some politicians do. I am fully aware of the threat to our planet. But just as the subject has been talked down for decades, it seems that people want to turn everything upside down overnight.

The biggest polluters in the world community, China, the USA, Russia and India continue to burn increasing amounts of coal as if there were no climate problem at all, while Europe imposes all kinds of restrictions on its citizens in the name of climate protection. The European environmental system is supposed to help the world climate to regain its health. We are supposed to give up flying, conventional cars, meat consumption and well-heated homes. The purchase of electric cars is allegedly the only way to reach a state of green bliss, which is disputed by some well-known scientists with good arguments, and our modern fuel-powered vehicles should end up on the scrap heap as soon as possible.

With such advice, some European optimists believe they can save the world climate. But what about the massive slash-and-burn clearances in the Amazon, Russia and Africa? Nobody seems to be able to stop this gigantic destruction of the environment. The forest fires in Siberia alone are polluting the climate with the same amount of carbon dioxide as Germany's total emissions in one year, as a research group recently calculated.

We Europeans should set an example, that makes sense to me, but everything needs to be done with a sense of proportion. Europe is currently strangling its relatively clean industries and the rest of the world continues to pollute the globe undaunted. And who is picking up the bill for these European ambitions to save the world? Of course, as always the so-called middle class, that is people like me, via higher prices for everything, for housing, heating, electricity and petrol. I admit I suffer from disenchantment with politics, like many of my contemporaries. But that is not a reason for me to run after political populists. On the contrary, they repel me with their opportunistic cries.

The weather map on the screen interrupted my train of thought. I flicked through the television programs for a while. There was nothing interesting to watch and I switched off.

After dark I intended to go and get the diaries. Until then there was still more than an hour left and I decided to go for a walk. The weather was dry and mild, and some exercise and fresh air would do me good. After a long walk through my residential area the night was setting in so I marched briskly towards the east end of the city, directly to Alexander's apartment. A church bell struck ten o'clock, and I was still about five minutes away from my destination.

The street called 'Fischerstrasse' was deserted at this time, with only a few pedestrians here and there. An elderly lady with a dog, then shortly afterwards a group of four young men with a Mediterranean appearance, perhaps Arabs, all dressed uniformly in jeans and hooded jackets. They made a sinister impression as they passed me, silent and threatening. The neighbourhood had not improved in the last few years. One met all sorts of shady characters here, who instilled little confidence. Further down the street there was apparently a homeless shelter, from which individuals often walked up to the supermarket in the evening with plastic bags full of rattling bottles to stock up on alcohol for the night.

Alex had moved here about twenty years ago. Back then it was still a residential area where a middle class dominated the scene. In the meantime, many apartments had been resold, and the old buildings in particular were increasingly being sold to buyers from more modest backgrounds. Malicious tongues already spoke of a newly emerging district of proles. Alex had often complained about this. Two years ago a rude young woman had moved into his building. She lived alone, but always brought some nasty-looking guys home. They then spent the nights with her and partied and made a lot of noise until late.

The whole neighbourhood was slowly falling into decay, Alex sometimes said, making it more and more attractive for people of the lowest level. I had contradicted him back then and criticized him for his somewhat arrogant manner of expression. But after walking around several times, I developed a certain understanding for his views.

The apartment building where he lived was now in sight. The street was empty. There were six flats in this building. On the ground floor the lights were on, on the first floor, too. Alexander's apartment was on the second floor on the right. Everything was dark there. I opened the garden gate. It squeaked, which annoyed me, because I did not want to attract attention and if possible not be seen.

Carefully I went up to the front door, took the key and opened it. Alex's name plate had already been removed and there hung a temporary sign with the name 'Kimmich'. I walked slowly and carefully up the stairs to the second floor and then stood in front of his apartment door. Music came from the apartment opposite and one could hear scraps of conversation between a man and a woman.

Nothing could be heard from Alexander's apartment. I opened the door as quietly as possible, entered and gently closed the door behind me. The lamp in the hallway had been removed, only a naked light bulb was still hanging from the socket. In the hallway I could see immediately that the apartment was no longer occupied. All the furniture was gone. I walked carefully and quietly through the apartment because I knew that Mr Fleischer, who lived in the apartment below Alex, had very acute hearing and I didn't want to be surprised by him now.

In the bathroom everything had been cleared out, the same was true for the living room. There was no more furniture, only a box tied with red string in the middle of the floor. I turned on the light switch, but it remained dark. The bulb had been removed.

I picked up the box and carried it into the hallway under the lamp to read the attached note. It said:

Dear Mr Kimmich, these documents are intended for my friend Winfried Alumno. This package contains teaching materials and books which I should urgently send to him. If you find the package here, I did not get around to delivering it to him. Please call him so that he can pick up the things here. His number is 0178-9252017.

So I guessed this was the package Alex had been talking about. In the hallway I also saw the two boxes that he had left for the next tenant. After I had made sure again that there was nothing else in the apartment that could have been of any importance, I decided to leave.

I carefully opened the apartment door and listened for a moment when I suddenly heard the front door open and someone come in. Two people were talking loudly to each other. That was not the right moment to go down the staircase. I had to wait until it was quiet again. I could hear footsteps coming up the stairs. Luckily they only went up to the first floor, then an apartment door was unlocked and then slammed shut with a loud bang.

Apparently it was the Afghan family on the first floor, which Alex had often complained about because they were in the habit of slamming their door. After a while it was quiet again, and I put the box outside and closed the apartment door. I went downstairs carefully and left the house, gently closing the front gate.

The box was quite heavy and I thought about the best way to take it home. My apartment was more than a mile away and walking through the city at night with such a package was very conspicuous and also tedious. I walked down the street to the main road and called a taxi by phone. Five minutes later a beige Mercedes stopped at the side of the road. I was glad when I arrived home shortly afterwards and could close the door behind me.

16 A Search Warrant

It promised to be a very warm Tuesday. From a midsummer blue sky a hot sun shone down on the two uniformed police officers standing in front of the house, one of them holding a toolbox. Inspector Rohloff searched in vain for the name Strasser. A nameplate made of paper hung from a doorbell with the name of Kimmich. Inspector Sauer had applied for a search warrant and received it, under the condition that Strasser was initially suspected of being involved in a murder.

As expected, nobody opened the door of the Kimmich apartment, and the officers rang all the neighbours' doorbells. Finally the door opened and the men went into the building and up the stairs. On the first floor Mr Fleischer stood in his apartment door and called theatrically:

"Help, the police! What do you want at ten o'clock in the morning? Are you real police officers? Have you got badges?"

The officers stopped, pulled out their IDs and held them in front of him.

"I was only joking," said Mr Fleischer. "You need to see the funny side of things now and then, am I right or am I wrong? Besides, it's obvious you're policemen."

Inspector Rohloff grinned. "Well, you're absolutely right to ask for our ID. Lately there have been quite a number of cases of fake policemen creeping up on citizens."

"Yes, that's what I heard. Just last night there was something about a case on TV. But where are you going, gentlemen? Are you going to arrest my wife? She deserves it. She was bothering me all day yesterday."

Inspector Rohloff laughed, his colleague Widmann grinned.

"No, we don't want to take your wife away from you. We actually want to see Mr Strasser. He lives in this house, doesn't he?" the Inspector asked.

"Well, he lived here until recently, but I think he has already moved out," replied Fleischer. "Last week there was a lot of banging and thumping, furniture being moved to and fro, and there were three powerful guys who carried all the household goods downstairs. As far as I know, the apartment is already completely empty."

"Is there a new tenant now?"

"Yes, a Mr Kimmich was here last week and he'll probably move in on August 1st. His name plate is already downstairs."

"Do you happen to have a key to the apartment?" asked Inspector

Rohloff.

Fleischer hesitated and looked suspiciously at the police.

"As a matter of fact I do, yes. Mr Strasser gave me a key in case anything should happen like a burst water pipe or something."

"Wonderful," said the officer. "Then we won't have to break the door down and save on repairs. Would you let us in?"

"Of course I don't know whether I'm allowed to," the man said thoughtfully. "I don't want to get into trouble. Maybe I will be charged for trespassing!"

"Come on, we're the police, you've seen our IDs and we have a search warrant. I'll show it to you." He pulled a document out of his pocket, which Fleischer skimmed over.

"I can't see a thing without my reading glasses. You might be holding a contract for a washing machine in front of my nose. But what has poor Strasser done to make you come after him like this?"

"I can't tell you about that, but you may have heard about the murder at his school."

"What, Strasser is wanted for murder? Well, I'll be damned! I would not have believed him capable of that," marvelled Mr Fleischer.

"No, he's not wanted for murder, he's wanted as a witness, there's a big difference! So, let's have a look inside now?"

"Wait a moment, I'll just get the key, unless my wife forbids me," laughed Fleischer and disappeared into his apartment. The officers stood on the landing and waited. A short time later he came back.

"Fortunately my wife is asleep," he grinned and they went upstairs together. Fleischer unlocked the apartment door.

They went through the rooms and immediately noticed that the apartment had been completely cleared out, only two removal boxes were standing in the hall against the wall. Other than that all the furniture and the curtains were gone.

"Everything seems to have been removed," said the officer with the toolbox in his hand, which he no longer needed.

"And what about these two boxes?"

"I don't know," said Fleischer. "Look inside, I don't know what's in them. Maybe he hid a dead body in there."

Inspector Widmann put on rubber gloves and rummaged around in them. In the first one there were pots and sauce pans. In the second one they found a hotchpotch of small objects; office utensils of all kinds, some dictionaries and also a pocket calendar. Inspector Rohloff took out the calendar and leafed through it. It was a calendar of the current year with numerous dates.

"We'll take this box of bits and pieces with us," said the policeman.

"Our forensics team will search it for DNA traces. I think we've seen enough, Mr Widmann, don't you?"

The colleague nodded in agreement and the Inspector then turned to Fleischer.

"If you should see Mr Strasser, please tell him to get in touch with us urgently. We would like to speak to him. That would be the easiest way to clear things up."

"Yes, of course I will tell him," replied Fleischer, "but I don't know if I even want to see him again if he is so dangerous. Well, if he comes, my wife can talk to him. She can handle herself, if necessary." He grinned again.

"Well, we've seen everything," the inspector said. "We thank you, and will now get back to the station."

The policemen left the flat. Fleischer locked the door and then said goodbye.

"Well, take care, folks, and get things done. There are too many idlers and thieves here in Lundenburg! Just last week there were two more burglaries right in our street. You have to watch it, otherwise we get our stuff stolen from under our noses. And if my wife annoys me again, I'll call you and expect you to take her into custody, at least for one day, so she gets a fright and leaves me alone."

The policemen laughed and Inspector Rohloff said, "Well, we'd rather not mess with your wife, but you're right, burglary is really a big problem. We'll keep at it and do our best, and with neighbours like you keeping your eyes open, well, it´s half the battle. With that in mind, take care."

17 Conversation among Teachers

The ladies and gentlemen of the teaching staff sat together in small groups in the staff room of the Schiller Grammar School, which had been released by the police for use again, and talked about the recent police interviews.

A holiday mood was in the air. It was the penultimate day of the school year and today the lessons ended after the fourth period.

In the afternoon there would still be projects that had to be prepared but the predominant topic at the moment was the interrogation by the police, which had taken place the day before and, for the latecomers, that morning. The colleagues reported to each other about what the police had wanted to know.

Just then, Mr Pobler came in to the teachers' room. The colleagues at one of the tables raised their heads and Mr Beerwisch called over to him with a grin. "Hello Peter, how did it go? Did they tear you apart?"

Pobler snorted contemptuously and walked towards the table where his clique was waiting for him. "Those cops are a bunch of sleepy wimps," he rumbled.

"And the type of questions they ask! I had to explain our new system 'Schiller FIX, fantastic, innovative, excellent' three times before they finally seemed to understand it."

"That's not a sign of your pedagogical skills," said Ms Tetzer sarcastically.

"Anna, stop teasing all the time. Of course you always know better. After all you are Teacher of the Year!"

Pobler had spoken the last words with exaggerated sarcasm.

"You're jealous, aren't you?" she replied with a grin. "The pupils must have had their reasons for choosing me. You'll just have to polish up your teaching technique a bit. You still have time, you don't retire until next year!"

"And you'll get an early retirement this year, I'm going to propose it today. By the way, the cops wanted to know if there was a colleague I suspected of murdering Lochberger and I made it quite clear that there was one colleague, and her name is Anna Tetzer."

From the neighbouring table, Mrs Matten-Degen called over in her shrill of voice:

"Mr Pobler, don't shout! Nobody here is interested in your vulgarity. Besides, I find it shameless the way you are making jokes here while we are all still shocked by the murder, but you don't seem to have noticed it yet."

"Mrs Matten-Degen, don't act up now. Even if your husband is the deputy headmaster here, that is no reason for you to constantly think you have to rebuke everyone. Besides, you are interfering in a private conversation that is none of your business. So please, kindly stop eavesdropping."

Mr Pobler was angry and snorted like a bull that was about to be let into the arena. The colleagues at the table tried to calm him down.

"Well now, don't get so upset," Mrs Woller tried to calm him down. "Better tell us what else the police asked."

"They asked about Alex. They asked me what I thought of him and how he behaved towards the headmaster. I told them that Alexander was one of the few people in the staff who spoke his mind to the old man. You have to give him credit for that. Apart from that, he is such a loner, actually quite a boring guy."

"Not everyone can be the life and soul of the party like you, Mr Pobler, always so entertaining and friendly. There's only one like that in every school" said Mrs Woller.

"Maybe so,'" Pobler continued unperturbed, "but in any case, I definitely believe Alexander might be a murderer. He always has such a sneaky expression, you never know what he is really thinking."

"Well, that really is the limit," Mrs Gross exclaimed. "I hope you didn't say that to the police. I don't agree with you. In my opinion Mr Strasser is a decent guy, and he gives his opinion about the school management, even if it gets him into trouble. Many others here don't do that but always consider carefully whether they might risk their future chances. That's why there is so much moral cowardice here among the staff, and not all those who are now sounding off are exempt from it."

"Mrs Gross, why are you butting in? You have only been at this school for three years. You still have no idea what is really going on here."

Mrs Tetzer intervened. "It doesn't take more than three days to notice that you're constantly ranting and raving and playing the alpha male. But if there is anyone here in the college who deserves to be considered a murderer, it is the one who started a brawl in the American student exchange last year and proved how violent and brutal he really is."

All the teachers at the neighbouring tables had now become aware of the raised voices and pricked up their ears. A noticeable silence set in. Mrs Tetzer looked triumphantly at Mr Pobler, whose face had turned bright red before he screamed loudly:

"I will not put up with your insolence any longer, you liar!"

Mrs Tetzer had caught him off guard: "The only one who is impertinent here is you! And it was you who last year in Denver in a restaurant punched my partner in the face because you could no longer stand up to his arguments. If I hadn't intervened and held you down, there would have been a huge scandal and you would have ended up in an American jail, you pompous old swine."

Mr Pobler yelled out once more "You lying old bag. Hysterical bitch," turned around and marched quickly to the door, which he slammed loudly behind him.

The colleagues all started whispering and talking at the same time. Anna Tetzer was asked whether this had really happened. She told them in detail the course of events at the time and that Pobler had gotten so upset over a little thing that he flew into a violent rage with her partner and then punched him in the face.

"He is a primitive, that's all I can say. And it gets on my nerves when he always acts up here as if he were the head of the school."

A few tables away, Erika Campos-Mimados sat beside Sabine, a young student teacher. Erika acted as her coach and mentor and guided her with lesson planning and the like. The young woman had only been at the school for a few days and had listened carefully to these arguments between Pobler and Tetzer.

"Tell me, Erika, is it always so aggressive here? It's pretty intense."

"Well, there are cliques that more or less like each other. You must have heard about the murder of our headmaster last week. Of course everyone is still quite excited, especially because yesterday and today there were police interrogations where all the colleagues were questioned. So far the police have no idea who the murderer might be, but basically everyone who has anything to do with the school is under suspicion."

"That's awful! So teachers and students alike are suspected?"

"I haven't heard anything about students so far, but they are looking for motives among the teaching staff at the moment, but I think that's pretty nonsensical. I can't imagine that any teacher would sink to such a level that he could commit murder. I wouldn't even suspect old Pobler. He always yells a lot, but apart from a big mouth, there's not much behind it."

"Was there real hostility between the staff and the headmaster?"

"Well, of course there are always arguments with different colleagues, but in my opinion there was nothing really serious. However, it seems that Alexander Strasser is now suspected because he was late at the school on the evening of the murder and because he did not appear for police questioning. That was of course quite stupid of him. He called in sick yesterday."

"And what was the headmaster like, in your opinion?"

"You know the saying 'De mortuis nil nisi bene'. So I'll stick to that and only speak well of the dead. He was a good organiser, but he lacked sensitivity. Perhaps he was more of a manager type. As a teacher, however, you sometimes need a little advice and encouragement, because there are often conflicts with pupils or parents, and then you look for the support of the headmaster. But that was usually wishful thinking with us because, for him, the parents came first, then the pupils, then the pupils again and finally us, the teachers. And that frustrated some of the staff, including me, sometimes."

"Of course, these are things you don't learn about at university. That's a big shortcoming of our educational system, that we can only gain practical experience after our studies by actually working at a school."

"Yes, that's what happened to me when I came from university and saw a school from the inside for the first time after five years of studying. You have to get over quite a few shocks. That starts with the equipment. At the university and in the teacher training seminar they told us a lot about modern media in the classroom, and then I was standing at a dusty blackboard with a piece of chalk and had to manage with a broken overhead projector. Hardly anything has changed at school for forty years it seems. Small overcrowded classrooms with thirty pupils. I experienced this in my own student days, and today it is no better. All the politicians have been shouting 'education, education' for many years now, and we sit here with the same miserable equipment as in my childhood. Soap, for example, is not available at school. We teachers bring it from home, just like towels. There used to be soap dispensers in the toilets for a while, but then they disappeared again, regular filling was too expensive for the state. It is a real shame how schools are treated in this country by the same politicians who boast that the education of our children is their main concern."

"It's really awful, you're absolutely right."

"And then there's the competition among the staff. You are not prepared for that at all and nobody talks about it in the teacher training seminar either."

"Is that a big problem?"

Ms Campos-Mimados lowered her voice and made the young colleague understand that one had to be very discreet on this subject. "Of course this is a huge issue," she said softly, almost in a whisper. "A headmaster has his favourite teachers, and they are those younger colleagues who always say what he wants to hear and are prepared to do whatever he asks. As a reward for such people, there is an early promotion. On the other hand, if you ask too many critical questions or drop comments that challenge the headmaster's views, you can wait for your promotion until the cows come home. Or you can change school, which happens quite often."

"It doesn't sound very good," Sabine said.

"This was also roughly the same with the introduction of our new 'FIX' model. In the first discussion before the vote the headmaster's favourites all emphasized in detail the positive aspects of the reform and thus had a very strong influence on the general mood. Anyone who spoke out against it had to expect that this would have a negative impact on their careers. That's how simple and primitive these things are."

"And do you think this could have anything to do with this murder?"

"I don't think so. The teachers are all too well provided for to exchange their gilded cages for the prospect of living behind bars. What advantage could anyone gain from a murder? The only conceivable motive would be revenge, and there are other means of achieving that than murder, I think. I can't imagine a teacher did this."

"Anyone could walk into this building though, couldn't they?"

"Exactly. Which is why some mugger could have come in at night looking to steal. I told the police that they should rather search in the criminal milieu than interrogate the teachers for days on end."

"Actually it is an impertinence to think we are all potential murderers, isn't it?"

"I agree, Sabine. You should tell them that. But we've made it through now, and the holidays are just around the corner, so let's not let it spoil our mood now, eh?"

"Of course not. The day after tomorrow I'll be in the car and on my way to Rügen island. I hope the warm weather will last for a while."

"Oh, you're going to the Baltic Sea. How nice! I'll be at Lake Constance for a fortnight first, and then we'll see. By the way, I hope I didn't frustrate you too much before when I talked about our everyday school life. It may have sounded negative, but on the whole, working at school is fun, and there are many nice colleagues. I definitely don't want to give you a negative overall picture."

"No, you didn't, don't worry. Oh, look, it's already half past eleven. I have another appointment with Mr Degen. I'll see you this afternoon, okay?"

"Okay, I'll be back shortly before three, so see you then, bye."

18 Insights

I flicked through the diaries of my friend Alexander. Normally I do not read other people's diaries. But things were different with Alex. He expressly recommended these diaries to me and also encouraged me to read them. He said that as his best friend I should know all the details of his life story.

Of course I had a strange feeling about it now because I could not quite shake off the impression that he had given me the box of diaries when something seemed to be going wrong in his life. Could it be that he was involved in this crime after all and feared a bitter end? I was nervous as I rummaged around in the box.

There were an estimated thirty diaries in various colours and sizes. Also smaller books with imitation leather covers, probably from his childhood, with locks to keep the secrets safe. Each of the diaries had a label on the outside showing the period of the entries. After a long search I had roughly sorted them and picked out the most recent one. The older entries did not interest me at the moment. Finally I found what I was looking for and began reading the entry which referred to the start of the summer holidays.

I skimmed over the pages that reported on everyday impressions, school experiences or even conflicts with his current girlfriend, Ulla. For the first ten minutes I found nothing particularly remarkable, just reports from my friend's everyday life. I turned the pages and after a while I came across an entry that left me puzzled.

July 2, 2017
My colleague Friederike no longer talks to me, she is obviously offended and ignores me. I noticed this a few days ago, and for several days she wasn't even in the teachers' room. She has obviously barricaded herself in her classroom. This may have something to do with the conflict she has had with my class for some time. The class is complaining that she calls students to the blackboard and makes them look ridiculous in front of the whole class if they don't prove their knowledge. Apparently they are then also given exaggeratedly bad oral grades. When I cautiously touched on the subject, she reacted rather dismissively, even aggressively. I advised her to have a discussion with the pupils, and if she wished, I could also be present as a moderator. She rejected these suggestions, eventually accusing me of being on my students' side rather than hers. Since then all communication has stopped. She avoids me, neither greets me nor returns my greetings. She ignores my presence. I wouldn't have thought that a

colleague with thirty years of school experience could react in such a way.

I was astonished by this entry and wondered why the cooperation between the teachers apparently didn't work out as well as one usually imagines from the point of view of an outsider. Of course, this also raised the question of whether these personalities were really capable of leading our young people to university entrance qualifications. I read on.

July 27th
Today was the last day of school and I handed out the reports. Nothing special happened, except that the class was very noisy. I had to call them to silence by shouting loudly over and over again. I tried once again to make an appointment with the boss. It is about the student Albert Vogel, who complained about his mark in the Spanish oral exam. Lochberger has asked me to present him with documents concerning his final marks. Another bad joke, he will of course make deals with the student again and turn against me, possibly trying to force me to change my grade. I have submitted the requested documents to him. From these it is quite clear that the student cannot be given a better mark in Spanish. Lochberger saw the documents, but did not offer me an appointment for a meeting.

Let him do what he wants. As far as I'm concerned, the matter is settled and I'm fed up with him constantly trying to interfere with my grades. That seems to be the norm with him. Franz Baum told me a few weeks ago that Lochberger forced him to repeat a class test in German. A pupil had approached the headmaster with the claim that the subject had not been agreed upon or something similar. The man is a scandal. He should know that as a boss and superior he has a re-sponsibility to his staff. He obviously can´t get that through his thick skull.

So his relationship with the headmaster was obviously quite tense, as I could tell from this entry. I turned the pages and opened the diary at the back of the book.

April 23, 2018
Today I met Monika again. She explained to me the situation of the software market in the school sector. There is tough competition and the Lochbergers have had the best sales figures for a long time. Mess-erschmidt would like to improve his market position and is interested

in internals and program code from Lochberger's software. Monika apparently wants to separate from her husband and before that she is planning to get his latest software modules in order to continue the company after the divorce, in cooperation with Messerschmidt. Her husband keeps his software development under lock and key. The new modules are on the school computer and on his SD data card, which he always carries with him. She asked me whether I would dare to get hold of these documents, adding that Messerschmidt would appreciate that very much. I have promised in part. I can't refuse this woman anything. She fascinates me more and more.

What did that mean, I wondered. Apparently Alex had a suspiciously close relationship with Lochberger's wife, which he had previously kept from me. And apparently this Monika Lochberger had incited my friend to steal her husband's data and sell it to the competitor. Then Alex had apparently only got into this criminal affair through this woman's urging.

But how can a wife, who is also the owner of a business, find no other way to get her husband's data than theft by a third party? That was not quite clear to me. And what did this data theft have to do with the murder? Had she possibly given the order to murder her husband? And had she perhaps commissioned Alex to do it and found in him a willing tool because he hated her husband and adored her?

All this seemed to me quite worrying and at the moment rather hard to see. I closed the diary and didn't feel like reading any more because it was late and I didn't want to risk losing a night's sleep by pondering these strange revelations.

19 Another Visit

Monika Lochberger opened the door and let Commissioner Sauer and his colleague Schmelzer in. The Commissioner had arranged the meeting the day before.

He had announced the meeting as 'purely routine', but Monika Lochberger was of course aware that she, as the sole beneficiary of her husband's estate, was counted among the group of suspects.

She invited her guests to sit on the couch and had also provided a bottle of mineral water and three glasses.

"Please help yourselves. You will probably refuse alcohol, but mineral water is certainly not a problem, especially with this heat."

"Thank you very much, that's very thoughtful," said the Commissioner.

"Anyway, a few days have passed since your husband's murder. Have you got any ideas or information that might help us?"

"No, unfortunately. Absolutely nothing," Mrs Lochberger said. "The whole thing is still completely mysterious to me."

"Mrs Lochberger, as the wife of a school headmaster, did you attend events at your husband's school from time to time?"

"Yes, of course, it can't be avoided."

"Perhaps you may have had private contact with various members of the school? If so, with whom?"

"My husband's deputy, Mr Degen, was with us two or three times with his wife. Two other members of the extended school management, Mr Meinhard and Mr Reier, were also with us a couple of times, but otherwise we had no private contact with the rest of the staff."

"We invited all of the staff members for interviews and wanted to know whether there were any hostilities between them and your husband. Do you know anything about that?"

"Well, my husband sometimes told me about trouble he had had with one or other of the teachers. But hostility, no, that would be going too far. He never mentioned it."

"Does the name Pobler mean anything to you?"

"Yes, I remember that name. My husband reported that this teacher had caused some trouble. He said he was one of the older members of staff and liked to play the leader of the opposition."

"Some teachers have stated in their description that this Mr Pobler is a man with a lot of potential for aggression. Do you think he could be somehow connected to your husband's murder?"

"Well, I can't answer that, I hardly know the man. I've seen him two or three times and he was always friendly to me. My husband never said he felt threatened by him."

"Does the name Baum mean anything to you?"

"Yes, I remember that name too. My husband occasionally reported some difficulties with this teacher, but I don't remember the exact details."

"So, if I understand you correctly, you personally did not have much contact with the staff. Were there any teachers to whom you occasionally spoke by telephone?"

Mrs Lochberger paused for a moment and seemed to think. She then said that it was possible, but at that moment she could not remember talking to her husband's colleagues on the phone.

"What about Mr Alexander Strasser? Did you know that your husband received a very unfriendly letter from him?"

"Oh yes, he told me at the time. It must have been about a year ago. He invited Mr Strasser to a meeting during the holidays because of some disagreement and then this teacher freaked out and wrote a rather impertinent letter to my husband."

"And how did your husband react? What was your husband's attitude towards this individual?"

"You know, he has so often experienced minor conflicts. It happens regularly if you have eighty employees. But he was always very matter-of-fact. He was basically a manager type and never took such conflicts personally but was always oriented towards ensuring that the school continued to run as smoothly as possible. He didn't like Mr Strasser. He didn't say anything positive about him, but it wasn't a big issue for us either."

"Did you at any time have any personal contact with Mr Strasser?"

"I don't remember, I don't think so."

"Your husband's staff-members have been questioned by the police already. Of course there are other potential suspects. These could be petty criminals from the drug scene who happened to meet your husband. Or any pupils, perhaps? What do you think about that?"

"Well, I don't think so. My husband was very popular with the pupils. He took care of each one of them, especially the problematic ones."

"Okay, we can probably rule out the pupils then. Are there any people who might have gotten some advantage from his death? For example, professional competitors. Your husband was a software producer, you are the owner of the company. To our knowledge there is only one company competing with you in this limited market. What contact do you have with this competing company?"

"You are obviously talking about the Messerschmidt company. We have little contact, except at specialist conferences where we meet once or twice a year, but the contact has always been limited to business. My husband developed the better software and we therefore have a slightly higher market share than Messerschmidt. That's why he was never particularly responsive to us, and that's also why we never had any close contact."

"Do you think it is possible that your competitor could benefit from the current situation? I mean, your husband is no longer available as a developer, so it could be that your lead in product development has diminished."

"That would be conceivable in principle, but we also have freelancers. And I believe that they are now so well trained that we can continue to develop our software packages even without my husband."

"What do you think about the idea that your competitor Messerschmidt might be behind the murder?"

"Well, come on, that seems pretty far-fetched. What could he possibly hope to gain from it? As I said, we have freelancers who can replace my husband, so murder would certainly not be a sensible way for a competitor to gain an advantage."

"Have you spoken to Messerschmidt recently?"

Mrs Lochberger's face now showed a distinct uneasiness.

"Where did you get that idea?"

"As a policeman, I am used to asking questions. Sometimes it may sound nonsensical to the interviewees but nevertheless I beg you to answer, yes or no?"

"I can't remember at the moment, but I don't think so."

"I'm in no hurry. I can wait until your memory is refreshed. Think again calmly, it will come back to you."

Mrs Lochberger's discomfort had obviously increased. Suddenly she said abruptly:

"Yes, it just came to me. We spoke on the phone a few days ago and talked about the new rules and laws on data protection. These are things that concern both of us, competition or not."

"I see. Have you spoken to Mr Strasser recently?"

"Well, you know, all these questions, I'm not sure! I work fifty hours a week and phone a hundred times a day, so it's a bit much to ask that I should remember every single phone call."

"Mrs Lochberger, I don't want to overburden you in any way, but after all, Mr Strasser is not just any telephone contact from your department, but a member of your husband's staff, whom we suspect may be connected with the crime against your husband. I would therefore like you to try to remember whether you spoke to him on the phone or not."

The woman was obviously nervous and thinking hard. The Commissioner had the impression that she was unsure how she should act now. After some moments of hesitation, she suddenly said:

"Yes, I have spoken to Mr Strasser on the telephone. He called me on the night of the murder, around ten past nine. What he said to me, however, confused me quite a bit. I didn't really know what he meant."

"What did he say to you?"

"He said: 'Mrs Lochberger, your husband is still sitting in the office at work. I really feel sorry for him, I think you should take more care of him. He works too much. It's not good for his health'. Those were his exact words. At first I thought he was pulling my leg and wanted to ask him what he actually meant by that, but then the connection was cut. He'd hung up."

"Strange," said the Commissioner thoughtfully. "But why didn't you tell us this earlier when I asked you if you had had any personal contact with Mr Strasser at any time?"

"By personal contact I understood something else. That was an extremely short phone call, it didn't last a minute."

"After the call, what did you think and how did you react?"

"I found it impertinent that a complete stranger should take the liberty of giving me advice on my husband's health. I wasn't sure if he wasn't just making fun of me, because I had heard that Strasser didn't like my husband. Anyway, shortly before I called my husband at the office, which must have been just before nine, and asked him when he would be coming home. He said he was about to leave, but had a few things to do. Of course I knew what that meant. When he's really involved in a task, time just flies and he doesn't even notice."

"Have you had other conversations with Mr Strasser?"

"No."

"Mr Strasser was indeed at the school until shortly after nine o'clock. Apart from your husband and Mr Strasser and two other colleagues, there was nobody else in the building. Did your husband mention this in his phone call to you?"

"No, he didn't say that."

"Didn't you suspect Strasser immediately after the crime?"

"Not at first, but when I came home I thought about it."

"Do you suspect Strasser of murder?"

"I don't know. I hardly know this Strasser. I have no idea whether he would be capable of doing such a thing."

"Yes, that is indeed a difficult question, and we cannot answer it at the moment. But for today we are finished. If anything else comes to your mind, please call me, here is my card. Every little thing can help us, and that's in your interest, I am sure."

"Yes, of course," said Mrs Lochberger, visibly relieved about the end of the interview.

The two policemen said goodbye. Monika Lochberger showed her guests to the door, then closed it behind them, took a deep breath and lit a cigarette.

The Commissioner and his colleague walked next to each other without a word for some time until they were sure they were out of earshot.

"Well, what do you think, Schmelzer?" he asked his colleague curiously.

"I got the impression that the woman has something to hide. She also lied to us when she said she hadn't talked to her husband's colleagues. Now finally, she reluctantly admits to having spoken to Strasser, but the story of his phone call to her sounded incredible to me."

"That was my impression, too. If Strasser called just before the murder, it was hardly to whine to her that her poor husband had to work so late. It's quite ridiculous."

"What other reason could he have had?"

"I was about to ask you that question, Schmelzer. Let your imagination run wild. What could have happened?"

"Well, if Strasser is indeed the perpetrator and he calls Lochberger's wife just before the murder, it is certainly not for nothing. I would rather suspect that he is making common cause with the wife, that the two have agreed on something. Perhaps about the exact execution or timing of the murder."

"Very good combination, Schmelzer. I see you're making progress. Now we just need to find out when and how often the two have communicated with each other, or perhaps still do. I'll make sure all phone calls and email contacts are tapped. The prosecutor will not object, I have reasonable suspicions of foul play."

"Shouldn't we also place Mrs Lochberger under surveillance?"

"Yes, I think that would be the right thing to do. Arrange for that to be done. Perhaps Mr Schulze can do it together with our new trainee."

20 Increasing Suspicions

In the meantime Alex had now been away for forty-eight hours and I hadn't heard from him. At that particular moment I had no way to reach him either. I had to wait until he got in touch with me. However, I planned to look into his diaries again and tonight I had time and no appointments. So I got the box that was in the room next door and took out the diary from the day before.

August 1st, 2017
Spent the first few days of my holiday relaxing and will go away this week. This year to England. I have already put almost everything I need in my RV and I can set off soon.

Just now I checked my letterbox, it's 1 pm, and there was a letter from Lochberger in it, without a stamp, so obviously he has put it there personally. He claims that I prevented him from reaching an appointment on behalf of the pupil Vogel, and that I have done so several times, and so he feels compelled to invite me for an interview during the summer break. The date he gave me is on a Tuesday in the fourth week of the school holidays. What an idiot! I will pay him back for this. If he thinks he can go on bullying me, he is mistaken. I'll get my own back soon enough.

August 3rd, 2017
Wrote a sarcastic letter to Lochberger today. The fool should know that my early retirement has a lot to do with him.

Ah, I thought. That was the letter the Commissioner was talking about. It was pasted as a copy on the next page and read as follows:

Dear Mr Lochberger
You sent me a letter at the beginning of the summer holidays claiming that despite several attempts, it was not possible to make an appointment with me regarding the concerns of the student Albert Vogel.

This is incorrect. I have pointed out to you several times in recent days that this matter should be resolved before the holidays, and you have claimed each time that we must find another day for that conversation. In this respect, the cause for the failure to make an appointment lies entirely with you.

Apart from that, you summoned me in the middle of the holidays to discuss this student's complaint about his oral grade in Spanish. Do you seriously believe that I will interrupt or shorten my vacation in order to discuss my oral marks for any student?

Your request is sheer impertinence. I will not interrupt my long-planned holidays to pay for your inability to make reasonable arrangements. I reject the appointment you have set for me and I will not attend. If necessary, I will refer the matter to the school's Staff Council.

Incidentally, I wonder why you are always meddling in things you cannot possibly understand. As a mathematician, you will hardly be able to judge the content of my subjects, English and Spanish, but you have nevertheless interfered in my grading on several occasions. As soon as a student is dissatisfied with his or her grade, he or she need only knock on your door and can safely assume that you will decide in his or her favour and against the subject teacher. I find this scandalous. As a headmaster, you have a responsibility to your staff first and foremost but you don't seem to care about that. You are constantly ingratiating yourself with pupils and parents and then, in case of conflict, you turn against your staff. Officially you are obliged as a superior to take care of your teachers first. Also on a human level, of course. But to try to address this with you is probably a waste of time.

I'm glad that the coming school year will be my last, because it really is not at all pleasant to work under your authoritarianism. You think you have to run a school in the style of an autocrat. It seems to have escaped your esteemed attention that a lot has changed in the last fifty years in terms of staff management. I leave it up to you to look into the subject occasionally.

Incidentally, you may also be concerned that at least seven colleagues have left our school in recent years and sought employment elsewhere, always for 'personal reasons', of course. However, you can always hear the whisperings that the overwhelming dissatisfaction with their boss was the real reason.

I am looking forward to my retirement and to the time when I no longer have to deal with you. Moreover, some of my colleagues are wondering how long you actually want to stay in office. You too could actually step down earlier and do the whole school a big favour. Best wishes and looking forward to learning of your early retirement,

Alexander Strasser

Here the entry for that day was over and the next diary entry was already from his holiday, which he had started on Thursday of the same week. This action of the headmaster seemed to me rather authoritarian and hostile. If I had been in Alexander's shoes, I would have been just as upset about this insolence. The headmaster apparently wanted to force him to interrupt his vacation in the middle of the holiday period to discuss this minor topic of a pupil's oral assessment. That was really nasty of his boss, I must say. I didn't know him as a supervisor but only as a customer whose computer I had to maintain. But now I understood my friend Alex very well, who had apparently fallen victim to his boss' arbitrariness, despotism and bullying on several occasions.

I only hoped that he had not allowed himself to be influenced by this provocation to such an extent that he might actually have committed an act of violence, as revenge for the humiliations he had suffered. The letter, however, was unnecessarily provocative in my view, but that only showed how much Alex had been boiling with rage.

That evening, I was suddenly no longer quite sure that Alex was not involved in the murder. Maybe he had lost his head in the heat of a violent altercation. Maybe there was an aggressive exchange of words with the boss or some other unforeseen event that triggered a rash act of violence. There were many possibilities. Or maybe he had been ordered by Monika Lochberger to kill her husband. After everything I had read so far, that no longer seemed impossible either.

I was now seriously worried because if my fears were correct, Alex was a murderer on the run, and therefore his chances of remaining free for a long time would probably be slim. Also, I might be charged with helping to cover up a crime, and in the worst case, that could mean the end of my professional life and I might possibly even go to prison.

I spent that evening restlessly, thinking over and over again about what to believe and how I could try to contact Alex without putting the police on his trail. As the evening wore on, the more my attention started to wander. I decided to go to bed. Tomorrow would be another day.

That night I had bad dreams, some of which were quite alarming. Once I saw Alexander arguing with a policeman. Suddenly he said:

"Yes, I killed Lochberger, and you want to lock me up now, but that won't happen. I have a remedy right here." Then he pulled a pistol out of his pocket, pointed it at the policeman and pulled the trigger. I heard a loud shot and the policeman fell over. I woke up drenched in sweat.

It was half past three in the morning and I still had three hours to go before I had to get up. After a sip of chamomile tea from the thermos I went back to bed and fortunately I was able to get back to sleep.

21 Evidence and Assumptions

"Welcome everybody," the Commissioner opened the service meeting with the seven members of the Schiller Special Commission. "We are here to discuss the state of the investigation and to exchange information. The murder of headmaster Lochberger is now only a few days old and we have some initial results. First of all, perhaps the summary of the forensic medical examination. Mrs Faller, could you briefly present them. Thank you."

The addressed person, a stout woman of about forty years of age with dark brown hair and horn-rimmed glasses began to speak.

"According to the examination report, the cause of death is a skull fracture with severe brain injury caused by the impact of a blunt object to the head. It may have been a wooden club or similar object. Death was most likely instantaneous. The time of death was determined by forensic medicine to be between 9:30 and 10 pm. The dead man was apparently robbed, as no personal effects were found on him. According to his wife, he always carried a wallet with money and credit cards. In this context, we can assume a robbery-homicide. Forensics have recovered various DNA traces on the body. These can be used to convict the offender as soon as we have arrested a suspect. Thus far this is the conclusion of the forensic report. Are there any questions?"

"How promising are these DNA traces likely to be?", Mr Kugler wanted to know. "We often find that these traces come from family members or people in the daily environment."

"Nothing conclusive can be said about this yet. There are traces of several people but we cannot yet say anything about a link to single individuals or family members."

Commissioner Sauer took over the conversation again. "Our next item on the agenda is to narrow down the suspects. We have questioned around eighty teachers at the school and have not received any clear indications of possible perpetrators. However, there were numerous indications that the person killed was an extremely ambitious person and that he was carrying out educational reforms, sometimes against the will of the staff, which the majority of teachers felt were a burden. We can therefore assume that there were certainly a larger number of teachers who were in clear opposition to the headmaster. As possible suspects we have short-listed two people. A teacher by the name of Pobler was described by several people as very irascible and violent. We will take a closer look at him. During the interrogation he was rather sociable and cooperative. He is also a year away from retirement and the teacher enjoys a certain freedom to do whatever he wants, as he is considered to be the most senior teacher. Under these circumstances, I regard his involvement as unlikely.

The second candidate is Alexander Strasser, who has already distinguished himself in word and deed by relatively strong reactions to the headmaster. There seem to have been several major confrontations and Mr Strasser has also written a very direct letter to the headmaster, in which he called on him to retire early and expressed himself very negatively overall. Unfortunately, we were unable to question Mr Strasser in person. He called in sick on Monday and was summoned by us by email for Tuesday with the express request to appear or risk a forced interrogation.

He also ignored this request and apparently went into hiding. Our officers were unable to locate him, neither at his flat in Lundenburg nor at his new home in the Bavarian Mountains. The flat in Lundenburg is already empty, as Mr Strasser is retiring next school year and has probably already completed his move. The man is extremely suspicious because of his behaviour. After all, he could have come to the interrogation like the others. The fact that he has now disappeared without a trace places him under serious suspicion. I have therefore requested an international arrest warrant for him this morning. The suspect may already be abroad."

Now Inspector Rohloff gave his report.

"In addition, I can perhaps add that I was with officer Widmann at the suspect's old address this week. We did not find him, but a neighbour from the house allowed us access to Strasser's apartment which was empty. Of course we could have placed the flat under surveillance, but Strasser probably won't go back there. In any case, the neighbour who let us in knew nothing about his whereabouts and said that he had already said goodbye."

"I don't think there is any point in watching the flat and we don't have enough people for that kind of thing," said Commissioner Sauer. "Besides, it is not as if Strasser is the only possible suspect. Mrs Knoblauch will tell us in a moment what other suspects there are. Please, officer Knoblauch."

"Thank you, Commissioner. We must indeed take a closer look at another group of people besides the teachers. Firstly, family members. Secondly economic rivals and thirdly, random criminals from the criminal milieu, such as those often found near the crime scene in the area around the station."

"On point one, family members. The murder victim has a wife and no children. His wife is the owner of Lochberger School Software Ltd., which specializes in and distributes a software package used in many schools in various federal states of Germany. The author of this software is her husband. She also benefits from a large life insurance policy worth three hundred thousand euros. This could of course be a possible motive for murder. We have already had murder cases for much smaller sums.

The spouses had appointed each other as sole heirs. The wife of the murder victim could also be considered a beneficiary under this aspect. The family's financial circumstances are very good. There are bank deposits of almost one million euros."

This information triggered an astonished murmur among the officers. "You should be a school headmaster," said Inspector Widmann. His colleague Faller added, "And have a company on the side, otherwise you will never make your fortune."

"Silence please colleagues. Mrs Knoblauch is not quite finished."

"So Mrs Lochberger will experience a significant increase in her wealth as a result of her husband's death, which is why she is considered a suspect in the narrower sense of the word."

"I suggest we place her under observation immediately and tap her telephone," Faller said.

"Please let's talk about possible measures at the end," continued Inspector Knoblauch. "If we include another group of suspicious persons in the observation, namely the commercial competitors, then an interesting constellation emerges: Lochberger has only one serious competitor, Messerschmidt Software. Both supply the same market. Messerschmidt, with a forty percent market share, is smaller than Lochberger, who dominates around sixty percent of the market. We have found that in the last two weeks there have been numerous telephone calls between Messerschmidt and Mrs Lochberger, during the day, especially in the mornings, when Mr Lochberger was normally at his school. It can therefore be assumed that his wife made these telephone calls. There were ten calls in total. Such frequent conversations between competitors are conspicuous and we should include this fact in any future questioning of Mrs Lochberger."

"By all means!" the Commissioner interrupted his colleague. "At the last hearing, she claimed that she had only spoken to her competitor once. That is more than suspicious."

Mrs Knoblauch continued with her report.

"It is possible that the two company owners want to cooperate and then monopolise the market. And that would significantly increase the profit expectations of both parties."

The speaker looked directly at her listeners, who signalled approval.

"Another subject, and this brings us back to Mr Strasser. When we checked the telephone connections, we found that a call had been made from the Lochberger phone to a Ms Ulla Schulze the morning after the crime, at six in the morning. Since the woman was completely unknown to us, we did some research and found something surprising: Ms Schulze and Mr Strasser have been in a relationship for two years."

A murmur went round and the Commissioner exclaimed in amazement, "Really?!"

The Commissioner waited a moment until the general excitement had subsided and Mrs Knoblauch continued:

"Yes, and this is of course very suspicious. And, listen to this, a call from Mr Strasser's mobile phone to the phone of the Lochberger couple took place at 9:10 pm on the evening of the murder, but the call lasted only twenty seconds."

Voices were raised at this moment. "That's incredible", "Madness", "Well, well", were some of the exclamations and the Commissioner immediately burst out in high praise of his colleague.

"Excellent work, Mrs Knoblauch, that is what I call intuition."

Inspector Knoblauch was obviously flattered by the Commissioner's praise and smiled contentedly.

The Commissioner took charge of the meeting again.

"During our visit yesterday, Mrs Lochberger admitted that Strasser called her on the evening of the murder. However, she told us a strange story about this. Namely that Strasser had accused her of making her husband work too hard. That sounded rather confused and not very credible. From my point of view it looks more like Mrs Lochberger hired Strasser to kill her husband. Why else would she have phoned him twice and so close to the time of the crime. What else could this woman have to do with this teacher? Of course we will have to ask her that at the next interrogation."

Mrs Knoblauch had not yet finished her report.

"Hold on, please. We do not want to jump to conclusions. Perhaps our suspicions are correct, but as I said before, we have three potential suspect groups and I would like to come back to the third group now, namely petty criminals and drug addicts. These petty criminals have been making trouble in the area around the station for years. It is not impossible that one of these people entered the school in the evening in search of cash and accidentally came across the headmaster and subsequently killed and robbed him."

The Commissioner had now taken charge again.

"Many thanks, Mrs Knoblauch. I believe you have provided us with valuable information. I think we will now concentrate on Mrs Lochberger and her relationship with Strasser and Messerschmidt. I will immediately apply to the public prosecutor for permission to tap all relevant telephones and all electronic communications, as I believe there is a strong indication of involvement in a murder. It is possible that Mrs Lochberger may also have contact with the fugitive Strasser, who apparently collaborated with her."

"These results of tonight must remain top secret, everything is strictly confidential. Under no circumstances should you pass on any information, especially not to the press. This could jeopardise our entire investigation. We will meet again on Monday afternoon at two o'clock. Perhaps by then we may have some new leads. I wish you all a good weekend. Until Monday."

"Same to you. Bye boss," said the officers as they packed their things and filed out of the room.

22 The Father

The next day I came back from my work assignment with a customer in Stuttgart at around three o'clock. I made myself a cup of coffee and then could hardly wait to continue reading Alexander's diaries. I flipped through the one from the day before and as I turned the pages, the headline 'Letter to Father' caught my eye. I knew that Alexander's father had died about ten years ago, so it couldn't have been a letter in the traditional sense. I began to read with great curiosity.

Dear Father,

You have always maintained: "Man alone cannot solve his problems!" God would have to intervene, and he would cause apocalyptic destruction before a completely new, heavenly world would be created. That was your vision of the State of God, which supposedly had been foretold for mankind in the Bible. I could never get anything out of this idea and was always very distant from your Old Testament views. That was one of the reasons why we could never really understand each other.

But apart from that, our life is first and foremost something that has to do with personal experiences for each and every one of us. It is the events and feelings of childhood that deeply shape us as persons and these are the things we remember later on, even into old age.

Some of my childhood experiences still weigh on my mind today, after more than half a century, and there are a number of things that I never dared to say to your face personally. As long as I was a child, I could not do that, because you were a merciless tyrant as a father, and rigorously suppressed any criticism. Your threatening exclamation "Don't argue!", combined with a grim and frightening expression on your face, accompanied me throughout my entire childhood and youth.

Many years have passed in the meantime. Childhood is a long time ago, but nevertheless some of the images and events of that time are still as present in my memory as if it had been only yesterday.

There are some fond memories too. For example, of the long walks in the summer through the vineyards near Stuttgart, where we often spent entire days, roaming through meadows and forests. I was only four or five years old at the time and we would walk long distances, and sometimes we would stop in an orchard under a shady tree and fortify ourselves with a fresh apple for the way home. You yourself were sometimes surprised at how far I was able to walk as a little boy. When my strength ran out, you carried me on your shoulders or on your back, as on that day when we marched up the steep path to the Rotenberg-Hill in hot weather.

When I see one of the few photos today of the little boy I was then, I see a child smiling at me with confidence, with children's eyes that apparently as yet had seen nothing bad. But the evil had already entered my life and the child's basic trust had already been considerably disturbed.

For the first two years of my life we, that is you, mother and I, lived in extremely cramped conditions in an attic room that was part of your parents-in-law's flat.

It was the post-war period, Germany was destroyed and housing was scarce. Living in a space of about twelve square metres was a burden for all of us, especially for you, as you had to get up at five in the morning to go to work in the machine factory. I screamed and cried a lot when I was a baby. Especially at night I would often cry for hours without anyone being able to calm me down. The cause was not really clear, one suspected indigestion or colic. The constant lack of sleep became a problem for the family.

You, father, sometimes told me later about this difficult time and how exhausting it was to have to get up at five o'clock after a night with little sleep. Your nerves were stretched to breaking point and your attitude towards me was not very loving: "I sometimes felt like flinging you against the wall", you told me later, literally, more than once. The first time I heard that from your mouth was when I was thirteen years old. It then became frighteningly clear to me that my father, that giant of a man, had shown me great mercy by simply not bashing that poor little soul's brains out.

Whether and to what extent I actually experienced violence from you as a small child, I don't know from my own memory. My grandmother, who otherwise spoke of you only in glowing terms, once told me, when I was already thirty years old, that you beat me black and blue several times when I was a small boy. As a consequence even she, who was a firm believer in corporal punishment, rebuked you in the strongest terms one day. "You shouldn't beat a little child like that, it can cause permanent damage," she said to you in order to protect her grandchild.

I felt unpleasantly touched by this reading. Alex had never spoken to me about his childhood, I had always assumed that he had grown up under quite normal circumstances. After I had read these notes about his father, a completely different picture emerged. Apparently he had experienced child abuse and at that time there was no public awareness to put such parents in their place and no laws to protect children. I got up, went to the coffee pot and got myself a refill. Then I read on.

My childlike trust in my father was unfortunately betrayed too soon. The great powerful man could become very angry. I had to learn this lesson early.

Once in early summer, when I was about four years old, I incurred your wrath again. I was put to bed very early to go to sleep, but I was not yet tired. Outside there was still bright sunshine, and I heard through the window the happy voices of the adults, you, my mother and a couple from the neighbourhood, enjoying yourselves playing badminton.

I started to cry because I felt left alone, I wanted to be there too. Nobody reacted to my screaming, so I finally came up with the creative idea of pulling up the roller shutter a bit, opening the window and shouting out my misfortune. You heard my crying, but the result was quite different from what I had intended.

You, father, were very angry about this disturbance, came into my room furiously and scolded me for behaving so impossibly. Then you grabbed me with an iron grip and laid me over your shoulder like one of those potato sacks which you had carried around on your father's farm every day when you were a young boy. I remember you taking me down to the cellar, which smelled musty and damp. There was a big box of potatoes in our cellar shed. It was partly filled with the last remains of the winter supply and the tubers had almost all sprouted.

You put me into this box. All my frantic screaming and pleading was of no use.

You said something like, "Well, you can keep screaming here as long as you want." I screamed like a pig. The cellar had always frightened me. I knew that there were rats there. Your footsteps were receding. The lights went out. The door slammed shut. I screamed with all my might in mortal fear and I was all alone in this dark and mouldy place, locked up in the box. I couldn't climb out. It was pitch black and I felt the rotting potatoes under me. Around me the horrible smell. I screamed. An eternity went by in which I felt only fear, panic and abandonment.

You later explained the whole thing to me as the just punishment for my naughtiness. My fear of you and your irascibility was hardened by such traumas and has been burned deep into me .

I was downright shocked by this entry from my friend. So he had grown up under such a father? Of course that worried me a little in

111

view of the suspicion of murder. Had Alex's traumatic experiences with his father developed in him a hatred for men who were dominant towards him, as was probably the case with his boss? In a recent article I had read that such cases are not so rare.

But I did not want to speculate too much here. First of all, I was really shocked by what Alex reported about his old man and the unpleasant experiences he had had as a child. Secretly, I was glad that I had grown up without a father. It seemed to me the lesser evil not to have one at all than one who behaved so brutally and callously towards his little son.

I had read enough for today and closed the diary.

I'm not a psychologist, but Alexander's letter to his boss seemed to indicate that he saw in this headmaster a kind of father figure. Was he therefore capable of a murder, a proxy murder, so to speak, which was actually intended for his real father? The whole thing gave me a headache and I now realised that my preoccupation with these diaries was starting to have a very negative effect on me and might deprive me of my peace of mind.

23 Plotting Revenge

Monika Lochberger was a good-looking energetic woman in whose name the software company "Lochberger School Software" had been registered ten years ago. Up to now she had not been too concerned with the business, which was basically her husband's company. Reinhard Lochberger discovered a passion for programming at an early age and developed very efficient school software. However, a state civil servant was not allowed to have a second job on such a large scale. So the idea was born to register the company under the name of his wife Monika.

Thus it came about that Monika Lochberger's company became one of the two leading software companies in the country. Since its foundation, the turnover had multiplied and the profit of the company was now several times higher than Mr Lochberger's income as headmaster of the Schiller Grammar School.

However, this was not a monopoly market. The company Messerschmidt Software offered similar products and the competition for school contracts was quite fierce. In the last financial year Lochberger was able to expand strongly and win some of Messerschmidt's customers. This was partly due to the fact that the competitor had had a greater number of errors in its software updates over the previous two years and dissatisfaction among its customers was growing.

Lochberger took advantage of this and gradually shifted market share to around sixty percent in favour of his company. He also had better contact with his customers and with the help of a well-trained sales force he registered all the wishes and suggestions for changes of his clientele very precisely. He then announced improvements again and again, which corresponded exactly with the wishes of his customers.

Monika Lochberger was more than satisfied with this development and, together with her husband, was delighted with the joint successes and growing prosperity.

This changed abruptly when she suddenly and unexpectedly received a shocking anonymous letter in which she was told that Reinhard had a lover and had been cheating on her for some time. In support of this allegation, the letter was accompanied by three photographs showing Mr Lochberger in close embrace with an attractive young woman.

Monika Lochberger was stunned and did not know how to react.

She decided not to confront her husband at first. If these accusations were true, he would certainly deny everything. Secretly, she hoped to expose these allegations as slander. In the following weeks, however, she unfortunately found several indications that her husband was indeed having an affair. It was then that she decided to take revenge quietly, without engaging in lengthy arguments with him.

In the meantime she had become painfully aware that her married life had been reduced to a minimum over several years. Their love life was practically non-existent and Reinhard threw himself into his work with unbelievable energy and tenacity. Even during the holidays he was mostly at school so that she hardly ever got to see him. At home, too, he concentrated very much on working on his software projects. When they went on holiday together once a year, they spent two weeks at a golfing resort where her husband was so active in sports that he was tired early in the evening and only wanted to sleep.

She could hardly remember how their sex life had been in the past. They hadn't even exchanged caresses for such a long time. Apart from his programming, the most important thing for him were his ambitious goals at school, where he competed with the other headmasters of the city and wanted to show off with the best and most successful school.

All this led to Monika feeling more and more cheated. She was an attractive woman in her so-called prime, five years younger than her husband and was quite dissatisfied with her present life. Of course she did not lack anything materially. She could basically fulfil every wish, but little by little a nagging feeling had crept in that something important was missing in her life. She felt increasingly lonely.

Now and then the novel Madame Bovary came to her mind, which she had only recently read again. Certain parallels with the character of Madame Bovary could not be entirely denied. Both she and the novel's protagonist felt rightly neglected by their husbands, although their characters were very different. The novel's Charles Bovary, the husband, appeared to be a rather naive and somewhat sluggish person, who, with a bit of luck, had made it to a country doctor's surgery, where he carried out his tasks in a mediocre manner. Her husband, Reinhard Lochberger, on the other hand, was by no means modest, but a very successful headmaster of a grammar school, with a great deal of ambition, who apparently now in his old age was also becoming a philanderer.

Basically, the only conceivable answer from Monika's point of view was that she also had to get a lover, which was probably the most appropriate lesson she could teach her husband. If she honestly examined both situations, the apparent parallel to Flaubert's novel was actually not there, because in the novel the woman broke the marriage, and in her own case it was her husband. And certainly, unlike Emma Bovary, she would not, at the end of an affair, even if it ended unhappily, resort to poison to take her own life. Rather, she would hand her unfaithful husband the poisonous drink.

Oh, when was the last time she had gone to the theatre, she sighed inwardly. Reinhard was not a fan of theatres or concerts, and her two girlfriends were both cinema-goers, and they could not be persuaded to see a theatre play. It was high time she gave her life a new direction, a thought she had often had lately.

Soon after the traumatising revelation of her husband's fling, an opportunity arose for Monika to make a charming acquaintance. Her husband had taken her to a lecture evening at his school, and afterwards some colleagues and the school management had gone to a pub for a drink. There she met the teacher Alexander Strasser, who happened to be seated next to her. During the evening, her husband oriented himself more to the other side of the table and was involved in lively conversations while she chatted to the man next to her and soon discovered that this Mr Strasser was a very likeable guy. They had a very animated conversation that evening and when Monika Lochberger finally went home with her husband, she had the tingling feeling that the little adventure she had longed for had begun that night. Alex also had felt a spark that evening, and he could not get this charming woman, with whom one could talk about everything including literature and theatre, out of his head.

A short time later, a new opportunity arose for the two of them to meet again, on the occasion of a school concert at which the student orchestra of the Schiller Grammar School played in St. Mark's Church. Like Monika, Alex had secretly hoped that they would see each other that evening, and indeed their wishes came true. The two, secretly in love, exchanged furtive glances while still in church, and again after the concert there was a small convivial reception at a nearby restaurant, where the school management and a group of about fifteen teachers came together. Monika and Alex had another lively conversation, and towards the end of the evening they managed to exchange their telephone numbers and email addresses, and they agreed to meet again as soon as possible.

A certain fondness grew between the two lonely hearts, which quickly turned into a love affair. For the first time in many years, Monika enjoyed the feeling of being loved by a man and feeling completely a woman, while Alex was fascinated by the intelligence and erotic charisma of this woman with whom, unlike his eternally quarrelsome partner Ulla, he finally experienced a feeling of over-whelming harmony.

Alex developed a passionate love for Monika and let it show. Of course they had to be very careful to keep their relationship secret. After a few months they started to make plans for the future and Monika thought aloud about a divorce and then had the idea to sell her company's software to the competitor.

From a purely legal point of view, this was not a problem because she was the owner of the company. There were no agreements between the spouses that somehow limited the power of disposal of the company owner Monika. Mr Lochberger had not thought of this when he registered the company in his wife's name.

Under normal conditions Monika would never have thought of this idea either, but she wanted to take revenge for her husband's infidelity, and besides, she had now acquired a taste for love and passion, and she had the feeling that she had finally broken out of a cage after many years and could enjoy life again. From time to time she caught herself planning journeys together with Alex, who dreamed more and more passionately about a future together, which Monika then dampened a bit, referring to her still existing marriage.

During this time, she contacted Karl-Heinz Messerschmidt and lured him with the remark that she was interested in a cooperation. Karl-Heinz Messerschmidt was suspicious at first, but when he learned of the Lochbergers' planned divorce, he recognised the opportunity and declared his willingness to work with Monika Lochberger.

Messerschmidt had already got wind that Lochberger was working on a new, greatly improved module that would give his software an even stronger advantage in the market. Some customers had spoken openly about this and hinted that, as Lochberger's technological edge increased, they might refuse to follow Messerschmidt. This threatened him with the loss of further market share and, in the longer term, the end of his company.

In this situation, Monika Lochberger's offer seemed to him to be a lifeline and he did not hesitate to take her up on the offer, especially as Monika also made clear advances and coquettishly let it be known that she did not intend to spend the rest of her life alone after her divorce, but could possibly imagine a man like him as a partner.

Monika knew from her husband that the new software module of the Lochberger company was largely completed. But it was still a well-protected secret, because he was the only one working on it. Every evening he took the current data home on his SD data card and put the card in a wall safe immediately after his arrival. Only he had access to it.

In recent weeks, Monika had shown her husband increased professional interest and had the innovations in his programme package explained to her in detail. Therefore she was now able to give detailed information about the new functions of the future software. Monika offered Messerschmidt the chance to obtain her husband's secret and thus enable him to launch an ultra-modern new version of his own software within a few weeks. For the procurement and delivery of the new module, she demanded a one-off payment of thirty thousand euros. A modest sum considering the necessary development time of half a year, she told Messerschmidt. She also demanded to be entitled to a half share in the profits of Messerschmidt in the future.

The two of them reached an agreement as Messerschmidt not only hoped to regain the lost market share, but also to take over the market, especially since Monika agreed to cooperate with her freelance software developers, who had previously worked for Lochberger. In intensive talks with her two programmers she had been able to convince them that the conditions and income prospects would improve if they were prepared to continue working for Monika under the new company arrangement, after the divorce.

This led to Monika Lochberger developing a plan as to how she could come into possession of the data for the new software module. Since the data card disappeared every evening into the safe immediately after her husband's arrival, to which she had no access code, she came up with the idea of stealing the data card from her husband's office.

The exchange for a data card of the same type was to be carried out by Alex, who accepted the task with great zeal, especially since Monika promised him a remuneration of ten thousand euros. Once she was in possession of this data, the way would be clear for further cooperation with Messerschmidt and she could then file for divorce.

For several days, in the evenings, Alex lurked at the school near the headmaster's office, waiting for a suitable opportunity for access. But either there were too many colleagues in the building or the headmaster was not alone in his rooms, so that Alex slowly lost patience and began to doubt whether this plan would ever succeed.

But on Thursday, July 19th, the moment finally arrived, and around nine o'clock in the evening he was able to exchange the SD card, introducing a virus on the headmaster's computer at the same time. Alex was especially proud of that little trick, which should distract the headmaster and prevent him from realizing the exchange of the data card

The stolen card was later handed over. He had parked near the school and had had to wait almost an hour for Messerschmidt's assistant Daniel, who briefly inspected the card on his laptop and then handed him an envelope with the agreed amount.

When the headmaster's body was found later that evening, the supposedly harmless case of theft had turned into a shocking violent crime.

24 An Abyss

My reading of yesterday's diary had upset and frightened me quite a lot, and I sat down on the balcony immediately after work to continue reading the 'Letter to Father'.

I must have been about five years old when I had another of my first shocking experiences. At that time we were still living in Waiblingen, it was before we moved to Stuttgart. One day I heard my mother screaming from the next room and opened the door. She was sitting on the bed and her head was bleeding. You were standing next to her, holding a frying pan in your hand. You tried to calm me down and I don't remember what you said to me. The images spoke for themselves and any comment was unnecessary.

Actually I am almost unwilling to trust such a memory. An absolutely surreal picture, my mother bleeding and my father beside her with a frying pan in his hands. If I hadn't later seen with my own eyes the extent of your brutality and your irascible violence, I would perhaps dismiss this memory as a figment of the imagination. I was still very small at the time and the memory fragments from early childhood may not be entirely reliable. However, I have had enough experiences of a similar nature with you in later life, and so there is no reason not to trust my memory and the images burned into it.

It would be unfair and dishonest for me to say that you only had negative sides. The opposite is true. You have also meant a lot of positive things for us children.

First of all, you were the only parent who was involved with us children at all, our mother obviously had no interest in this. You took your time to sit with us and read to us, especially the stories from the children's bible. The stories from the Old Testament particularly fascinated you and you read them to us during our lessons together, especially at the weekend. Admittedly, the ulterior motive with you was to educate us in the spirit of your fundamentalist religious attitudes, but that is a different story. Mother also knew how to prevent this by her strong rejection of all religious indoctrination.

It was also you with whom we played board games and I remember that it was always very nice and exciting for us when you sat down at the table in the children's room to play Snap, Rummy or other card games with us. Our mother never did this. She was always absent. Either she watched TV after housework or she immersed herself in her reading. Playing with her children hardly ever occurred to her. She had a certain coolness or even coldness in her nature, and it is diffi-

cult for me to judge whether this was an original trait of hers, or whether it was the result of experiencing your brutal violence over so many years that made her withdraw from the family to a large extent. For this is certain: you treated her cruelly again and again, and did not shy away from letting your children become eyewitnesses to it.

You were a narcissistic person. You wanted to be admired by those around you. Outwardly you liked to portray yourself as the caring husband and father to whom nothing was more important than the welfare of his dear ones. Every parents' evening was very welcome to you. You were also a keen visitor in the consulting hours of the class teachers, but not because it was necessary with me or my sister. No, you just wanted to hear what good pupils your children were and then bask in the glow of the teacher's praise.

Even when relatives came to visit us, one of your favourite subjects was the very good school results of your children, and you listed their grades in detail and boasted about them, which was often very embarrassing. It was actually quite dishonest because my achievements at school were solely due to my efforts. I did everything on my own, despite the permanent psychological strain of your regularly recurring violence. In fact, you should have said in front of the relatives:

"Surprisingly, my boy has excellent grades, even though I make a constant and sustained effort to break him down psychologically."

It was always important for you to give a good impression on the outside, the facade had to be right. A white shirt, a suit and tie and a Mercedes in front of the house: that's how you incarnated the middle-class citizen of that time. Only the residents of the apartment building, who heard the shrill cries of the Strasser family again and again, soon realised that behind the shiny exterior was a rather morbid existence in which violence was part of daily life.

From my physical inferiority to you I have suffered all my life.

That was also because you had always ruthlessly played off your advantage of greater physical strength. You even threatened to beat your teenage son, and occasionally you put it into practice, mostly when in a violent rage.

Things went badly for me shortly before my final A-Level exams, two days before the deadline for my German essay. For weeks the marital war had been raging at home and on that day the situation came to a dramatic head. After an hour or two of the usual screaming, you, Father, burst into the living room and said:

"Alex, I'm going for an hour's walk. Take care of your mother, she turned on the gas tap a moment ago."

I was shocked by this revelation and speechless, but you were already out of the front door. You just walked away while your wife and the mother of your children was suicidal and had tried to take her own life. She wanted to end her life out of despair over the breakdown of her marriage and your brutal and violent behaviour towards her, which was the sole reason for this breakdown.

The next day you came up to me and spoke to me. Not about the previous day's incident but about the fact that I urgently needed a haircut because I looked terrible with long hair. Like a hippie, you said. That was the epitome of an antisocial and despicable youth for your generation back then.

I defended my hairstyle, pointing out that young people's tastes today were different from twenty years ago. Then you got angry and said that it was not right that I did not want to follow your instructions. As long as I lived under your roof, I was obliged to obey the rules you had set down. I replied that there were a lot of things not right with us. For example, that the day before, you had put me in charge of mother in this difficult situation and then just walked out of the house.

It was after that sentence that it happened. The frightening metamorphosis to wild fury that I had to experience so often from you was particularly terrible that day.

Your face turned red with rage within seconds, your eyes stared at me, wide open and hateful. You jumped up and roared: "What! You want to tell me what to do? We'll see about that!"

And already the blows were pounding my head. I was sitting on the sofa and under the force of your first blows I fell to the floor, sideways into the corner, where I lay on my back. I held both arms in front of my face, but it didn't help much. You beat me in a blind rage, then you ran out of the room and left the apartment.

When I looked in the mirror, my lower lip was bleeding. It had been split. The whole right side of my face was swollen and I was very frightened by my appearance.

The next day I went to the German essay test anyway. Of course everyone - classmates and teachers - asked what had happened to me. I made up a story that I had fallen down the stairs, making it sound as credible as possible. I don't know if anyone believed that. I didn't really care. The final examination was only important for me in so far as it marked the end of my time under your brutal tyranny. It was absolutely clear to me that after the exam nothing and nobody would keep me in your house.

We never talked about this incident later on and you never said a word about it. On the one hand this is understandable - who wants to talk about such brutality in the first place. But on the other hand it would have given you the chance to feel remorse and maybe even ask for forgiveness.

A few years before you died, you once told me with conviction: "I have always loved your mother." Today I painfully regret that I was not brave enough at that time to contradict you decisively and to ask you if it is a sign of love to mistreat and regularly beat the person you pretend to love.

I regret that I missed the chance to tell you all this to your face, to confront you with the fact that you darkened my childhood with your violence. And that the ruthlessness with which you treated mother still haunts me today, even after decades, occasionally in dreams and even in a waking state.

Many of my experiences with you were traumatic. Your fits of pathological raving and frenzy went as far as death threats. Several times you shouted loudly through the flat at night, "I'll kill you!" You meant our mother, and once you even kicked in the door to my mother's bedroom. These are all sad facts and memories that I still suffer from today. With you these memories seem to have disappeared completely, but you have always been a master in the suppression of reality.

You came from a peasant home. Your father was an extremely strict man who used a riding whip to punish his sons. With me you used whips from plaited willows at first, later in Stuttgart you used only simple bamboo canes. According to your own statements you were often beaten by your father. Your comment was very simple-minded, and I had to listen to it many a time: "My father beat me, so what? Anyway, it didn't do me any harm!"

How you reached this conclusion I do not know. You had to kneel for hours on sharp logs in the shed as punishment and were whipped like a beast by your father. So all this has not harmed you? Didn't it change your personality, pushing you towards violence and sadism? Did you not have any thoughts of revenge against a father who so sadistically tortured you?

I did. And also my sister. There was a time when we talked about how to do away with you, once and for all. What kind of murder would be the least risky and what such a plan would have to look like to be successful. Thank God our desire to carry out such an act was not great enough and the fantasy was lost after a while. But mentally you made us become patricides.

At this point I stopped reading. These last pages had shocked me, and it was hard to believe that my friend Alexander had grown up under such extreme conditions. The last section affected me deeply.

So Alex had, by his own admission, been toying with the idea of murdering his father as a teenager? What did this mean for the present situation? I suspected that he had fallen back into his old ways of thinking and feeling and that those dark, murderous thoughts had returned and had been directed towards his boss instead towards his father. I was terrified to think of it.

I had to try to make contact with Alex and talk to him. However, this was difficult to do at the moment as I didn't know where he was or whether I could reach him by email. But what should I write to him? That I could understand him, that he would remain my friend even if he had committed a murder? I couldn't think of anything. I was at a loss as to what to do.

25 Accomplices

"I have missed you so much," Karl-Heinz Messerschmidt whispered into the ear of the blonde woman he was holding tightly in his arms.

"So have I, my love," she whispered back to him.

The two of them were inside a luxurious mobile home that Messerschmidt had parked by Lake Waldlach all year round and where he occasionally spent his leisure time. Here he was able to meet Monika without having to fear being recognised by anybody from Lundenburg. She had just arrived after a short fast car trip.

"I haven't seen you for ages," Messerschmidt muttered and hugged his lover once again more fiercely.

"I feel the same way," she murmured. "It's been terrible, all these days without you."

"I'm sorry about what happened to your husband, what a terrible thing."

"You can say that again. The police now have me under suspicion, they showed me that quite openly. It is clear that I am profiting from my husband's death. Firstly because of the life insurance and secondly because I inherit all the assets."

"Yes, they will be watching you very closely now, so it is very, very important that we don't call each other and are not seen together. Otherwise that would cause suspicion."

"I have got an idea, Monika. I have two business mobile phones that were used by my sales representatives until recently. The employees have left, so from now on we'll use these phones for our calls."

"That's an excellent idea, my love." She hugged him and gave him a kiss.

"Well, out here we're reasonably safe, anyway, I don't think the police are snooping around. However, there are some people from the Lundenburg area who like to spend their weekends here. But on weekends we can go somewhere else. What's the matter with Mr Strasser?"

"The police are watching him. They think he's the killer, but I don't believe it."

"Why not? You told me he hated your husband. Besides, he was apparently at school until late at night, so it could be that he did indeed hit your husband in a fit of rage, without the intention of killing him. Perhaps he just wanted to teach him a lesson, and went too far."

"Well, I don't think that's very logical. He stole the data card from my husband's notebook with a lot of cunning and effort, and it was his intention to collect the ten thousand euros. He would have to be crazy if he attacked my husband afterwards. I think that's unlikely."

"I agree with you, it wouldn't make sense. But a teacher who is willing to steal important data from his headmaster may have a different approach and may not necessarily follow the laws of logic."

"In any case, he is now on the run. The police seem to be looking for him. They asked me if I thought he was suspicious. I was rather reluctant, but then I told them that it was theoretically possible. The problem for us is if he is caught and if the story about the theft is revealed, then we are in for it. Then we might even be considered the instigators of the murder."

"I know, that worries me too. Why didn't this Strasser go somewhere where he would have been seen by people immediately after the theft. Then he would now have an alibi for when the murder happened. Anyway, why doesn't he have an alibi?"

Monika raised her eyebrows and looked at Messerschmidt accusingly.

"Because he waited in his car for an hour near the school for your employee Daniel, who arrived late. The two of them hadn't finished making the deal until a quarter to eleven, and the murder is said to have taken place between half past nine and ten."

"If necessary, we could of course provide an alibi for Strasser if Daniel testified that he was with him, but that could become a problem for us. It's no secret that Daniel works for me, and then there would automatically be suspicion that Strasser stole the data from your husband's computer to sell it to me."

"Yes, it's a real dilemma. We can either provide an alibi for Strasser and spare him the suspicion of murder and incriminate ourselves in the process, or we do nothing, and he may be arrested and charged."

Messerschmidt frowned, a new thought had obviously just occurred to him.

"There's something else that comes to mind. How do we know that Strasser was really just sitting in his car for an hour waiting? He could have left his car at any time, walked the few metres over to the school and committed the murder there, thinking it was the right time for revenge. Afterwards he could have quickly gone back to his car, nobody would have noticed. Or he could have committed the murder before he got in his car and then called you."

"I hadn't thought of that. This means that we could possibly provide him with a false alibi and then Daniel would be liable to prosecution for false testimony or even perjury."

"That's exactly what it looks like. We do not know whether Strasser is involved in the murder or not. If he was in the vicinity of the crime scene for so long, it was quite possible for him to have done it."

"Oh, my God, this is really complicated. Anyway, he's on the run, but we have to prepare for him to resurface. If he were to confess to the police about the theft, we would have to deny everything."

"Yes, absolutely. For example, I could claim that I had only once spoken to him about the possibility of supplying me with your husband's business secrets. Or I could say that he himself offered to get me the information and asked me if I would honour that."

"Yes, that would be plausible, and of course it would be important in such a case that our close relationship was not mentioned at all. If the police find out that we are in this together then I am of course immediately a suspect and could even be accused of murder," said Monika.

"I know, darling. That's why it's so important that we are not seen together."

"All right, but suppose he is indeed interrogated and claims to have stolen the data on our behalf, what do we say?"

"I don't know right now. We'll have to think about it, but we aren't at that point just yet. Who knows if they'll ever find him, maybe we'll be spared all this."

"I don't share your optimism. In a case of suspected murder, international searches are conducted. Sooner or later they will catch him. Besides, we must be prepared for the police to interrogate us both again extensively. Let's make sure we don't contradict each other."

"If we had known that your husband was about to die, we could have done without that stupid theft. But anyway, we now have the source code and I can get my programmers to install the new modules and then our new software version will be ready in two months and will be a great success."

"Okay, but before that we'll finish our contract. I sell you the rights to my software, we said for a hundred thousand, and you guarantee my company income of fifty percent of the profit."

"Yes, darling, that's what we agreed upon, and that's what the contract will say. Now let's just relax a bit and do the business later."

They embraced and enjoyed a long, passionate kiss.

Outside the summer sun was shining brightly, it was absolutely quiet. Through the window you could see the lake. The camper van park was now quiet because it was lunchtime, and the two lovers took the opportunity for a short nap.

26 The Last Resort

It was Friday morning and I was working from home, so no visits to customers were planned. But I was on standby because a customer could always call about some problem or other.

The previous afternoon I had gone to the funeral of the murdered headmaster. Lochberger was one of my best clients and so it was only natural that I attend the ceremony.

A large crowd of people had gathered in front of the North Cemetery to give the headmaster his final farewell. About fifty teachers had come from his school, as well as some of the older students, many parents and of course important officials of the city of Lundenburg, such as the Mayor. Representatives of the press were also present as Lochberger had been a public figure.

After the burial, the visitors walked in long lines past the group of family members one by one and gave their condolences to the wife and relatives. I joined the line and waited impatiently until I could finally shake hands with Monika Lochberger and express my commiserations. I did not attend the subsequent reception at the nearby Café Waldesruh. Some professional appointments were waiting for me in the late afternoon.

In the evening I had picked up the fake papers for Alex. The scrap dealer had delivered good quality. Everything looked impeccable. The photos of Alex seemed a bit strange to me as he had shaved off his beard and wore dark horn-rimmed glasses, whereas he had always worn rimless glasses before.

On my table now lay the new ID, the passport and the driving licence. I would take them to the post office later. At breakfast, I leafed through Alexander's diary again, rather randomly, and my attention was drawn to one page, on the word 'Werther'. I was aware that Alex was interested in literature. That was normal, so to speak, for a philologist, but so far, when I looked through his notes, I had hardly noticed any literary references, unless, and this came to my mind at that moment, one could interpret the 'Letter to Father' as a literary reference to Franz Kafka, who became famous with a text of this title. Spontaneously, I decided on the Werther entry and began to read.

October 15, 2017
I have read Goethe's Werther again for the umpteenth time and am fascinated by this book. The narrator is a young man with an amazing understanding of all varieties of human existence. Here are a few sentences:

<<When I see how all effectiveness boils down to the satisfaction of needs which again have no purpose but to prolong our poor existence, all this, Wilhelm, leaves me speechless.

I gladly confess to you that the happiest are those who, like children, live into the day. They are happy creatures.

They are also happy who give their miserable occupations or their passions splendid titles, and sell them to the human race as gigantic achievements for its progress and welfare. Happy is he who can be so!

But he who in his humility recognizes where all this leads to, who sees how undaunted even the unhappy man under this burden is, and all are equally interested in seeing the light of this sun for a minute longer, yes, he is silent. And then, limited as he is, he always keeps in his heart the sweet feeling of freedom, and that he can leave this dungeon whenever he wants to.>>

Yes, the busybodies of public life, like certain pompous superiors, have existed at all times and of course they could not and cannot understand what the narrator has to say. What fascinated me about this text is the reference to the 'freedom that one can leave this dungeon' of earthly existence whenever one wants.

This was the diary entry of Alexander on 15 October of the previous year. I was not exactly reassured by that note. Of course I knew that Alex read a lot and that he was familiar with many standard works of world literature. But the fact that he picked out these passages about the idea of putting an early end to life made me feel insecure again. And here again he was unmistakably alluding to his boss. That was not a good omen.

He obviously had certain tendencies to take something positive from the idea of suicide. All this made me increasingly perplexed and worried. How could I help him?

He probably needed psychotherapy. That might be a way to regain his balance. But now he was on the run and he might have committed a murder. And if not, he was very suspicious and in danger of being arrested and then disappearing in prison.

I doubted whether he could survive such a detention. Instead I saw the danger that he might prefer to commit suicide in such a situation.

It was high time to make contact with Alex. I could email him and ask him to call me back, although I didn't know whether he was even able to read emails at the moment. Anyway, I had to try. But first I wanted to talk to his partner Ulla. After all she had been with Alex for two years, so perhaps she could tell me something that would help.

27 A Love Letter

Alex had now been on the road for four days, and I was increasingly worried about him and wondered where he was headed. I had called his partner Ulla, but she was apparently on holiday. Her answering machine said she would be available again from the fifteenth of August. So I couldn't find out anything from her at the moment and I wanted to send Alex an email to find out where he was and how he was doing.

When I checked my emails, I discovered a message from my friend, which he had written the previous night around 11 pm. I felt relieved as I eagerly opened the message.

Hi Winfried, have arrived safely. For more details see 'Appendix 1'. Please confirm briefly reception of my email. Best wishes Alex

Now I felt reassured by this sign of life from him. I opened the attachment. It was a Word file that required a password when opened. This was what Alex and I had agreed upon for such cases. I typed in the password and I quickly skimmed through the text. Alex was in Catalonia, near Blanes, about fifty kilometres north of Barcelona. He was fine, he said. Everything there was crowded with holidaymakers and the weather could hardly be more summery. Until now he had always spent the night in the car. He was afraid that if he presented his identity card at a guesthouse or camp site he would be reported to the police. He asked me urgently to send him the new identity papers. I should send everything by registered mail and express 'poste restante' to the post office in Blanes. He would then pick it up there.

He then talked about 'attachment 2'. This was a letter to Monika. He asked me to deliver the letter to her personally and as soon as possible. He did not dare to send an email directly to her, because her telephone and mail traffic might be tapped. The file was also encrypted. My instructions were that I should open it, print it and then take it to Monika. With great curiosity I opened this file and read the text.

My dear Monika, I hope you're okay. I'm doing as well as can be expected. I'm now on the Costa Brava, in the middle of the holiday hustle and bustle. There are thousands of German holidaymakers here at the moment, so one more German doesn't really stand out. We have great summer weather here, and the beaches are full.

Is there anything new with you? Did the police visit you? I miss you a lot. Write to me, but not via email, I'm afraid it's under surveillance. Send a letter 'poste restante' to the post office in Blanes.

Oficina de Correos, En lista de correos, Plaza de la Solidaritat 9,
E-17300 Blanes, Spain
I long to see you and send you a kiss - Your Alex

I was perplexed and could not believe my eyes. Alexander was having a love affair with his boss's wife? From his diary entry I had only concluded that there was a friendly and business relationship between the two of them. The whole thing seemed more and more confusing to me.

I decided to call Mrs Lochberger immediately. At the other end of the line, a woman's voice answered.

"Am I speaking with Mrs Monika Lochberger?"

"Yes, speaking."

"Mrs Lochberger, we met briefly yesterday at your husband's funeral service. Once again my sincere condolences."

"Thank you very much."

"I worked with your husband on a professional basis, my name is Alumno. Your husband had concluded a maintenance contract with me for his school computers and we therefore had frequent contact. But apart from that, there is one thing that I urgently need to discuss with you. I also have a document to hand over to you. It will only take five minutes, but we can't do it over the phone. Is there somewhere I can speak to you privately today. I think it is relatively urgent."

"You make me curious, Mr Alumno, but could you not send me this document by post?"

"I'm afraid I can't do that, I have to say a few words about it. But I promise you it will only take a few minutes."

There was a short pause, she was obviously thinking about how to proceed.

"Then come and see me. You have my address?"

"It's 12 Faraday Street, isn't it?"

She affirmed and we agreed to meet at two o'clock.

Until the meeting I had ninety minutes left. I packed the personal papers for Alex in a padded envelope, addressed it and added a short handwritten letter in which I wished him good luck and all the best on his further odyssey. On the way to Mrs Lochberger´s I would stop at the post office and send the letter by registered mail to Spain.

28 An Innocent Lady

At 2 pm I parked my car in front of Lochberger's house. I had never been here before, I had only visited the headmaster at school. It was a very exclusive residential area with beautiful, detached villas with well-kept front gardens and many expensive cars. That was my first impression of the neighbourhood.

I rang the bell and shortly afterwards the door opened and Mrs Lochberger smiled at me. I had already seen her at the funeral service, but was surprised nevertheless to see such an attractive woman.

"You must be Mr Alumno?" she asked politely.

"Yes, that is correct," I replied somewhat awkwardly. "I really don't want to keep you long, and if you prefer, we can have our conversation right here in the doorway, it's...."

"No, no, I beg you, please come in."

She led me into a room, which was obviously her husband's study. The walls were crammed with books and at the desk were two chairs on which we sat down.

"So, what exciting news do you have for me," she asked with a hint of irony in her voice.

"I have received a letter for you, which I am to deliver to you personally, from my friend Alexander Strasser."

While I was saying this, I watched her face closely. She seemed a little worried, but she managed quite well to disguise her surprise.

"Where is he, our friend?" she asked curiously.

"As you know, he was still at school for a relatively long time on the night of the murder, and for this reason he is among the suspects."

"Yes, of course I know that," she replied. I noticed that she was obviously uncomfortable about it.

"So you have a letter for me?" she then suddenly asked. "Then please be so kind as to give it to me right away."

I wanted to ask her a few questions beforehand but now I could hardly counter her direct request, so I handed her the folded letter.

She quickly skimmed over the letter, and then murmured, "So he's in Spain. And he sent you the letter by email. Isn't that risky for him? It could be that the police read his emails."

"We have agreed on an encryption with password protection."

"Oh yes, that was a good idea. But what is Alex doing in Spain? He can't hide forever." Serious concern showed on her face.

"I would have preferred he had stayed here, but I think he had a legitimate fear that he could be taken into custody on suspicion of murder. The big question for me is of course why he has no alibi to prove his innocence."

Mrs Lochberger nodded her approval.

"I asked him about the alibi too but he only gave me evasive answers. He also told me that he would try to explain the seriousness of the situation to his partner and hoped that she would give him an alibi. Unfortunately, that didn't work out. I think that's why he left in such a hurry. He didn't say goodbye to me, by the way."

"Alex explained the problem with the alibi to me very vividly. That was the reason for his leaving here so quickly. But what he didn't tell me was the close relationship he had with you."

Mrs Lochberger smiled embarrassedly.

"Well, we handled it relatively discreetly. I'm still married after all, even though my marriage has been a formality for many years. My husband and I have remained together more or less pro forma but we were planning to divorce soon. And then a few months ago I met your friend Alex and we became closer and fell in love. That makes it all the worse that he now has to hide abroad. Do you have any idea how we could help him," she asked and looked at me expectantly.

"You should be the one to come up with these ideas," I said somewhat irritated. "After all, you're the one who got my friend to commit this data theft."

Mrs Lochberger now looked at me in shock.

"How do you know that," she asked me, very unsettled.

"Alexander left his diaries with me for safekeeping, and in one of these diaries he described in detail how the contact with Mr Messerschmidt was arranged by you. From my point of view, it is quite clear that you persuaded him to do it."

A kind of stubborn defiance showed on her face.

"You are completely wrong. Even if that is what his diary says, it is still not correct. What is true is that I talked to Alex about my future plans and my intention to divorce my husband. For the time after the divorce, I had planned to work with Messerschmidt and since I am the owner of the company, I am allowed to decide independently about the fate of my company. Together with my competitor Messerschmidt, I came to the conclusion that it would be more advantageous for all of us if we did not supply the market with products as competitors, but together. It was clear to me, however, that my husband would not agree to such cooperation. That is why I decided to take possession of the new software modules, which I am entitled to anyway."

I was surprised at the cold-bloodedness of this woman and could not do much about her arguments at the moment. As she was the owner of the company, it could not be denied that she owned all of its products. In this respect, the theft of a data card from her husband's computer could perhaps not even be legally considered theft.

"What you say may be true, at least as far as your role as owner of the company is concerned. But you have involved Alex, and he is not an employee of your company. He is an employee of your husband's school and an employee of the country. If he is arrested, he will be charged with theft or embezzlement of a superior's work. This data card not only contained program modules of your company, but also other information relevant to the school. So it won't help Alex much if you go to court and say that you put him up to it. Misappropriation of a superior's data is a criminal offence in any case."

"Now don't exaggerate. The data card did not contain any school secrets. Only some worksheets and overhead transparencies for the next teachers' conference."

"Do not try to make light of this. The main thing is of course that a murder has been committed, otherwise we wouldn't be talking about the whole matter. And the only reason Alex is on the run is because he is a murder suspect now. Nobody would have been interested at all in a simple data card."

"You're right," she said thoughtfully. "I know that I am to blame for this mess."

I interrupted her.

"And as for the alibi, it is quite clear that the only reason he doesn't have one is because he was waiting in the car for Messerschmidt's employee Daniel at the time of the crime and did not want to be seen by anyone during that time."

Mrs Lochberger was now becoming increasingly nervous.

"OK, I'll try to help him. I already do miss him very much and I can't imagine sitting here for weeks or even months without seeing him."

"And I am seriously worried about him," I said after a brief pause. "At the moment he must feel that he has lost everything; his job, his right to retirement, his very existence. He is all alone and on the run and if the police arrest him, I fear that he could possibly commit suicide. From reading his diaries, I have the impression that he is far from being as mentally stable as he may appear on the outside. Don't you think that you yourself could somehow provide him with an alibi?"

"Yes, that will probably be the only viable way," said Mrs Lochberger thoughtfully. "I'll think of a way to present this plausibly."

"Then we should hurry. Maybe we can find some creative solution together," I said.

"Yes, you are right. Why don't you give me your phone number and I will get back to you shortly. If there is any news or if one of us has an idea, we can get together and keep each other informed."

I agreed to her suggestion and gave her my business card.

"It was a pleasure to meet you and I hope we can find a way to get poor Alex out of this."

"Yes, I hope so too," she said. "Now that my husband is gone, I miss Alex more than ever. We had already made plans for the future together, and all that is in danger now. It weighs heavily on me," she said with a look of sadness. "Call me if you hear anything new from him. I will also send a letter to Alex right away so that he knows that he is not completely alone and forgotten."

"That's good of you," I answered with a touch of emotion and we said goodbye with the prospect of calling each other again as soon as possible.

On the return journey I thought about the conversation. The woman seemed ambivalent to me. But if she really loved Alex, she would surely be able to conjure up an alibi for him. For the first time in days I felt confident and relieved. Besides, I was now looking forward to seeing Susanne again tonight and to discussing everything that was on my mind.

29 A Pleasant Encounter

After a cup of coffee I called Susanne, who was already on the Intercity Express from Hamburg and was due to arrive around 7 pm. The train had left on time, she confirmed, and she was looking forward to seeing me again. I told her that I could hardly wait to be with her. At ten past seven I would pick her up at Stuttgart main station.

A little bike ride in the fresh air would do me good now. I took my bike and rode out over the fields. About an hour later I arrived back home, perspiring but content. After a refreshing shower there were about two hours left before Susanne was due to arrive. I decided to take another look at Alex's diaries, although I felt increasingly less inclined to do so because I found my friend's revelations about his past and his mental state too gloomy and disturbing. I picked up the book with the most recent date and opened it at random. The first sentence that caught my eye appealed to me positively and I began to read.

May 15, 2017

Yesterday I had a nice encounter. The weather was warm and sunny and I walked into the park with a book and sat down on a bench. It's a beautiful season, everything is blooming and green and the sound of birds chirping lets you forget everyday life.

A young woman and her little daughter, perhaps eight years old, sat down on the bench next to me. My granddaughter Corinna will be about the same age now, I thought. I haven't seen her since my daughter emigrated to Australia. That was many years ago. I'm going to visit her after I retire. That's my firm intention.

The two of them were having a lively conversation about this and that and the mother patiently answered all her daughter's questions. After a while the little girl asked for her ball and started running wildly around the park. The mother called her over immediately and explained to her very calmly but firmly that she was not allowed to run into the flowerbeds under any circumstances. She then sent her to a piece of lawn where no flowers were planted.

Later, the child came back to her mother and wished to have a story read to her. Her mother took a book of fairy tales out of her rucksack and started to read it aloud.

It was good to watch the two of them enjoying each other's company. Also later the two exchanged words calmly, when the girl asked for an ice-cream, which the mother refused, pointing out that she had already had one.

The communication between the two touched me . I clearly felt the mother's love in every one of her utterances, even if she refused her daughter's wishes.

Secretly I envied this girl for her happiness with such a loving mother. Most parents today understand that their children are human beings, not things to be managed. And that these little people have the right to recognition, care and love and that it is a crime to humiliate them, to frighten them and to damage their self-confidence.

You only have to read nineteenth century novels, such as David Copperfield or Oliver Twist, to realise that the whole of the so-called civilised world abused children in an appalling way until very recently. The beating of children was not uncommon in my own childhood, and I myself enjoyed enough samples of it.

My mother could have been a protector in my difficult childhood. Instead, I painfully remember her as a constantly nagging, criticising and scolding person. The irascible, but basically also warm-hearted father was ultimately an easier burden to bear, despite his violent behaviour, than the loveless and callously bossy mother with her disparaging comments, which shaped the everyday life of my childhood. Of course there are mitigating circumstances in favour of my mother. She herself had had a hard childhood and experienced the war years with all kinds of traumas. But as a child I knew nothing about this and only felt that she must have regarded me as a nuisance because she constantly treated me in such a cold, harsh and humiliating way.

Later, when I was an adult, she was completely unwilling and incapable of even the slightest involvement with this subject. She nipped in the bud any attempt on my part to talk to her about my childhood experiences and feelings by adopting an icy silence and displaying a pained expression. In the past she would have sacrificed herself for us children day in, day out, and this was the thanks she got! She maintained this attitude until her death, and refused point blank to ever talk about it.

I closed the diary and was once again discouraged by what I had just read. Everything in these notes was leadenly heavy and depressing. The happy encounter mentioned at the beginning of the entry had made me hope to find something pleasant and enjoyable, but for Alex it was merely an occasion to pursue the bleak memories of his childhood injuries.

The whole thing gave me the impression that he was mentally unstable, maybe even ill. But in any case it seemed advisable to recommend psychological counselling to him.

The fact that a grown-up man at the age of retirement has nothing better to do than to constantly deal with his childhood traumas and those dreadful parents, I could only take as a serious disturbance. Against this background I also thought of the possible dangers of suicidal tendencies.

I wanted to discuss the subject with Susanne afterwards. After all she was a professional and had been working in her own psychotherapy practice for twenty years. I was curious to see how she would judge the matter.

30 Susanne Is Shocked

Ten minutes before the scheduled arrival of the Intercity Express from Hamburg, I was already at the station as parking space was always very tight there. I was lucky and threw some coins into the parking meter. The station concourse was very full at that time. The arrivals board indicated that Susanne's train would be five minutes late.

I was very happy to see Susanne again. We had last met three weeks before. The previous week she hadn't been able to come because of a professional obligation and the week before that, she had been prevented from coming by the surprise visit of an old friend.

So much had happened in the last ten days alone, it was almost dizzying. I recalled the events, the murder of Mr Lochberger, the revelations about my friend Alex's data theft, then his desperate cry for help because of his lack of an alibi and the suspicion of murder. His break-up with Ulla, and finally his hasty escape, in which I had helped him by obtaining forged identity papers.

It was basically unbelievable what an adventure I had suddenly become involved in. In retrospect, I now had serious doubts as to whether I had really rendered my friend a good service. And if he was the murderer, then I had helped him to escape and probably made myself liable to prosecution, which worried me increasingly.

But then there were moments when I was completely convinced of Alexander's innocence. However, I was seriously concerned about his state of mind. What I had read in his diaries was very alarming. I was glad that in Susanne I had a partner with whom I could not only talk about this subject, but who would also make some well-founded observations on it from her own professional perspective and experience.

A glance at the clock showed me that the train from Hamburg would arrive immediately. Large crowds of people hurried in and out of the station. My patience was put to the test. Finally, after a few minutes of waiting, I saw Susanne's striking face in the crowd coming towards me. I waved to her and immediately she also recognised me. Moments later we hugged and greeted each other with a loving kiss. Then I took her suitcase and led her to the car.

"I am glad that you are here," I said contentedly. She smiled cheerfully and was also very happy to be with me finally.

"We haven't seen each other for ages."

"Yes, because you dumped me a fortnight ago in favour of your French girlfriend," I mumbled and played the offended one.

"Oh, darling," she said, also acting exuberantly. "I do regret that very much, and I will more than make up for it today."

"That sounds good," I said with a wink and we got into the car.

We hugged each other tenderly once more and then drove off and were at home after thirty minutes.

I had already prepared a small dinner beforehand and we sat down to it on the balcony, enjoying the last rays of the evening sun and the pleasant summer atmosphere. It was now around eight o'clock and still a warm and pleasant evening. Over a glass of red wine we told each other what had happened during the last few weeks.

Susanne told me about a female patient who had been with her for two years in psychotherapy and who had recently attempted suicide. This had affected her a lot and also put a lot of strain on her. She naturally wondered whether and to what extent she could have prevented it, or whether the therapeutic steps had been too much for her patient.

I listened to this case very carefully and then brought up my friend Alex.

"I told you about it briefly on the phone," I said, keeping my voice down so that none of the neighbours would be able to hear too much through the windows that were open everywhere. "Alexander has fled the country and is apparently in hiding in Spain because he is under suspicion of murder. His school headmaster was attacked and killed."

"Yes, you told me about the murder. It's terrible. But I didn't know he had left," she said in amazement.

"I was so confused I forgot to tell you. In any case, he had no alibi for the time of the crime, and since he was at school late on the evening of the murder, suspicion fell on him. But there is something else. He did something stupid that evening, before the headmaster was murdered. He had wanted to play a trick on him and stole and exchanged his data card. He considered that as an act of revenge against the headmaster he hated, and he apparently sold this data to the rival company."

"What? That's incredible. Why on earth did he do such a thing?" Susanne was upset.

"Well, I asked him the same question. After leaving school in the evening, he met with his clients, who of course want to remain anonymous, so he has no alibi for the time of the crime, which was probably between 9.30 and 10 pm."

"He really stole the data from his headmaster? This is madness!" exclaimed Susanne.

"That's what I said when he came out with the confession. He was paid ten thousand euros for the stolen data."

"I wouldn't have believed that your friend could have done such a thing. That's a serious crime."

"You're right, I'm disappointed in his behaviour. He seems to regret it too, at least that's what he told me. He has no alibi for the time of the crime because he fell out with his partner. She was not willing to cover up for him, so he finally decided to go into hiding until the police find the murderer."

"This is really a wild story," Susanne said thoughtfully. We continued to speak in hushed voices.

"Are you in contact with him now?"

"I received an email from him yesterday in which he wrote that he is in Catalonia and feels safe there for the moment because the country is teeming with tourists."

"Do you think he has anything to do with the murder?"

"Not really," I replied cautiously, "but I'm not so sure now. Alex has moved out of his flat and has already taken all his things to his farmhouse in Dorflingen. His flat in Lundenburg has been cleared out, but he left a box of diaries there and asked me to pick them up. He was afraid the police might find them and confiscate them during a house search. He didn't know where else to put the diaries to keep them safe. In any case, he wanted to prevent his records from falling into the hands of strangers."

"And you took these diaries?"

"Yes, I went to his old flat on Monday and took the box. I also looked through it a bit, as he had expressly asked me to read them. But I must say that reading them made me very uneasy."

"Why?" asked Susanne with a sceptical look.

"He writes a lot about his unhappy childhood, his hatred of his father, who beat him often as a child and teenager and also abused the whole family, especially his mother."

"Of course that is terrible," Susanne said compassionately.

"And I could imagine that this experience made him oversensitive to authoritarian father figures. He probably saw his boss as such a figure. In any case, he had a very negative attitude towards his superior."

"It would be interesting if you could show this to me."

"Yes, of course, we'll do that later. Something else that worries me very much is a high degree of self-pity, which one finds in his entries. His general complaint about the undeservedly hard fate he had to suffer. All this has given me the idea that he might be suicidal, especially if this escape situation lasts for long or if he is arrested by the police."

"Such a sad and traumatic family history is of course always a burden. Has he ever had any psychological support before?"

"I have never heard anything about that. I don't think so."

"Do you get the impression that he's really in danger of committing suicide right now?"

"Not at the moment, no. It's just my fear that with this hopeless situation he will reach a point where he sees no solution. And if the police arrest him and charge him with murder he might be in custody for weeks or months. That could change the picture entirely."

"I see what you mean," Susanne said thoughtfully. "Is there a woman in his life? You said he had broken up with his partner?"

"Yes, he separated from his girlfriend Ulla. They had been together for two years, but he was never really happy with her, so he told me. But apparently he has recently fallen in love with a married woman."

"Oh dear, that too! And who is this woman?" Susanne could hardly hide her curiosity.

"Now get this. The woman is the wife of the murdered headmaster."

"What? Good heavens!" Susanne said, impressed. "All of this is pretty strange. Do you know her?"

"I visited her briefly yesterday because Alex emailed me a letter for her. I was supposed to print it out and take it to her. Of course I read it, and he writes that he loves her and that he is consumed with longing for her."

"And how did she react to the letter?"

"Her name is Monika, by the way. She admitted to me that she is having an affair with Alex, and she has also talked about the fact that her marriage had been on the rocks for years. She maintained that she and her husband were planning to get a divorce."

"Well, she wanted to get rid of her husband, and Alex apparently had a hatred for this man. Smells a little suspicious, doesn't it? Maybe they were in on it together?"

"I don't know, I'd rather not imagine that," I replied reluctantly. "All in all, this is a very mysterious situation, and my head is already spinning."

"I'm not surprised, Winfried," said Susanne and placed her hand on mine, soothingly. "I'll have a look at the diary entries you spoke of later. Perhaps I can get an idea of what's going on in your friend's mind."

"You know what," I said. "It's a nice summer evening. Let's just enjoy it now and put this whole thing off until tomorrow morning."

Susanne agreed with my suggestion and I refilled our glasses. We sat on the balcony for a long time, chatting about this and that, making holiday plans for the autumn and enjoying being together again after the long separation.

31 An Alibi

Monika Lochberger pressed the button on the remote control and the gate in front of Mr Messerschmidt's villa slowly opened. She drove along the driveway to the bungalow. Monika rang the bell. The door opened and she walked into the house, closing it behind her. Messerschmidt came towards her excitedly.

"What happened? Why did you come here? You know this is risky!"

"We need to talk, Karl-Heinz," she said with a nervous tone that worried him.

"I hope you weren't followed? What's wrong, darling?" he asked and led her into the living room, where they both took a seat on the leather sofa.

"Do you know a Mr Alumno?" asked Monika.

"No, can´t say I do," said Messerschmidt relatively indifferently. "Why, what about him?"

"I didn't know him before either, but he's a good friend of Alex. He came to see me."

"Oh, yeah? And what did he want?"

"He brought me a letter from Alex, who is now on the run in Spain, because he was afraid he would be arrested for murder if he stayed here. And he wrote a letter to his friend Alumno by email and asked him to deliver it to me personally."

"Well, well, I'm getting jealous."

"Now stop joking, Karl-Heinz, you know that I told Alex a little fib to get him to join us. But the problem is that now this Alumno also knows. He has Alex's diaries and has read in them that Alex stole the data card and sold it to you. Now he has accused me of being responsible for Alex being on the run because I set the whole thing up and persuaded Alex to do it."

"Oh, that's really unpleasant," Messerschmidt said with a critical expression on his face. "And what does this Alumno want now? I hope he's not blackmailing us."

"No, he didn't say that, but he wants me to help Alex find an alibi for the time of the crime so he can establish his innocence. He wants to help his friend, that's all."

"But how are you going to establish an alibi for Strasser?"

"Well, I've got to do it somehow or we're going to be in trouble. If they catch Strasser, he will of course testify and everything will come out, and in the end we might end up being charged as the people who arranged the murder. That would be the worst of all conceivable possibilities."

"That would be bad indeed! But what are you going to do about it?"

"I've thought that the only plausible alibi is that he was with me at the time in question. He came straight from school to my place and we spent two hours together."

"But it's going to be a scandal when they find out that you're having an affair with a teacher from your husband's school!"

"I don't intend to advertise this. The police will get my statement and I will of course insist that they treat the matter discreetly. The best thing would be for me to get my lawyer involved, so he can make sure that the police don't let anything get out to the press."

"That means you really want to tell the police that you're having an affair with Strasser? I don't think that's such a good idea," said Messerschmidt looking doubtful.

"That seems like the only solution right now, because where else is he going to get an alibi? We can't bring your employee Daniel into it, because otherwise we'd expose the whole story. As long as Alex has an alibi, he will not tell the police that he stole the data card. And I don't think that his friend Alumno will go to the police because he doesn't want to incriminate him."

"You might be right about that," Messerschmidt said with a thoughtful expression. "But I don't like the fact that you want to tell the police this intimate story. There's always the danger that something might get out. And that would probably lead to gossip and nasty rumours about the two of us. And if we got married later, it wouldn't be good for our reputation."

"That is why I want to involve my lawyer. Then he can put the necessary pressure on the police so that they know that my alibi is a very private matter and that we are threatening to sue for damages from the outset if these private statements are not treated with absolute discretion."

"All right, if that's the way you feel about it... but what exactly are you planning to do now?"

"I want to get Strasser back from Spain as soon as possible."

"What! You want to go to Spain to get him back? You can't be serious!"

"There is no other way, I'm afraid. I can't reach him at the moment. I'm sure an international arrest warrant has already gone out and he's sitting there in Catalonia in a tourist resort. It won't be long before the police find him and extradite him. And if he is interrogated and possibly talks, then we are screwed. That must not happen under any circumstances, so I want to get him back as soon as possible."

"Well, I don't like the whole thing. Where exactly is he anyway?"

"I only know that he is in Blanes, near Barcelona. As a postal address he has indicated the post office there, where he wants to receive letters."

"But that means you can't meet him there. You don't know where he is."

"That's true, but I will ask Alumno to send him an email and tell him that I'll come to see him and that I have an alibi for him."

"Be careful with emails, the police might read them!"

"Alex wrote the letter to me in an encrypted mail and Alumno also writes only with encryption."

"Okay, and what are you going to do when you get there?"

"Then I'll bring him back and we'll go to the police to give our statement and he can thus prove his innocence. Then the escape story will be over and we won't have to worry about him talking too much."

"That all sounds a bit adventurous, what you're up to," Messerschmidt said and frowned. "And when do you want to leave?"

"As soon as possible. Perhaps tomorrow. Anyway, I wanted to discuss all this with you before I make any decisions."

"At least I am happy about the fact that you thought to discuss such important steps with me first. After all we'll soon be in the holy state of matrimony, and it is only right and proper that we always discuss everything important together before making decisions."

"But of course, Karl-Heinz," said Monika flatteringly and tenderly kissed him. "Now let's forget the stress for a while and relax. But please don't be angry with me when I go back home in the afternoon to organise everything necessary."

32 Frightening Revelations

At breakfast we both complained of a slight ache in our muscles. Yesterday we had spent the day with a beautiful but very long hike in the Black Forest and arrived home exhausted. Today Susanne wanted to have a look at the diaries. I showed her some of the passages I had already read. She was speechless. We then turned the pages and towards the end of the most recent diary, we came across an entry with the title 'Nightmares'. I read it out loud with Susanne's consent.

I feel threatened and I am still haunted by nightmares. Again and again I experience dreams in which my father suddenly appears and puts our whole family in fear. Like last night, when I had another such dream. I saw myself as a teenager in the circle of my family and my father suddenly threatened us all. I was very afraid and when the situation became more acute and dangerous, I decided to knock him down. I knew that I would have to strike very hard, as only in this way could I eliminate the danger that he would kill us all in his fury. I felt responsible for my family. Unfortunately I couldn't find a suitable object and I felt paralysing helplessness and powerlessness come over me.

My childhood is half a century ago and I am still haunted by such dreams. This fear of being attacked by someone suddenly and without reason is constantly present in me, to a greater or lesser extent. That is why I bought a switch-blade years ago, which I always carry with me.

I have also seriously considered the purchase of a pistol, but so far I have only thought about it. I have to keep my fears in check. The fear of someone suddenly appearing out of nowhere and threatening me. Someone who is stronger than me and against whom I have no chance of defending myself with my bare hands. A firearm would be reassuring, and if I lived in the USA I would certainly get one.

Protecting oneself against everyday violence by gangs of robbers and criminals has been necessary at all times throughout history. Even in Friedrich Schiller's time it was completely normal to carry a loaded pistol with you when travelling. Modern society has taken away the right to carry arms and justified this with the state's monopoly on the use of force. But if the state does not help me, if I am threatened, what then? How often had I been beaten up in my youth or had to watch my mother being mistreated, but a policeman was never to be seen. I am neither a criminal nor a perpetrator of violence, but I never want to get into the situation again of being helplessly subjected to violence by someone.

I closed the book and looked at Susanne worriedly. There was an expression of horror on her face that I had never seen before.

"For God's sake," she exclaimed. "Your friend is really disturbed. In fact, he's dangerous."

"Don't exaggerate," I tried to reassure her. "He is only concerned about his own protection. After all the dreadful things he has experienced you can understand that, can't you?"

"Of course I can understand him. He has been severely traumatised since early childhood. He desperately needs therapy, but instead he is running around with a knife, fantasizing about firearms. That is really a danger, especially now that the police are looking for him. He has probably seen too many thrillers and now he's paranoid."

"I agree with you, I don't like it either. I had no idea he was carrying a knife."

"We do not always know everything about our friends. This dream he was talking about is very worrying. There is apparently a violent impulse in him that has been suppressed for decades. This is expressed in the dream in his desire to strike down his father. I immediately thought of the murder case. You said that the headmaster had been killed from behind by a blow to the head?"

"Yes, that's right, and I felt a little uneasy reading this dream sequence, I must admit. It's a good thing the police didn't get hold of the diaries. They'd see a connection to the murder."

"If a psychological report is commissioned, something like that can easily come out of it," said Susanne. "I've read such reports many times before."

"The whole thing is such a mess," I moaned to myself. "I hope that this Mrs Lochberger will keep her promise and find an alibi for him so that he can come back and not possibly do anything stupid while he is on the run."

"Yes, we can only hope so," Susanne said somewhat mechanically. "But even if that works, we still don't know whether he is really innocent. After what I read there today, I am at least a little sceptical."

"I'll talk to Mrs Lochberger this afternoon and see if she has any ideas about the alibi."

"Yes, I'm curious to see how things develop. You must keep me informed. But I've got a train to catch in five hours. Let's go out. A walk in the woods would be nice. What do you think?"

I agreed and a little later we drove out of town and enjoyed the fresh forest air on our leisurely Sunday stroll.

33 The Samaritan Woman

I drove Susanne to Stuttgart station at about 4 pm and we said goodbye after having arranged to meet in Hamburg the following weekend.

When I got home, the light on my answering machine was flashing. Monika Lochberger had called and asked me to call her back right away. She answered immediately.

"Hello Mr Alumno," she said. "I am going to see Alex and wanted to speak to you beforehand. Can you manage today?"

"If you have time, we could have a coffee together. How about the market place?"

"Okay, I can come now. Let's meet at Café Papillon, shall we?"

I agreed and twenty minutes later we were sitting together in the sunny market place of Lundenburg.

"So you really want to go to Spain?" I asked curiously. "Do you have an alibi for Alex now?"

"Yes, I have decided to testify that Alex spent time with me between nine and eleven o'clock in the evening. This will naturally raise questions and gossip, but I don't care."

"But of course it will look like you were having a secret relationship with my friend at a time when your husband was still alive."

"I am aware of that, and that is why I had not even considered such a possibility before. Of course everyone will be spreading malicious stories and I will be cut socially. But I don't see any other possibility, and I don't want Alex to be caught by the police and go to jail."

"That's a surprisingly positive turn of events," I said, somewhat perplexed. "Of course I'll be glad if he can end all of this, but..."

"What do you mean by that?" she asked me somewhat indignantly.

"Well," I said hesitantly. "Of course I don't want to say anything negative against my friend, but... but if he had anything to do with your husband's murder, what then?"

"I really don't understand you, Mr Alumno," she replied in a harsh tone.

"First you wanted to do anything to save him, and now you doubt his innocence! That really doesn't add up! What are you trying to insinuate?"

I realised that I had gone too far, because I could not and would not talk about what I had read in the diaries only recently.

"I didn't mean it," I said apologetically, "but still nobody knows exactly what happened on the night of the murder."

"That may be true, but you should stop suspecting your friend. What I actually wanted to discuss with you here," she added in a calmer tone of voice, "was a request. Namely that you inform Alex by email that I am coming to pick him up. And above all that I'll offer him a watertight alibi and that he can prepare himself for his journey home. And then, of course, we still have to solve the problem of where I can meet him and when."

"Yes," I said, "but that might be a bit difficult. Of course I can send him emails, but I don't know how often he actually reads his emails. He will probably do so in public internet cafés or similar places, because his mobile phone is not in use, for obvious reasons."

"Yes, that would make it too easy to trace him. Anyway I'm leaving tomorrow morning, spending the night in France and then I'll be in Catalonia on Tuesday in the afternoon, maybe around five. That would be the earliest time to meet him, preferably at my hotel."

She handed me a small business card. On the back she had written the details of the hotel.

"I just hope he reads his mail and comes to meet me."

I nodded and signalled my agreement.

"Well I am glad that you have decided to take this step. Hopefully it will change the whole situation now and above all enable Alex to lead a normal life again."

"I hope that everything works out, as I imagine it will, and then we will be back here in a few days and the matter will be settled."

We talked about this and that, drank our coffee and then said goodbye. I promised to pass on the news of Monika's trip to Spain to Alex immediately.

34 A Farewell

I don't usually go shopping on Monday morning because it's very crowded everywhere. This Monday, however, I made an exception and was in my favourite supermarket at 8 am, stocking up on the food I needed for the week. While I was shopping, I thought of Alex and Mrs Lochberger, who was going to Barcelona that day. In fact, I was so absent-minded while shopping that I repeatedly put items in the trolley that I didn't really want to buy.

The evening before, I sent Alex an email and told him all the important news and I was very happy when I received a reply less than an hour later. He wrote me that he was very happy and that he wanted to celebrate this turn of events with me when he came home.

On the one hand I was relieved that a solution to the tense situation had now obviously been found, but I was still not quite sure whether the alibi Monika had promised him would actually be accepted. But now was not the time to worry about it and I hurried to finish my shopping trip as quickly as possible.

Shortly before nine I passed the checkout, put my shopping in the boot of my car and then got behind the wheel. It now occurred to me that Monika Lochberger lived not far from here and I spontaneously decided to stop by to tell her that Alex had received my email and was looking forward to seeing her again soon.

With a bit of luck I might just find her at home, if she had not departed yet. I started the engine and was soon in Faraday Street, where her house was located. At first I was pleased when I saw, from a distance, Mrs Lochberger standing in front of a car. But when I saw a man next to her, I hesitated and was alarmed. I drove the car up to the right, and parked behind another vehicle so as not to be recognised.

I was still about a hundred and fifty metres from the Lochberger house. The two seemed to be arguing, the man was gesticulating wildly at her. She shook her head and made dismissive gestures. Finally, she looked at her watch, hugged him and they kissed goodbye before she hastily got into the car and started the engine. The man was standing next to the car, waving at her as she drove away.

In a moment she would pass by my car. To avoid being seen, I ducked sideways into the passenger seat. In fact, the vehicle roared past me and Mrs Lochberger had obviously not noticed me. I straightened up again and looked to the spot where she had just said goodbye to this man.

He was now also getting into a vehicle. It was a blue BMW, whose number plate I could not make out from my position.

His vehicle set off and quickly moved away from me. I started my car and followed him as I was very interested to know who the unknown man was. I was driving relatively fast and the distance between us was decreasing. Finally he stopped at a red light and as I approached him I was now able to decipher the lettering on his vehicle. I couldn't believe my eyes. The inscription on the car read 'Messerschmidt Data Technology'.

Monika Lochberger was possibly having an intimate relationship with her competitor. Why the two of them had just argued was unclear to me. But I suspected why Monika had instigated Alex to steal the data card. She had probably been involved with this man for a very long time, so it was likely a lie or false pretence that she was in love with Alex. So why was she going to Spain now, I wondered. She was probably afraid that if Alex were arrested, he would tell the police everything and then of course the question would arise whether Monika was possibly the mastermind behind the murder of her husband. But, I kept thinking, the whole thing could not possibly go well, because sooner or later Alex would find out that Monika was cheating on him and was only pretending to love him. Or was it possible that she had two lovers and that she actually loved both? How would Alex react if he found out about his rival? And if he then threatened to break his silence out of anger and rage, how would she react? Maybe she was a murderer and would not hesitate to kill Alex.

At that moment I felt a chill run down my spine. What if she was going to Spain for exactly this reason, namely to murder Alex there?

The traffic light changed and Messerschmidt turned left and I turned right. I drove home, and immediately wrote an email to Alex, urging him to be very wary of this woman. I also told him that Monika seemed to be romantically involved with Messerschmidt and that he should be aware of that. Hopefully he would read this message in time.

35 Shadowing

Following the police conference on Wednesday of the previous week, the telephone lines of both Mrs Lochberger and Mr Messerschmidt were monitored and both were under surveillance. Civilian police cars were parked near Lochberger's house and in front of Messerschmidt's property. The next meeting of the Schiller Special Commission was scheduled for the afternoon at three o'clock. Inspector Donner and his colleague Klar were sitting in the civilian Volkswagen Passat and both felt exhausted. They had been watching Lochberger's house since four o'clock that morning. Now it was just before nine and nothing conspicuous had happened.

"I don't know whether all this fuss is really worthwhile," Inspector Donner said to his colleague Inge somewhat irritably.

She made a cheerful face and said, "Now don't be in such a bad mood, Egon. It's quite comfortable to work a six-hour shift here. We sit comfortably in the car, listen to music, don't need to bother with drunks or crazy people, so I find this kind of assignment very pleasant."

"Well, I find it really boring. I'm glad it doesn't happen that often."

"I think we'll soon have something to do," said Inspector Klar and grabbed her camera with the telephoto lens. A blue BMW had just driven up to the house. A man got out and went through the garden gate to the entrance. Klar took several pictures.

"Boring as hell!" she rebuked her colleague. "You can see that there's something going on here. I think we're going to get some action now."

"Well, it's about time, and I hope they hurry up and do whatever it is they are planning to do. I'd like to finish my shift at ten."

"Don't be so dramatic, you can write down overtime and then celebrate. Now let's see who this car belongs to," said Inspector Klar and radioed the number plate of the BMW to her duty manager. A minute later the answer came: the car was registered to a certain company, 'Messerschmidt Data Technology'. Inge grinned triumphantly.

"Well Egon, what do you say now, we've hit the jackpot. Our two suspects are meeting early in the morning. Our colleagues will be very interested when we tell them this afternoon, don't you think?"

"Yes sure, you're right again," said the man reluctantly. "But my stomach is already rumbling, I must have breakfast soon. Otherwise I won't be able to stand it much longer."

"Now don't be so grumpy," Inge admonished him. "In the fight against crime, the eye of the law must also get along without breakfast. But I can give you a banana before you die of hunger."

"Oh Inge, just wait till you get to my age first, then you'll see."

"Don't exaggerate, Egon... Oh look, they're coming out."

Both policemen watched the scene very attentively. Mrs Klar took photos non-stop.

"The man seems to be upset about something. I don't think he likes her leaving," said Inspector Donner.

"In any case, we'll have to follow them for a while. And I don't think we'll be able to finish the shift at ten o'clock," Inspector Klar said mockingly.

"That's all I need. They're making such a fuss. But it seems the woman is going to travel alone."

"Yes, that looks like a goodbye," said Inspector Klar and eagerly took photos again. "If she's really going on a longer trip then maybe we should inform Sauer, but let's see what happens now."

"Yes, we should do that. I'd rather have the headquarters send another vehicle to follow her, I don't feel like driving around for hours. Maybe the woman wants to go to Hamburg! Then we'll be on the road all day."

"What a sourpuss I have as a colleague," sighed Inge. "Hamburg wouldn't be so bad, then you could take a walk along the Reeperbahn and do some sightseeing. You probably just hang around in Lundenburg all year round and never go anywhere."

"Don't talk nonsense, I was in Mallorca this spring. I travel abroad every year. I've probably seen more of the world than you have."

"That may be so," the inspector said somewhat absent-mindedly. She was still looking through the camera's viewfinder and taking pictures. "I think it's starting, Egon. The two of them are saying goodbye and she is getting into the car. Are you ready to go?"

"Of course, I am always ready. I've had more assignments in my life than you can imagine," said the policeman at the wheel and fastened his seatbelt.

"She's sitting in the car already. The guy waves at her. Well come on, what are you waiting for?" asked Ms Klar impatiently.

Inspector Donner made a grimace, started the car and followed Monika Lochberger's Mercedes.

"Call Sauer right away. He must be told immediately, we can't wait until this afternoon. We don't even know if we can be there for the conference at three o'clock."

"Yes, you're right." Inspector Klar called the number of Commissioner Sauer.

Inspector Donner reported. "Hello Thomas, this is Donner and Klar, we've been assigned to observe Mrs Lochberger and we've been doing so since four o'clock in the morning. Now things are moving, she has just had a visit from Messerschmidt. He said goodbye to her. She has now left. It looks as if she is going on holiday. What do you want us to do?"

"Morning Egon, just stay behind her. We want to know where she's going."

"Of course," said Donner, "but it could be that she'll be driving a longer distance. How far should we follow her?"

"Just follow her, and if she drives onto a motorway, we'll call someone else and you'll be relieved."

"I hope so, I don't want to follow her to Berlin or Hamburg."

"You won't have to. Don't worry, the important thing is that you stay with her until the other colleagues can take over. I'm going to ask around right now to see who is available, but I have to know first of all where she's going. Are you sure it was Messerschmidt who came to say goodbye to her?"

"Yeah, we checked his plates. The car belongs to his company."

"Well, it could be an employee, of course, but you're probably right. We already watched them meet last Thursday at a caravan park."

"Well, that's interesting," Inspector Donner said amazed.

"And did the surveillance reveal anything else?" asked Inspector Klar curiously.

"Yes, we discovered something else by tapping their phones. Winfried Alumno, a friend of the fugitive Alexander Strasser, had contact with Mrs Lochberger twice. I have the impression that something is going on there. And it could be that Lochberger is now going to a rendezvous with Strasser. So please stay close to her. You must not lose her under any circumstances. And give me the plate number of Mrs Lochberger." Inspector Klar did this immediately and said she had just taken lots of photos of the meeting between Lochberger and Messerschmidt, which she could bring this afternoon.

"All right, get back to me in about twenty minutes and then tell me what the situation is and where she's going, okay?"

Inspector Klar confirmed. Twenty minutes later, the civilian police Passat was driving on the A8 motorway in the direction of Pforzheim. About two hundred metres ahead of them, Monika Lochberger's white Mercedes Coupé was driving in the right-hand lane at a moderate speed.

"Now call Sauer again," Donner said to his colleague.

"Hello Thomas, we're on the A8 going towards Pforzheim. Where the woman actually wants to go is still unclear. Either north towards

Frankfurt or south towards Basel."

"Fine," said Sauer. "Stay on the line and I'll alert the emergency services in Karlsruhe. They are to provide one car on each side of the motorway, then we can follow her whether she goes north or south. Once these colleagues have taken over, you can go back and call it a day."

"That sounds good," Donner said with relief.

"Please contact me just before Karlsruhe. I'll need about five minutes so that we can carry out the switch as smoothly as possible."

"OK, we'll do that. Speak to you later."

At the motorway junction, the white Mercedes turned south and the Karlsruhe colleagues were able to take over the pursuit as planned. Donner and Klar drove back to Lundenburg, but before that they made a detour to Karlsruhe and had a hearty breakfast in a small café in the city centre.

Around noon the phone rang at Commissioner Sauer's office.

"Hello, Mr Sauer, this is Mehldorfer from Karlsruhe, we are following Mrs Lochberger and we have already passed Freiburg. She is now turning straight onto the route to Mulhouse in France. What should we do? Do you want us to drive over the border?"

"No, but keep following her until she actually makes the crossing. I will then ask the French police for help with surveillance. But don't pursue her through France. At the moment we have nothing on that woman either. She is a suspect, but we don't have any evidence yet. So let me know where she is actually going. If she leaves Germany, you will inform me immediately and then drive back to your location."

"Understood. I'll keep you informed."

36 The Reunion

Monika Lochberger was heading west on the motorway and she knew that she had a long and arduous journey ahead of her. However, in her comfortable Mercedes Coupé she had all the comforts a motorist could wish for. With the automatic air conditioning, she was largely insensitive to the summer heat, which was already noticeable in the morning. It was the end of July and the weather forecast had predicted temperatures of forty degrees for Central Europe.

Next to her in a large bag were her travel provisions and light snacks. She also had a whole series of podcasts with her for the trip, especially on the subject of nutrition, in which she was particularly interested. She liked to use road trips to listen to interesting texts. On the A8 motorway before Pforzheim, she got into a small traffic jam where she lost fifteen minutes. Already an hour on the road and only seventy kilometres! But today she had to be patient, and besides, she had only planned to cover half the distance to Spain on that day. She would spend the night in the city of Orange, where she had already booked a hotel.

Since there was heavy traffic, she made relatively slow progress. She turned on a podcast about medicinal plants and listened attentively. She had always been interested in medicine and natural healing and had often earned her husband's ridicule, who sometimes called her a witch. He had never understood how one could warm up to that kind of topic in such a way. His interest was exclusively in hard facts and figures, and this circumstance, too, had increasingly given rise to a certain distance in her marriage.

Now her husband was no longer there, and she could not feel any real sadness about it, at best a certain regret. She saw her future with Karl-Heinz Messerschmidt in a brighter light. He was a man of stature, had a wide range of personal interests and was by no means as narrow-minded as her husband. With him she could also talk about natural healing and alternative medicine from time to time. He had opinions on these things and had also informed himself about such topics. But above all he was a tender man who always remained open for personal and loving contact with her, despite his dedication to his company and long workdays. This made him seem extremely attractive to her and while she thought of him, she smiled happily to herself.

Then she remembered her present mission. What should she do with Alex? The best thing would be for him to disappear forever. He had made himself a fugitive and had basically chosen the way that she thought was best for everybody concerned. The man was a burden to her. He somehow thought of himself as a lover and believed in all seriousness that she wanted to spend her future life with him. It was not yet clear how she could dissuade him. Would an open conversation with him be enough to open his eyes? It was possible that he would answer this rejection with anger and indignation, maybe even aggression. But she would not accept violence from him, she had already made provision for that. He should not get the idea of threatening her or forcing her to do anything, she thought determinedly. Otherwise he would get to know another side of her.

Around half past eleven she passed Freiburg, and it wasn't far to the turn-off to France. Suddenly she noticed a beige Audi, which had been driving behind her at the same distance for some time. Looks like I'm being followed, she thought. She accelerated the car to one hundred and forty, although only one hundred and twenty kilometres per hour was allowed here. The Audi did the same and stayed at about the same distance behind her. Monika got nervous. Maybe the police were after her. She wanted to know exactly what was going on and slowed down to one hundred, then to eighty, the Audi behind her always doing exactly the same and keeping a fairly constant distance behind her.

This could not be a coincidence, and while dozens of cars overtook her, the Audi was constantly following her. Monika panicked. What could she do? She accelerated back up to one hundred and twenty and persuaded herself into thinking that it was just a coincidence. Maybe a scared novice driver who didn't dare to overtake her. Around twelve she crossed the French border and was extremely relieved to see that the supposed pursuer had left the motorway before the border and drove into the car park.

Thank God, so the whole thing had been harmless! She took a deep breath. She had to be careful not to panic or become paranoid. The events of the last few days had obviously burdened her more than she had previously admitted to herself. A little later she passed Mulhouse and then, after hours of driving and a few short breaks, she arrived in the city of Orange at about six pm. She went to her hotel and treated herself to an expensive meal before bedtime.

Early next morning the sun was shining from a cloudless blue sky. It would be as hot again as yesterday, even hotter. For the south of France, the voice on the radio predicted temperatures of up to forty-one degrees Celsius.

At about half past two she crossed the French-Spanish border at La Junquera. The traffic was backed up for about a kilometre due to road works in the area. Nevertheless she soon saw the coastline of the Costa Brava in the distance and arrived quite exhausted in Blanes at about four o'clock.

The liveried hotel employee of the Plaza Paris Spa drove her car into the underground car park and took her suitcase upstairs. At the reception she gave the instruction that she didn't want to be disturbed for the next two hours. Anybody who might show up should be told that she would probably arrive around six pm. She took a shower and then made a short phone call to Karl-Heinz. Afterwards she went to bed to rest.

She fell into a deep restful sleep for about thirty minutes. It was half past five when she looked at her watch. She was getting ready to go out, it was to be expected that Alex would show up soon. Monika called the reception and asked if anyone had asked about her. The receptionist told her in fluent English that a gentleman had asked for her at about five pm and he had replied as ordered that Mrs Lochberger was expected at about 6 pm. So Alex had received the mail and would be there shortly.

Around a quarter past six her telephone rang and the reception reported the arrival of a gentleman. She gave the instruction that he should please wait downstairs in the hotel lobby. She would come down.

On arrival in the red-carpeted lobby she immediately saw Alex in one of the massive chairs not far from the reception. When he noticed her, he jumped up in delight, rushed towards her and almost crushed her with his embrace. He tried to kiss her but she fought him off and whispered, "Not here please, let's wait until we are outside."

"I am so happy to see you," he said overjoyed and she hugged him and whispered in his ear. "Me too. Let's go for a walk, I've been sitting in the car all day, I need some exercise now."

"With the greatest of pleasure," he replied and they left the hotel together hand in hand and walked through side streets leading down to the beach. At some distance from the hotel Alex suddenly stopped and kissed Monika passionately. She was surprised by his outburst of emotion, but did not resist.

"How long have I waited for this moment," he said.

"I feel the same way," she sighed, "but let's go on, people are coming."

From far away you could already see a lively scene of many holidaymakers, swimming in the cool water or sunbathing on the golden sand.

"Did you bring swimming trunks?" she asked Alex and he nodded.

"We could go for a swim afterwards, that would be refreshing."

"All right then. We'll go for a walk first and then swim later," Alex said. "And I know a very nice restaurant here where you can have a delicious dinner."

"That sounds good," said Monika, "I'm really hungry. On the way I only ate a bread roll and some fruit."

"I still can't believe that you're really here," said Alex and looked lovingly. "And you really have an alibi for me?" he asked uncertainly.

She pulled him to her and gave him a kiss. "I've thought about it for a long time. We'll say that you came straight to me after leaving school and that we spent the whole evening together."

"That's great," said Alex touched, "thank you very much for that."

"You're welcome darling, after all we're both interested in you not having to wander around here, hiding from the police."

"You were originally concerned about your reputation."

"Of course it will reflect badly on me, and above all we must be careful that we are not seen as accomplices in the murder of my husband. But on the other hand, the police will find out that my marriage had been on shaky ground for years and that I had intended to file for divorce. From which point it is not a big step to admit to an extramarital relationship."

"Well, that makes sense to me, and of course I am very glad that you have decided to do so," said Alex beaming with joy.

"I couldn't have put up with it any longer without you," Monika whispered tenderly into his ear. "I missed you so much."

"Me too, I thought of you every day, every hour, and the worst thing was that I couldn't get in touch with you."

"Thank God we've put all that behind us now. I suggest we have a nice evening and then a trip tomorrow. Maybe to the mountains, they're supposed to be very beautiful here, I read. And the day after tomorrow we'll go back together."

"That's great," Alex said. "I'm the happiest man in the world today."

The two of them enjoyed a leisurely walk along the beach, then later went for a swim. The beach was still full, but by half past seven there were far fewer people there. The water was at a pleasant temperature and they enjoyed this short refreshment very much and then lay next to each other on the sand. Alex was overcome with tenderness and hoped to spend the night with his lover. But when he asked her, she robbed him of this illusion. She said that unfortunately she had only got a single room, everything else was full. But tomorrow they would have a double. It was already booked. She asked him to understand that they would have to postpone spending the night together for one more day. Alex was disappointed to hear that, but on the other hand he didn't want to contradict Monika's suggestion.

Around eight they left the beach and Alex took her to a small restaurant where he had eaten before. He had reserved a table there and while they were eating they could see the sea with numerous sailing boats cruising. It was a very warm summer evening, the temperature was still over thirty degrees and they found the cool breeze, which now occasionally came up, extremely pleasant. They had a fish platter with side dishes and enjoyed a wonderfully relaxed evening. Monika held back on the wine and drank very little. She too seemed relaxed and satisfied and nothing indicated that she was not quite as happy and satisfied as he.

After a coffee they left the restaurant at eleven o'clock and shortly afterwards approached the hotel. Alex made another attempt to change Monika's mind and asked innocently whether she would like to show him her room. She smiled tenderly at him and said that she had a headache and that the day had been exhausting, after having spent so many hours on the road. She asked him to understand that it was not convenient now and that she needed to rest. They would have a double room the next day. Alex was satisfied with that. Not far from the hotel they said goodbye with a tender kiss and Monika disappeared into the building, while Alex walked a few hundred metres to his car.

He spent the night in his car, as he had done on the nights before, because he didn't dare to go to the nearby campsite until he had new identity papers. He rightly feared that his name would be on a wanted list and he might be discovered and then arrested if the police checked his registration documents.

37 Difficult Decisions

Monika Lochberger went to her hotel room at the Plaza Paris Spa and closed the door behind her.

She was glad that she had got rid of Alex so easily. The story about the double room was a lie, she had no intention of spending the night with him. And now she doubted whether it had been right to go to Spain at all. Alex was obviously head over heels in love with her and she had to think about how to liberate herself from him.

She fetched a beer from the minibar and took a sip. Then she took the company mobile phone she had got from Messerschmidt and called him.

"Hello, darling," she heard him say. "Well, how did the evening go?"

"So-so," she sighed. "The man is madly in love with me, and I'm not sure if my idea of coming here was such a good one."

"I'm not so sure either," Karl-Heinz told her in a worried voice.

"The police were here this afternoon. Shortly after we had spoken on the telephone, two plain-clothes police officers from the criminal investigation department arrived. They asked me if I had five minutes to answer a few questions. I didn't want to send them away, it might have looked suspicious. So I let them in."

"And what did they want?" Monika asked nervously.

"They have obviously requested documents from the phone companies and now know that we've been talking on the phone quite often lately. They wanted to know why. I explained to them that these were business calls and that we were talking about how we could work together to develop even better software."

"Yeah, that's good, they'll believe that, won't they?"

"Well, not exactly, because they asked if there was a private relationship between us. I categorically denied it. Then they wanted to know where I had been at the time of the crime. It´s getting worse and worse!"

"I hope you have an alibi for that time, Karl-Heinz!"

"I think so. I was in the sauna until nine, then I had a beer with a friend and went home at a quarter past ten."

"That really is the limit that they suspect us!"

"But if you come here with Alex and testify to the police that he was with you on the night of the crime, it will raise a lot of questions."

"Why, what do you mean?"

"Well, I don't know if it is really plausible that you are having an affair with a teacher, an employee of your husband. That's one thing.

Very risky, by the way, because if Strasser is suspicious, then the two of you together are all the more so. But the other thing is, if this guy is really in love with you, he won't keep quiet if you want to get rid of him. What do you want to do then?"

"Yeah, I've been thinking about that. I might be able to dump him after a short time, but if he finds out later that I'm with you, I'm afraid he'll be driven by thoughts of revenge and then, who knows!"

"I agree with you. He'll probably go to the police and reveal everything. And if it comes out that I bought the data he stole, then things will get dicey. As long as they haven't found a murderer, we'll automatically be suspected of having killed your husband."

"Yes, you're right, but what should I do now? I really don't know where my head is at the moment."

"How about telling him that the alibi won't hold up? You could perhaps say that a neighbour testified to the police that she saw you alone in the garden for hours that evening and that no one was with you."

"That might be an idea, I'll have to think about it. But in spite of everything, if I don't take him back with me now, I don't know how he will react. He is clinging to the idea that I am going to save him and he can then come home again. He won't let go of that so quickly."

"I can imagine. At the moment I don't know what else we can do." He thought for a moment. "What if he had an accident?"

"What are you suggesting, Karl-Heinz?"

"That was not a suggestion, just a consideration. Why don't you take him on a mountain hike in the Pyrenees. Maybe he'll get careless and falls off a cliff."

" That's enough. I understand what you're trying to say, but that's going too far. Let's talk again tomorrow. I need to clear my head and think a bit about the whole situation and then decide how I'm going to proceed."

"Darling, I don't want to put you under stress. You're going to do it right. I'll say good night. Speak to you soon."

"Yes, tomorrow night, when I'm through with the hardest part."

"Take care, darling. Sleep well. I love you."

She switched off her mobile phone completely. She wanted to think clearly about the difficult task that lay ahead of her.

On the one hand she found Karl-Heinz's insinuations outrageous, what was he actually thinking? She wasn't a killer! On the other hand, he might not be wrong with this idea. If Alex refused to accept her request for a separation from him, there was always the danger that he could blackmail her and Karl-Heinz or even simply testify to the police out of revenge. That was a risk not to be underestimated.

161

Perhaps Karl-Heinz had instinctively judged her correctly as far as her ability to murder was concerned, she thought. After all, she had brought an old pistol, inherited from her mother, with her on the trip as a precaution, because you never knew what could happen.

Her mother had been the owner of a small jewellery shop and always kept the weapon there. Only once in her life had she really needed the gun, when a man armed with a knife came into her shop and demanded she hand over the jewellery and cash. The robber allegedly laughed stupidly when her mother suddenly took the gun out of a drawer and pointed it at him. He is reported to have said, "Put the toy gun away, granny," and when he then approached her mother, a shot was fired and the man fell to the floor, dead. The press at the time praised her mother as a heroine, who had faced the criminal with great courage. Monika was ten years old at the time and had been very proud of what her mother had done.

She now had the gun with her. It was loaded. She had been able to try it out at the shooting range when she was invited to a rifle club a few months before. But she didn't want to kill Alex. No, she definitely didn't want to do that.

She would tell him the truth tomorrow, namely, that she no longer loved him and did not plan a future with him, but that she would give him an alibi to enable him to return home. Then she would wait for his reaction and adjust her own behaviour accordingly. A peaceful solution would be possible if he accepted her confession and made no demands. Then they could go back to Germany as friends and everything could be put right again.

But if he reproached her, or even insulted or threatened her? If he said he would go to the police? What should she do then? For a long time all sorts of thoughts went through her head without her finding any answers. It was shortly after midnight when she finally came to a decision. She would tell him tomorrow that her feelings for him were only friendly. If he accepted that, it was fine. If not, she would have to say goodbye to him forever.

38 In the Mountains

The morning began as badly as the night had been. Monika woke up early, it was only half past six and she felt exhausted. She hadn't slept well and had had terrible nightmares. Breakfast was not served until half past seven, so there was no point in getting up too early. She thought about what she had to do. She wanted to go to the mountains with Alex, but which route exactly and where? Into the Pyrenees? That might be too far, she didn't know exactly. So she took her tablet and started to search the internet for places to go in the area. She noted down a few destinations that seemed interesting to her and took screenshots of the corresponding pages. At seven she got up and after washing she went downstairs to the breakfast room, where two other guests were already sitting. The breakfast buffet was well stocked, just as she expected for such an elegant hotel.

Contrary to her habits, she ate a little more than usual. Gradually the breakfast room filled up with more guests, most of whom were probably holidaymakers who could afford the luxury of getting up late. After breakfast Monika asked a waiter if he could give her recommendations for a trip to the mountains. However, it should be somewhere that was not overrun with tourists. She would like to experience a romantic trip through the hills and forests with a friend. Monika asked in particular about a spectacular view she wanted to enjoy.

The waiter smiled understandingly and considered. Then he told her of two destinations, which he apparently knew personally, and which were no more than about seventy kilometres away. The waiter affirmed that in both cases there were wonderful vantage points available and that one could enjoy wonderful vistas far into the country. But he emphasised that these places were actually secrets known only to the locals and that hardly any tourists knew about them. Monika thanked the waiter for his extensive advice and gave him a generous tip.

When Alex arrived in the hotel lobby at about ten thirty as agreed and asked at the reception to inform Mrs Lochberger of his arrival, she had already worked out her excursion plans. One of the waiter's recommendations coincided with her own research. On the map she had bought at the reception, the winding route included several viewpoints which could be seen in great detail.

Arriving in the hotel lobby, she walked straight towards Alex, took him by the arm and led him outside where she kissed him.

"I'm glad you're here, darling," she said. "I've thought about our programme for today. You like the mountains, don't you?"

"Of course," said Alex. "We'll really see a bit more of the country, because here on the beach everything is always the same. And where exactly do you want to go today?"

"Let's sit on a bench for a while so I can show you what I have planned on the map."

"There's one over there," said Alex and pointed to a bench fifty metres away under a pine tree.

"Wonderful, then we can look at our route right away."

Monika explained the destination she had chosen to Alex and he was surprised at how well she had planned everything.

"When are you actually going to move from your single room to our new double room," he asked incidentally.

"The chambermaids will do that later, they'll carry my things into the new room. I already have everything in my suitcase, and when we come back we can move into the double room, which will be ready from two o'clock in the afternoon."

"Fine," said Alex, but something in Monika's expression seemed to indicate that she was obviously not as happy about it as he had hoped.

"You don't mind us doing it this way, do you?" he asked nervously.

"But of course, darling," Monika said somewhat forced. "We've agreed on it and I want you to be happy after all."

"And I want you to be satisfied too. So if you're not quite content, it doesn't necessarily have to be this way," Alex said in a slightly offended tone.

"Come on, Alex, let's not talk about such nonsense. Of course I'm looking forward to spending the night with you. But now we're going on our trip. It's great weather today and we'll see some beautiful scenery."

She laughed encouragingly at him.

"Are we going in my car or yours?" Alex asked.

"If you don't mind," Monika said slowly, as if she had to think about it first, "better take mine. The car has a navigation system we might need. But you are welcome to take the wheel if you like. You would be doing me a favour. The two days on the motorway were exhausting."

Alex agreed and was content to get behind the wheel. Twenty minutes later they were sitting in Monika's Mercedes and drove off.

The conversation between them didn't seem to be going very well this morning. Alex thought he detected an element of rejection in Monika's facial expression. Since he had read the latest email from Winfried in an Internet café earlier this morning, he was worried and filled with apprehension.

In this email, Winfried had expressed suspicions about Monika, even warned him about her. He told him that he had seen her together with Messerschmidt in an intimate situation and that they had kissed as Monika was leaving. This news had deeply concerned Alex. He was initially not prepared to believe this allegation. But it preoccupied him so much that he lost the usual feeling of ease he always had when he was with her. She obviously noticed that and asked him:

"What's wrong with you, you're so silent today?"

"Sorry, I slept badly. The last few days have been very emotional. And now that you have come and we can finally go home, there.... It's just been too stressful for me, and so I'm still pretty tired this morning."

"I can completely understand that," said Monika. "I didn't sleep well either, probably the long drive and of course the excitement and joy to finally see you again."

She smiled at him and put on the most seductive smile she was capable of at that moment. This did indeed have a positive effect on Alex.

"Oh yes, I am happy that we are going on a trip together and then go home tomorrow. I am..... I can't tell you how happy I am that everything has turned out this way."

"I'm really glad too, Alex, and I'm sure everything's going to be fine."

Her last words sounded surprisingly soothing and believable to Alex again. Perhaps his fears and mistrust were completely out of place, perhaps Winfried had misinterpreted something. Now he did not want to let this beautiful day be spoiled and decided to put all gloomy thoughts aside. It was a beautiful summer morning with an azure blue picture book sky, and it promised to be a very hot day. A light, cool breeze blew in from the sea and made one feel pleasantly refreshed. The two of them drove northeast towards Tordera. The country road led over green hills and through farmland. Now and then they saw tractors in the fields. Beyond Tordera the landscape became increasingly mountainous.

About ten minutes later they came to a long valley through which a motorway passed with the C35 expressway running alongside. Alex joined this road and after five minutes they came to the Hostalric exit, where he turned north following Monika's instructions.

"We are going to San Feliu de Buixalleu now. That was a secret tip from the waiter in my hotel. He said there are very nice hiking trails there and an outstanding view of the mountains."

"I think it's great that you have prepared everything so well, Monika," Alex said appreciatively.

"I want us to enjoy our trip, Alex. And while we're here, I think we should see some of the beauty of this country, too."

"You're absolutely right, and I find the scenery here very attractive. I'm very eager to see our destination."

"Let's take a short break now," she said. "I'd like to smoke a cigarette."

"No problem," Alex answered and they got out of the car.

They had been relatively silent during the whole journey so far, and Alex kept thinking about the email he had received that morning from Winfried. In fact, he had got up at half past seven, which means that he had wriggled out of his sleeping bag in his car. After a walk and a breakfast with croissants and coffee in a small café he had read his emails in an Internet café. There he discovered the sobering email from Winfried, which culminated in the sentence:

I don't know what Monika is actually planning or intending, but be careful. This woman seems increasingly suspicious to me. Perhaps she is even behind the murder of her husband? Please keep your eyes open and be prepared for anything.

His friend's words alarmed him greatly. What did it all mean? Was it possible that Monika had not come with honest intentions? Was it possible that she was having an affair with Messerschmidt? He decided to be careful. On the other hand he didn't want to snub her, nor to risk his return home and the alibi she had promised him.

He recalled this morning once again. After visiting the Internet café, he had gone to the post office and asked for his mail.

After a quick glance at his identity card, the official had briefly disappeared into the next room before returning with a lined envelope. Alex recognised Winfried's handwriting immediately. He had left the post office with the envelope still closed and had returned to his car, in eager expectation of his new ID card. He tore open the envelope with some excitement and found a small package in a plastic bag with a note bearing Winfried's handwriting:

Here are the documents you wanted, my friend. All the best and get in touch again soon. Best regards Winfried.

He opened the small parcel and took out the long awaited documents, namely a driving licence, a passport and an identity card, all in the name of Peter Miller.

"So now my name is Miller, Peter Miller," he said to himself with great satisfaction, knowing that a new life could now begin. From tonight onwards he no longer needed to spend the nights in the car, but could book a hotel at any time without having to fear being arrested in the process. Peter Miller was a completely unsuspicious new identity. In the meantime it was almost ten o'clock and he would soon meet Monika. He had gone down to the beach with bathing trunks and a towel, where he took a short morning swim. Having returned to his vehicle with that feeling of freshness and cleanliness that only bathing in the sea can provide, he shaved and left just before half past ten. The walk to the hotel took only three minutes and he had arrived on time at the Plaza Paris Spa Hotel, where he met Monika.

Now they were standing in this small car park in the mountains, Monika was smoking and seemed to have a cold expression on her face. He was uncomfortable, the mood between them had been strange all morning. Something heavy was in the air, and his suspicion of this woman was growing stronger by the minute. The unpaved car park, about twenty metres in diameter, lay in the shade of eucalyptus trees and was empty except for a parked vehicle that stood on the other side to their left in the blazing sun. In front of them was a magnificent view of the Catalan mountains with its patchwork of forest and fields in between. While Monika was still smoking, he strolled to the edge of the square towards the slope. It was a steep descent of more than a hundred metres over rocks and only partly overgrown with trees and bushes.

"Not very beautiful, this slope here. Let's get back in and drive a little further," he said as Monika put out her cigarette.

39 Speaking Frankly

They got back into the car and fastened their seat belts. But Alex didn't drive off but instead turned to Monika and said with a serious expression:

"I think we should talk."

Monika's expression brightened, as if she had been waiting for exactly this and was happy about the upcoming discussion.

"All right," she said. "Let's talk."

"I don't know if you're being honest with me."

"What makes you think that?"

"Is it possible you have a relationship with Mr Messerschmidt that is as close as the one you have with me?"

She gave a slight sigh.

"I've been meaning to talk to you about that, Alex. I actually felt very lonely towards the end of my marriage and met you and Karl-Heinz at about the same time. You could say that I fell in love with both of you simultaneously."

"Well, that happens sometimes," Alex said with a slightly ironic expression. "But what is your relationship to him and to me now? I have so far assumed that you are planning your future together with me? Is that really still the case or has something changed?"

"No other man has this meaning for me as you do," she said and smiled encouragingly at him.

"But isn't it true that the day before yesterday Mr Messerschmidt said goodbye to you and kissed you?"

Monika turned pale and immediately afterwards blushed.

"How could you possibly know that," she asked in amazement.

"My friend Winfried happened to see you. He wanted to drop off something for you for the trip here, and that's when he happened to witness your rather passionate farewell."

"I think your friend meddles too much in our private lives. Mr Messerschmidt actually came to see me in the morning before my departure and brought me something and then we said goodbye as friends, nothing more."

"I don't know why I can't trust you Monika," Alex said with a grim face. "My gut feeling tells me that something is wrong and that you are not telling me the truth."

"What would happen if our relationship didn't develop as happily as we both once thought? We are both adults and we know that in the early stages of falling in love you can fool yourself. On closer examination you sometimes find out that you are not as compatible as you had once thought."

"So that's what you want to tell me," Alex said, increasingly irritated and in a slightly aggressive tone. "So it is obviously correct, what Winfried wrote to me. Namely that you have an intimate relationship with Messerschmidt."

"And if that were so, what then? After all, I am not your property, but a free person. You increasingly behave like my master who thinks he can order me around and decide for me."

"That's utter nonsense," he said angrily. "The fact is, however, that you have obviously lied to me. You have recently tried to make me believe that you were in love with me and wanted to spend the rest of your life with me. But in reality you have already made plans for the future with Messerschmidt. The question now is, why did you come here in the first place?"

"I wanted to help you get out of this damn situation."

"It was you who manoeuvred me into this situation. You probably set me up from the start. You talked me into this data theft that ultimately turned out in Messerschmidt's favour, because he will now continue to run the software your husband originally developed and he will no longer have a competitor. So you both have a glorious future ahead of you. I am the necessary sacrifice. And if it suits you, you can report me to the police and accuse me of theft. Then I might even be a murder suspect."

Monika interrupted him angrily. "Stop this now, you're talking nonsense."

"I don't trust you any more, Monika, and I don't think you mean it honestly. And I won't go back with you either. Who knows what you're really up to. In the end I'll wind up in custody because the two of you are going to join forces against me and make corresponding statements to the police. But of course I could also make my statement, and my friend Winfried knows all about it."

"I really think that's enough!" said Monika with a cold expression on her face and pulled out the little pistol from her handbag.

"You are a fool, and apparently you do not want to accept the help I am giving you. I came here to assist you, to provide you with an alibi. But I want to continue my life at home according to my own plans. We don't owe each other anything. You got me the data from my husband's computer, you were paid for it and in return I am willing to give you an alibi. We're even, got it? I neither love you nor will I be there for you in the future. When we get back, we are old acquaintances and nothing more. Do you understand?"

Alex stared at the gun in her hand in astonishment and was speechless for a moment.

"Are you going to shoot me? And my friend Winfried, who knows everything, will you kill him too?"

"If you force me to and there is no other way, then it may happen. Besides, I still don't know to this day if it wasn't you who killed my husband. Then it would only be just revenge for what you did."

"You must be completely crazy. I have nothing to do with the murder of your husband, but you probably had him killed to get his company and his software. And then be able to enjoy your escapades with Messerschmidt & Co. unhindered. You are a snake."

"It would be better if you kept your mouth shut now, otherwise I'll forget my good manners," said Monika, when suddenly a loud noise of squealing tyres behind them startled her. In the rear-view mirror Alex saw a green and white police car of the Guardia Civil.

"It's the police, better put the gun away," Alex whispered to her. She hid the gun in her handbag and laid it on the floor in front of her. There was already a knocking at the driver's door from outside. A corpulent policeman stood next to the vehicle and looked at Alex questioningly. Alex let down the window and the policeman, addressing him in English asked for his passport. Alex immediately replied in Spanish: "I can speak your language." The policeman's face brightened and he replied:

"Very well, then please show me your driving license and identity card. What are you doing in this area?"

"We are tourists and we are on a little trip. The mountains here are very beautiful," Alex answered in fluent Spanish as he groped for his identity card, which was not in the breast pocket of his shirt.

"Do you have the car papers, Monika?" he asked, but she was already busy getting them out of the glove compartment.

"And the lady's identity card too, please," said the policeman. In the meantime, the second policeman, a slender young man, had also got out of the patrol car. He stood next to his older colleague, watching the scene with a searching look. Alex was still going through his trouser pockets, but apparently could not find his ID.

"I have to get out of the car for a moment, my papers are probably in the boot."

"OK," said the stout policeman, "then get out."

Alex got out and told Monika that he had his papers in his rucksack in the boot. She watched him suspiciously. He went to the back of the car and opened the boot. Now he was not visible to Monika, the boot lid covering him. Alex took out his backpack and at the same time waved to the policeman and let him know that his female companion should not notice anything. The policeman approached him and Alex said quietly to him in Spanish:

"You must help me. This woman has a gun and she is going to shoot me. Arrest her!"

The policeman looked at him in disbelief. He obviously thought it was a joke.

"I am absolutely serious," Alex said very insistently. "This is not my wife, she is only an acquaintance of mine. I hardly know her and she invited me on this trip, but now I am in danger. Pull out your pistols, because she might shoot."

The policeman did not want to believe it and said quietly to his young colleague: "Listen, Jaime, I think this tourist is pulling our legs. He claims that the woman in the car wants to shoot him. Maybe he has had too much sun."

The younger one looked angry.

"Juan, let's get out of here, we're just wasting our time with these weird people. I want to be home in time for lunch," he growled moodily.

But Alex heard that and quickly said: "No, it's no joke, believe me. The gun is in her handbag. Be careful! That woman is dangerous!"

The corpulent official was still not convinced, but he now reluctantly walked forward to the driver's door, leaned forward and said to Monika:

"Señora, salga, por favor!"

Monika had not understood and called out through the window.

"What did the policeman say, Alex?"

"That you should get out of the car," he said.

"Come out of the car," the policeman translated now and Monika made preparations to obey this request.

"Give me your bag, please Señora," he policeman demanded, pointing to her handbag and making a gesture of handing it over.

"Have you been talking to him, you fool," Monika now shouted angrily in the direction of Alex, who stood behind the two policemen, as if he wanted to hide from her.

"Be careful," Alex said in Spanish to the policemen. "I told you she has a gun in her handbag."

"Give me your bag, please," the stout policeman now insisted.

She made a gesture of agreement and seemed to give in. She took the bag in her left hand, as if she wanted to hand it over, and then in a flash, put her right hand into it and pulled out the weapon. Her gun was now pointed at the three men.

"Hands up," she yelled energetically. "Hands up or I'll shoot!"

171

"Maldito sea!" cursed Juan. "Damn it, Jaime, this woman is crazy."

"No speaking! Do not talk!" cried Monika angrily and continued to point her gun at the group.

"Alex, get into the car now!"

"What does she say?" the older policeman asked Alex quietly.

"She wants me to get into the car." Alex replied in Spanish.

The Guardia now spoke to Monika in his poor English and tried to calm her down.

"Señora, we are Spanish police, no pistol contra police, please!"

"Stop babbling and hold your hands up," shouted Monika, and when the policeman Juan lowered his arms, she fired a shot into the air, over his head. The guard realised that this lady was not to be trifled with and immediately put his hands up again.

Suddenly another vehicle could be heard approaching. A heavy motorbike came around the bend. It braked and drove slowly past the car park entrance. It was a police motorbike. The driver had understood the seriousness of the situation with a single glance. His colleagues were apparently in extreme danger.

Monika had only looked over to the left for a moment. She had to keep the two policemen at bay, and only saw that the motorcyclist accelerated again and drove on. She didn't notice that he stopped after a few metres behind the next bend and turned off his engine. With his pistol at the ready, the motorcyclist ran back to the car park, always taking advantage of the cover of the bushes and trees.

"Alex, get in the car now or I'll shoot you all," cried Monika, who gradually fell into a state of hysteria. "Put that guy into the car," she shouted angrily to the police.

At that moment the motorbike policeman suddenly stood in the car park entrance, pointed his gun at Monika and shouted out loud, "Manos arriba! Hands up!"

Monika was startled, her nerves were already strained to breaking point. Reflexively she turned the gun to the left in the direction of the newly arrived policeman and fired. The shot of the motorbike policeman went off almost simultaneously. In a flash the two Guards had also pulled out their pistols and opened fire on Monika. Everything happened at breakneck speed and lasted only seconds. Monika staggered, fell and collapsed, then rolled backwards on the ground in a pool of blood, hit by several bullets. The motorbike policeman had also apparently been hit and was down.

Jaime, the younger policeman went over to the woman lying on the ground. He crouched down next to her, saw her gunshot wounds in her upper body, felt her pulse and then said coolly, "She's dead."

Juan was already kneeling next to his colleague, talking to him. It was Pedro. He worked in the neighbouring town and they knew each other well. Pedro was breathing heavily. He was conscious, but in shock and had severe pain in his left arm. The sleeve of his motorbike jacket had been torn to shreds by the bullet. He was responsive, briefly passed out and then regained consciousness.

"Man, you were lucky," said Juan.

"Yes, I think I'm okay, it's just my arm," said Pedro. "She shot me in the arm. What about that woman?" he asked.

"She is dead. We had to shoot, or she would have killed us all. Lucky for us that you came at that moment, otherwise we would have been pushing up the daisies by now. She must have been crazy."

The younger colleague Jaime now spoke: "Pedro, let's see whether you can be transported in an ambulance or whether we need a helicopter. Can you stand?"

They helped their injured colleague carefully to his feet. He could actually stand alone, and even walk a few steps. So he apparently had not suffered any other serious injury, but he complained of severe pain in his arm.

"All right, we'll call an ambulance." Jaime went to the patrol car and radioed the headquarters. "Hello, this is Jaime Montero. We urgently need an ambulance. Our comrade has a gunshot wound in his arm, and there is a dead woman. She shot at us, we fired back in self-defence."

He gave the necessary information about the location and the course of the incident and then went back to his colleagues. "The ambulance will be here soon."

Alex stood next to Monika's car the whole time. The boot and driver's door were still open. Behind the car Monika lay on the ground. The shock of these unexpected events was still written all over his face. That woman must have been insane, he thought. I loved her, but she would have shot me without batting an eyelid. How could it have come to this? He was confused. Only yesterday he had dreamed of spending his future life together with her, and now she was dead. A cold shiver ran down his spine.

He could not believe it. A single moment had changed his life completely. The woman he had loved so much had betrayed him, wanted to kill him, and now she herself was dead. His return to Germany had thus become impossible, and without an alibi he would have to remain on the run.

The policemen smoked cigarettes and now called Alex to their vehicle to question him and take down his details. They wanted to know what relationship he had had with this woman and how the whole thing had come about. He answered evasively, saying only that she was a brief acquaintance and that he had met her by chance on the beach. She had then invited him yesterday for a day trip to the mountains. Then here in this car park she suddenly threatened him and demanded money from him. Obviously she was a criminal. Perhaps also mentally disturbed. He could not say any more. He did not know her.

"We have to take your personal details," said the policeman. "Please give me your identity card." Alex now handed him his new ID card and the policeman noted down the data and then gave him back his credentials.

"Muchas gracias, Señor Miller. And thank you for warning us, we couldn't believe it at first. It's not something that happens every day."

Alex replied slowly and absent-mindedly, still trapped by the memory of the dramatic events.

"I could hardly believe it myself when she suddenly pointed a gun at me."

"In future, take a closer look before you get into the car with someone," said the policeman.

"I won't get into a car with a strange woman ever again, believe me," Alex replied with a resigned expression on his face.

"We'll need you as a witness, Mr Miller, can you come with us for the report?"

"Of course," said Alex, noting with a certain satisfaction that he was now at least travelling with a new identity and did not need to fear arrest for the moment.

40 Bad News

When I arrived home at about 7 pm, my answering machine was flashing. I immediately listened to the recordings and to my surprise there was actually a call from Alex. The text was short:

"I need to speak to you urgently, if possible today. Bad things have happened. Please call me at the number I have sent you by email. Alex."

That sounded worrying, and I was very curious to hear what Alex would tell me. I immediately sat down at my desk and switched on my computer. I had received an email from a sender 'Pedro Molinero', whom I had never heard of before. I smiled because it was the Spanish translation of Peter Miller. So Alex had opened a Spanish email account. In the attachment to his mail I found his new telephone number. I called the number and he immediately answered.

"Hello Winfried! Thank goodness it's you," he said with relief in his voice.

"Hello Alex. What happened? Has Monika turned up? Tell me."

"Oh Winfried, it's all over," he said in a depressed voice and told me the whole story in detail, from Monika's arrival in Blanes, through her planning of the trip, to the scene in the car when she had threatened him with a pistol and how the Spanish police came and how she finally died, shot to death by the police.

"I loved her, but she betrayed me. She probably would have shot me if the police had not suddenly appeared. I wanted to live my last years together with her, and now everything is gone."

I was both shocked and relieved that Alex had not been killed.

"Of course I am terribly sorry about all this. But I'm glad you're still alive." I said. "But you don't get an alibi now and your plan to return to Germany has been put on hold for a while, right?"

"Unfortunately, that's exactly the way it is," Alex said. "I have to stay here for the time being, perhaps they'll find the murderer soon. I won't come back before then. If you could fill up the visa card a bit, occasionally, that would be good. I'll probably have to stay here a little longer."

"I'll do that for you, of course. What are you going to do now?"

"I'm staying in Spain for the time being. Maybe I'll go further south, take some holidays, although I don't feel like it at all. But now I can afford a proper overnight stay again. While I didn't have the new documents, I preferred to spend the nights in the car. By the way, I would be happy if you could check on my house occasionally."

"OK, Alex, I'll get it done. I just hope the police finally find the killer and that you'll come back soon."

"I wish I could, but of course it could take months or more. There's little point in speculating about it. We'll see."

"Well, I'm keeping my fingers crossed for you and wish you a safe journey."

"We might phone and exchange emails if necessary, but only in emergencies. Your communication will probably be tapped."

"All right, my friend, that's how we'll do it. Wait, one more question, do you want me to contact Messerschmidt?"

"I'd rather you didn't. You would have to tell him about my new identity. That would be risky for me. The whole thing is risky. If the German police were to try to contact the real Peter Miller, because of a witness statement, for example, then I'd fear for the worst. I don't even know whether he really exists and if so, whether he's still alive. That could still become unpleasant. Better leave Messerschmidt out of it. He'll figure it out soon enough, and if he should contact you, it's best to claim that you know nothing."

"Well, I understand, you're probably right, take care. See you soon!"

"I hope so, too. Bye Winfried!"

I spent the evening brooding. In any case, it was to be expected that the Spanish police would send a report to their German counterparts. And then it was probably also to be anticipated that this Peter Miller would be summoned as a witness. Of course, it would soon turn out that this man had not been in Spain at the time in question. Perhaps he no longer existed, he might already be dead, and then the suspicion would quickly fall back on Alex. The whole thing went round and round in my head for hours, and I saw no way out of the confusion.

The next morning, when I went to get the daily paper from the letterbox, I saw the headline on the front page with the detailed article on page one:

Widow of murdered school headmaster shot dead!
Only two weeks after the murder of headmaster Lochberger, which has not yet been clarified, his wife has now also met a violent death. According to research by our newspaper, Mrs Lochberger was on holiday on the Costa Brava. On a trip through the Catalan coastal mountains near Tordera she came across a police checkpoint and was shot by police officers. According to reports in the Spanish media, Mrs Lochberger pulled a pistol during the police check and threatened the officers with it. She was accompanied by a German, whose name was given as Peter M.

I didn't really feel like breakfast any more. I made do with my coffee and then drove to a business appointment afterwards, so that I could get my mind off things and stop pondering the case.

When I got back home around three o'clock in the afternoon, I had a call on my answering machine from Mr Messerschmidt. He asked me to call him back and said that he would like to talk to me in private. It was about the death of Mrs Lochberger. I didn't really want to have this conversation, but I probably wouldn't have any other choice now. I made an appointment with him for 1 pm the next day in the restaurant of the Intercity Hotel in the main train station of Stuttgart.

41 A Sad Winner

I was a few minutes early as I slowly walked into the Intercity Restaurant. In my left hand I was holding a newspaper, whose garish headline 'Headmaster's widow dies in a hail of bullets!' had lured me into buying it.

I looked around. About half of the tables were occupied. The thought struck me that I had no precise idea of Mr Messerschmidt's appearance. The only encounter at Monika's farewell had given me only a fleeting impression from a distance. On the phone I had failed to agree on an identification sign. But I hoped that somehow we would recognise each other.

I walked slowly through the restaurant and looked carefully to the left and right, but I couldn't see anyone whom I might recognize as Messerschmidt. Finally I sat down at a table, facing the entrance.

The waiter came, I ordered a coffee and skimmed through the newspaper report. As expected, it was very sensationally exaggerated. I couldn't read in peace, because I wanted to keep an eye on the entrance. Less than three minutes later a tall man, about sixty years old, with an athletic figure, black hair and a very serious facial expression, came in, looking around searchingly. That could be Messerschmidt. I gave him a sign by waving the newspaper. He slowly came closer.

"Are you Mr Alumno?"

I nodded. We shook hands and he sat down. The waiter brought my cup of coffee. He ordered the same.

"I called you because there was very dramatic and sad news from Spain. I suppose you know about it?" he asked.

"Yes, I read the newspaper article. It is a terrible story. My condolences, by the way. I know that you had a close relationship with Mrs Lochberger."

"Thank you, that's true, and it hits me very hard. We had actually made plans together for the future. Well, while we're on the subject, I'll be brief, our conversation shouldn't take too long. We both know that Monika Lochberger also had a close relationship with your friend Alexander Strasser."

"Well," I replied, "that seems to have been a somewhat one-sided relationship. I don't think it was very serious on her part."

"Let's not get into that for now," said Messerschmidt earnestly. "The newspaper article mentions that Monika was accompanied by a Peter Miller on her trip through the mountains in Catalonia. I don't know any such Mr Miller. But I do know that Monika went to Spain to meet Alexander Strasser. She wanted to offer him an alibi so that he would no longer be a murder suspect and could return to Germany. You know all that, don't you?" he asked me.

"Yes, I am aware of that. I also know that the suspicion of murder against Alex would never have arisen if he had not stolen the data card at your or Monika's instigation, from his headmaster's notebook."

Mr Messerschmidt frowned.

"What do you intend to do with this knowledge? Monika told me that you are in possession of Strasser's diaries and in this way you got some information that he would normally have been better off keeping to himself."

"I don't intend to do anything," I said. "However, I have left the information you are talking about sealed with my lawyer with the instruction that it should only be opened and handed over to the police if anything should happen to me. This is just a precaution, someone might get the wrong idea and think they have to get rid of me so that these secrets never come to light."

Mr Messerschmidt made a defensive gesture and looked at me as if to say that this was a completely absurd idea. I continued.

"I don't want to have anything more to do with this, and I won't talk to anyone about it. But if Alex were arrested and suspected of murder, I would have to come to his aid. That at least must be clear to you."

"The man who was with Monika when she was shot by the police is probably your friend Alex. Monika had told me the night before that she wanted to go to the mountains with him."

"I don't know, but I'd advise you to keep that suspicion to yourself. I have just told you that the police will not get any information from me about the data theft. In return, I expect you to do nothing now that could get my friend Alex into trouble."

"So you admit that his name is now Peter M.?" Messerschmidt asked in a sharp tone.

"It's possible that he has adopted that name now, I don't know. Leave him alone, he's on the run. As long as you don't hurt him, he won't hurt you either, the same goes for me."

Messerschmidt looked indecisive.

"By the way," I said somewhat hesitantly. "This alibi that Monika had promised him, couldn't you possibly provide him with that?"

"Well, that's absurd," Messerschmidt was indignant. "Think about what you're saying! I am the only competitor of Lochberger's software company. How would it look if I said that the suspicious Mr Strasser was with me on the night in question, having a beer? I might as well hang a sign around my neck saying that I am the murderer!"

"Well, I don't see it that way. If you both keep quiet together about the fact that there has ever been a data theft, then the problem would be solved, wouldn't it? And if you both did not commit the murder, then there will be no DNA trace from either of you on the murder victim."

Messerschmidt took a long time to answer. "I'll think about it."

"I'd like to know something else," I said. "Why did Monika have a gun on her? It almost looks as if she wanted to lure Alex into a trap intentionally."

Messerschmidt turned red.

"I really don't know anything about that. I can't even explain it myself. I didn't even know Monika owned a gun."

His statement was not very credible. I paused a while.

"All right, so my suggestion is that we both keep quiet, and please consider the matter of the alibi, that would of course be the ideal solution. Think about it and let me know as soon as possible so I can notify Alex."

Messerschmidt looked undecided and thoughtful. We finished our coffee, paid our bill and said goodbye.

When I arrived home, I talked to Susanne on the phone for a long time and told her all about the events. She was appalled that Alex had apparently only narrowly escaped being murdered by Monika. Tomorrow I would visit Susanne in Hamburg for the weekend, and we would then continue to think about the case. Had Monika possibly been the mastermind behind her husband's murder after all?

42 An Unexpected Turn

On Friday afternoon I had flown from Stuttgart to Hamburg. This time I had decided against the train and in favour of flying. It is always fascinating how fast you plunge into a completely different world as soon as you get off the plane. Although I know Hamburg and its surroundings well enough by now, I'm amazed by this effect time and again.

The weather was warm and sunny and on Saturday Susanne and I enjoyed ourselves very much. We cycled, sat in terrace cafés on the Alster Lake and time flew by.

Sunday began rainy and at breakfast we talked at length about Alex and speculated about what he would do now. Mr Messerschmidt hadn't contacted me again, so my suggestion to provide an alibi for Alex had probably not convinced him.

After breakfast I remembered to check my email in-box and there was indeed a message from Alex on Saturday night. It was short and to the point and said that he would delete his email account completely that same evening. As soon as he had a new email address he would inform me. I shouldn't write to the old address any more as it would no longer exist. I could, however, expect a text message, which should reach me at about 11 am on Monday. He would send it with a time delay.

I shook my head and told Susanne what I had just read.

"I don't really know what that's all about. He's deleted his email account. Now you can't get in touch with him at all."

"That's probably exactly what he intended," Susanne said thoughtfully.

"Yes, but what does he want?" I asked somewhat helplessly.

"I hope he doesn't have any suicide fantasies. I don't want to worry you, but when people are tearing down their last bridges, and the email address is such a bridge, it's sometimes a sign that something bad is going to happen."

"Now you're really scaring me. I hope he'll be alright."

"Don't worry. We can't change anything anyway. Maybe he'll send you his new email address soon. He probably just wanted to make sure the police weren't snooping around in his old files."

"That could be the case," I replied and with that we ended this topic, which had become a constant burden for both of us.

Later we talked about the extent to which a person's life path was actually determined by childhood influences.

There are very different opinions and many open questions. Is a person's development mainly genetically pre-programmed? Or do childhood experiences shape the personality more than hereditary factors? Or is the so-called free will stronger than all these influences together and everyone is the architect of his own happiness?

We both agreed that nobody has been able to answer these questions in a universally valid way. But it was generally acknowledged that childhood experiences had a great influence on the development of a person. Susanne then started to talk about the importance of family relationships.

"A family can be heaven or hell," she said. "I have known that from my therapeutic practice for many, many years. And when you have parents who live in a broken marriage, as unfortunately often happens nowadays, then serious conflicts and also disorders are often pre-programmed in the children. Unfortunately, very few parents manage to show sufficient consideration for their children when they separate. And then there is often the problem of domestic violence. When I think of the case of your friend Alex, who regularly had to experience how the whole family was beaten up, then it is a very hard experience which is not without its consequences."

"Yes, I think so too, and one can only be surprised that he did not later become a violent offender as well. So far, at any rate. The suspicion of murder against him at first seemed completely absurd to me. But I must admit that after reading his diaries I am no longer sure whether he did become violent. Perhaps he gave in to this inner desire to take revenge and attacked his boss in place of his father."

"Yes, I also had an uneasy feeling when I read these entries in the diary," Susanne confessed. "Especially when he wrote that as a young man he and his sister were planning to murder their father. That is an extraordinarily explosive situation which has to be taken very seriously."

Then I remembered that I hadn't read this diary entry all the way through. I suggested we continue reading at this point. I had brought the diary with me. She agreed. I went to fetch it and we continued reading together.

You have been a very contradictory father to me. On the one hand, the violent one I was afraid of and who could strike, sometimes almost without reason. On the other hand, the warm-hearted father who played with us children, had conversations with us, played music and sometimes had a word of praise for us. These positive signals were important to me as a child. I also remember how you stroked our hair in the morning at breakfast with appreciative tenderness. At a certain age I didn't want that any more, something in me rebelled against the man who at times showed tenderness, at other times violence.

It was difficult for me to reconcile these two opposing sides of your character. They were so incompatible.

But because there were many positive elements between us, I always kept in touch with you later as an adult. Basically, all my life I have sought confirmation from you, your recognition, your positive encouragement. In the last fifteen years before your death, I saw you almost every week at your musical evenings, where often one or two of your friends played along with us. We made light music, dance music and played old classics, and you were a hard-working and passionate trombone and saxophone player, even more so in your time as a pensioner than before. Music was a strong bond of togetherness between us. I played alternately the drums or the guitar, and when you praised my performance I was happy about it. Sometimes it was just the two of us, and in the breaks between the pieces many a conversation developed. You told all kinds of anecdotes from your life, from your youth, from the war and the expulsion of your family afterwards, and about the struggle for survival in the first post-war years.

When you talked about mother, however, your memory was very one-sided. All the blame for the failure of your marriage lay with her. I was unfortunately too fearful and not brave enough to stand up to you, which I regret very much today. You intimidated me for years as a child, and as an adult I was still tense and not really outspoken towards you. Even as an adult, I was still secretly afraid of you and your irascible temper. That was ultimately one of the reasons why there was always a certain reserve between us, a nervous tension that I often observed in you, an inner watchdog, so to speak, that was always ready to fend off possible attacks. The violent experiences of my childhood and youth were too intense and lasting for me to develop an undisturbed trust in you later on. And you probably felt this distrust instinctively and also felt a certain distance to me on your part.

More than ten years ago you passed away after a short and serious illness. It is a pity that I never found the courage to talk to you about the painful experiences of my childhood. I don't know whether you would have allowed it. In any case, it would have brought me great relief if you had listened to me and perhaps even expressed regret or remorse about some of your actions. It could have been a bridge between us, a way to forgiveness and reconciliation.

But forgiveness requires that someone has the desire to be forgiven. It presupposes admitting that one has caused pain or wrong to an-

other person. That was not the case with you but rather quite the opposite. You found justifications for your actions in the Bible, such as the phrase: "He who loves his child chastises him". In the same way, you trivialised your father's violence towards you by claiming that the severe beatings had not harmed you. Therefore, real reconciliation between us has unfortunately not been possible.

In a thought experiment I would like to imagine now, however, what it would be like if you received this letter, there in the eternal hunting grounds where, according to the ideas of the Indians, the ancestors live on. I want to let my imagination run wild and imagine that in your present state of being you have a different view of your past life. You will probably feel remorse for some of your actions, and the desire for forgiveness and reconciliation has grown in you. This idea is comforting for me and makes me want to forgive you, Father.

On our common path in life, such as it was, there were beautiful experiences and there were bitter ones. There is nothing we can do about that in retrospect.

I am now at an age where I am increasingly aware of the brevity of life, and I find it more and more inappropriate to carry the burden of childhood. For me, forgiveness is an important step towards inner peace, and therefore a necessity.

I have now told you all that remains to be said and with that I declare our reconciliation complete. This does not mean that I can approve all your actions, but looking back I want to stop accusing you, regretting my childhood and regarding myself as a victim.

Basically, you were a warm-hearted person who was exposed to paternal brutality as a child and permanently deformed in the process. You were endowed with an excess of energy that you were not able to control at times. I also remember that your masculine energy always radiated strongly on me and inspired and spurred me on in my actions.

I have inherited your manual skills and the joy of making music from you. In view of the many positive things I have also received from you, I would like to thank you and tell you that I loved you and can still think of you today with appreciation and love.

Your son Alexander

Susanne and I probably both felt the same. For a long time we sat next to each other in silence.

"So Alex has managed to forgive his father! It's a pity I didn't read this earlier," I said with relief. "Then I wouldn't have had such gloomy thoughts after reading the first part of it."

Susanne agreed with me. "Yes, that is really wonderful. So he has actually managed to free himself from this burden and is thus also on the way to inner peace. I am very happy for him."

"The only thing missing now is that they find the murderer and that Alex can come back soon."

We were both very happy about this unexpected turn.

The rain had stopped and the sun had come out again. We decided to go out and walk a little. The wind blew from the west while we enjoyed a little harbour tour and talked about Alex again. All signs were now pointing to a positive solution and we were glad about it and enjoyed the summer scenery of sailboats, seagulls and the fresh breeze.

Around 6 pm I was already on the plane and arrived home shortly after eight. There was no message from Messerschmidt, neither phone call, nor letter, nor email. I could probably bury any hope of his help in finding an alibi.

43 Between Fear and Hope

On Monday morning, I worked from home on backups, and besides I was on call. In my routine tasks I was interrupted shortly before eleven by the ringing of the telephone. I was startled when I heard the name of the caller:

"Sauer, Crime Squad. Hello Mr Alumno, how are you?"

"Mr Sauer, this is a surprise," I said. "To what do I owe the honour of your call?"

"Have you received any news from Spain?"

"What exactly do you mean?"

"A Volkswagen with the registration LUN for Lundenburg PE 753 is registered at your address, to a Mr Peter Alumno?"

"Yes, that's right, that's my son," I said worriedly. "What's wrong with the car?"

"We have been informed from Spain, more precisely from Tarifa in Andalusia, that this vehicle has been parked in a private car park for two days. The driver was a certain Mr Peter Miller, who rented a surfboard on Saturday and was supposed to return it by 6 pm. However, he did not come back and, after the vehicle remained in the company car park, the owner of the sailing school called the police."

"What? That's..." I said in shock. The rest of the sentence stuck in my throat.

"I suppose you know this Peter Miller?" the inspector asked me with a certain undertone in his voice.

"Well yes, that is, no, I don't know him," I stammered somewhat awkwardly. "But the vehicle, the red Golf. It belongs to my son Peter."

"Could it be that your son has been impersonating Peter Miller?"

"No, my son is currently in the USA, he's studying there, he's certainly not in Spain. But...., I lent the car to my friend Alex," I said now, without wanting to conceal anything any longer. "He needed a vehicle because he wanted to take a few days off."

"A few days off! Really!" said Mr Sauer. "Surely you know that the man is on the run from the police?"

"I know that.", I said.

"So, you are sure that this vehicle, a red Golf with the registration number mentioned before, was not driven by your son, but by Alexander Strasser?"

"I am sure that my son has nothing to do with it, and I lent the car to my friend Alex a fortnight ago," I said. "He was apparently still in the Barcelona area a short time ago. I don't know if he's actually in the south of Spain now."

186

"At the moment there is no trace of the driver of the car. He pretended to be Peter Miller to the owner of the surfboard business. According to the description, Miller and Strasser are probably one and the same person. The surfboard has not been returned, and it has not been found anywhere either. This is the state of affairs. The owner of the surfboard is worried that there might have been an accident. At the moment we do not know anything else. If you hear anything, please let us know," said Mr Sauer.

"Yes, I definitely will," I said. "Please do the same for me. Alex is a very good friend of mine and if anything has happened to him, I would of course want to know immediately. I also have to think about how I can get my car back from there, if he doesn't pick it up."

"Yes, that is the next point. The vehicle can't be left there forever, the owner of the sailing school only has limited parking space. I hope that your friend turns up and brings the car back, otherwise you will have to take care of the return transport."

After the phone call with the Commissioner, I felt paralysed and immediately imagined the worst. So Alex had rented a surfboard and had not returned it! And that in Tarifa, which is known for especially high waves and strong currents. I knew that he had been on a surfboard a few times, but that he was an experienced surfer? That was new to me. Had he possibly overestimated himself and dared to do too much? Or had he deliberately put himself in harms way? Or was the whole thing just a trick to escape the police and go into hiding? I pondered these contradictory thoughts back and forth in my mind. At the moment I was not able to think clearly, let alone do anything.

While I was making myself a coffee, my mobile phone beeped. It was a text message from Alex. So that was the text message he had already announced to me in the email at the weekend. I proceeded to read it.

Dear Winfried, I could not have wished for a better friend than you. Thanks for everything. I want to start all over again. Rebirth is not an empty word. I'll be unavailable for a while. Do not worry! Everything will be fine. Alex.

That sounded very ambiguous. I couldn't quite make sense of this text. Rebirth was a term I only knew from religious contexts. Were these possibly the parting words of a man tired of life? Of course, it could also mean something else. Maybe he had plans to emigrate and remain in hiding But the latter seemed very unlikely to me. Where would a man want to emigrate to after reaching retirement age? He could hardly have his pension transferred anywhere to Asia or Latin America as long as he was wanted by the police.

I was quite confused. At two o'clock I had an appointment with a client. My visit there didn't take long, it was just a small repair to a network and I was back home around four.

In the evening I spoke to Susanne on the phone and told her in detail about the new developments. Like me, she was quite depressed and did not rule out the possibility of my friend's suicide. Basically, we were both equally helpless in our ignorance and it was some consolation that we were able to talk about this subject for a long time and to calm each other down.

The next morning I woke up in a bad mood. I hadn't slept well and had had confusing nightmares. In one dream, Alex was standing on a surfboard when suddenly a giant fish approached from behind. All you could see was the huge dorsal fin and a big fountain of water. It had to be a whale, I thought, and was horrified to see that it now lifted its huge head out of the water, opened its mouth and devoured Alex together with the surfboard.

I awoke from this in a state of alarm. It was four o'clock in the morning. After reading a little I fell asleep again.

My sleep did not last long, however. As early as five o'clock heavy thunderclaps sounded over the town of Lundenburg, and lightning flashed brightly. I quickly closed all the windows. A heavy thunderstorm broke out, which lasted for almost two hours. The cooling rain was sorely needed, I thought, but I couldn't fall asleep again, so I got up shortly after seven o'clock.

I went down to the mailbox and got the morning newspaper. While having breakfast I had already skimmed the political part when my phone rang. It was only eight o'clock. Who could it be?

"This is Commissioner Sauer. Good morning Mr Alumno."

When I heard the Commissioner's familiar voice, I took a defensive posture.

"Good morning Commissioner. You're up early today. Is there anything new?"

"Yes, you could say that," said Sauer apparently in a good mood. "We now know that Peter Miller was a cover name for your friend Alexander Strasser."

I flinched. "Excuse me? How do you know that?"

"Well, we have carried out our investigations and the data from the identity card is apparently from a man who has already died. The owner of a sailing school in Spain made a photocopy when he rented the boat. A certain Peter Miller from Dortmund died about six months ago and someone cleverly took advantage of this fact and sold your friend a fake ID."

"That's incredible," I said.

"You could say that, Mr Alumno, and frankly, I have some suspicion as to who might have assisted in obtaining these documents."

"Well, Commissioner, I don't know what you're implying. But tell me, are you actually calling me so early in the morning to tell me about your suspicions?"

"No, please listen. I'm seriously worried. Right now, we don't even know if your friend is still alive. The thing with the surfboard is a little worrisome....," Sauer took a short break. It sounded as if he was really concerned about my friend's fate. "But something else. Have you not read the newspaper today?"

"I was in the middle of doing so when you called."

"Well, take a look at the local section right now, you'll find it interesting."

Curious, I leafed through the paper. The local section started with the headline:

Robbery at Goethe School

I could not believe my eyes.

"What do you know about this robbery?" I asked excitedly.

The Commissioner briefly described the circumstances. The previous evening at about 8.30 pm, an unknown person attacked the deputy headmaster with a wooden club in the school building of the Goethe Grammar School. Although he was slightly injured, he succeeded in knocking the attacker down with a punch and then tied him up. The perpetrator was arrested by the police and would will be brought before the magistrate.

"That's crazy," I said. "Maybe it's the same guy as in the Schiller Grammar School. If this man could now be convicted as the murderer, then Alex would finally be freed from this terrible suspicion."

The Commissioner replied: "Now, there's something else. The DNA analyses have shown that yesterday's attacker is identical to Lochberger's murderer, there is no doubt about it!"

"This is wonderful news," I exclaimed enthusiastically. "So now there is no doubt about the innocence of Alex, right?"

"It looks like it," said Sauer. "We still don't have a confession from yesterday's perpetrator, but he's unlikely to be able to prove his innocence against the evidence available."

"Do you really think the DNA evidence is reliable?"

"Well, our experts are certain that the traces of this unknown person were found on Lochberger's body, and on the other hand, there were no DNA traces of Mr Strasser on the murder victim. From our point of view, the matter is one hundred percent clear. The international arrest warrant for your friend will be lifted today."

"That is a huge weight off my mind, Commissioner," I said euphorically. "Thank you very much for calling me this morning! This uncertainty has been terrible."

"I can imagine. Now you must tell your friend the good news as quickly as possible. I hope he shows up soon."

"I'll try to reach Alex and let him know what's happened. Thank you very much again, Mr Sauer. You have no idea how relieved I am now!"

"I am sure of that. Have a nice day."

"Thank you. The same to you. And thank you again."

It was incredible! Alex was innocently persecuted! But now he was rehabilitated and could return to Germany without any problems and enjoy his retirement. But he didn't know about his luck yet and the question was how I should reach him. I immediately phoned Susanne and told her everything. She was as relieved and happy about this turn of events as I was. But where was Alex? We decided to check with the Spanish authorities to see if there had been any searches that might give clues as to Alex's whereabouts. We also wanted to contact all his friends and acquaintances to ask them for advice.

I made many phone calls over the next few days. The Spanish police told me that they had found the surfboard that Alex had rented. A sailor had seen it floating in the water not far from the beach on Sunday and returned it to the rental company. Searches by the water police had taken place, but neither these nor the routine helicopter flights over the entire stretch of coast had yielded any findings.

My other investigations at all possible locations were all inconclusive. I wrote once again to Pedro Molinero's email address, from which I had recently received Alexander's messages. But this address had been deleted and no longer existed, as I has expected. Several days passed without me having any clue as to Alex's whereabouts.

On Friday a motoring club truck with my son's VW Golf parked in front of my house and unloaded the car. Some days before I had ordered the car to be brought back from Spain. I searched the interior of the vehicle and found nothing. No clues, no messages, no letters. However, there was a backpack belonging to Alex in the boot of the car, with a camera, a small toilet bag and pyjamas. Underwear, a shirt and trousers were also there. It looked as if he had already prepared these things for a trip and put them in the car. A mobile phone was in this backpack, too. The whole thing worried me. Had he perhaps planned to go somewhere after surfing, maybe even take a flight? The whole thing seemed prepared. Something had then prevented him from actually taking the backpack with him on the trip. One obvious conclusion was that he had had an accident on the surfboard and therefore had not been able to put his travel plans into action.

But perhaps he had set the whole thing up? Maybe he wanted to give the police exactly this impression, namely that he had prepared a trip, but then hadn't been able to set out.

The situation was depressing. Now Alex was cleared of suspicion of murder, but he probably didn't know about it. He was either still on the run or had been killed in an accident. The uncertainty was hard to bear and yet I had no choice but to continue to wait and hope.

Weeks went by. Four months have now passed. The probability that he is still alive is dwindling day by day. But again and again I read his last text message in which he had written that he would not be available for a while and that I should not worry about him.

In a way, I cling to this statement and at some moments I am convinced that he has acted very cleverly and is hiding somewhere, maybe even outside Europe, feigning an accident while swimming.

But at other times I find it very unlikely because he would have sent me some kind of message, wouldn't he? Nor have I received any positive signals from other acquaintances and friends. Nobody knows anything about him, nobody has heard anything.

In the meantime I have spoken to Commissioner Sauer on several occasions. He seems depressed and last time he spoke of a 'tragic accident'. He no longer seems to believe that Alex will turn up again. In his opinion the conclusion of a fatal accident is obvious.

So weeks and months have passed. Now we are in November and I really don't know what to believe any more. The uncertainty is the worst thing. The days go by. I work more than ever before so I can push back the recurring thoughts.

The weather has become cool and rainy. My walks in the woods become rarer and shorter. The trees are in their autumn colours and the leaves fall and drift in the wind. Soon the trees will be bare in the mists of winter and the fields will be under a blanket of frost. The thought of the next spring is comforting. Will Alex be back then?

I have decided to stick to the maxims of the ancient Romans: Dum spiro, spero - as long as I breathe, I hope.

Hope must remain. I am not giving up hope.

Contents:

She is friendly, punctual and has organizational skills. JUST GREAT!

Simone Ayodele

I am INCREDIBLY RELIEVED and COMPLETELY BLISSED after Frau Ordnung has practiced her clean-up skills in my basement. It helped me a lot to make myself clear and to decide what to keep, what to give away and what to confidently knock down because I would never miss it. With her super effective system, she has managed to conjure up a veritable "cellar oasis" from a totally overloaded cellar. Now I have so much space and air in the basement that I can have a cup of coffee with my husband and 3-4 guests and enjoy a nostalgic slideshow on our basement wall from our very first vacation in Canada in the nineties :-) How cool is that?! I never would have thought that cleaning up the basement could bring so much fun, happiness, relief and freedom of movement. That must feel similar for an overweight who has reached his ideal weight again. Thank you very much, Frau Ordnung :-)!

Claudia Tan

Ms. Ludwig helps with order in the office and thus also in the head. We recommend!

Andreas Graf von Brühl